# No Paperwork Needed...

**No Paperwork Needed...**
*Memoirs of an inept loan shark*

**Chapter Zero**

"Who, me?"

That was my quick-witted reply to the six-foot-three, well-muscled, dapperly dressed client who asked me, "Did you just grab my girl's ass, you asshole? Because if you did, I'm going to stomp your ass into the ground." One could add "expansive vocabulary" to his list of distinguishing features.

"Yeah, you."

I assumed he meant the girl in the very short yellow sundress. Now, let me tell you that any normal, healthy male would have seriously considered doing just that. She was absolutely stunning—raven-black hair, the greenest of eyes, and a figure—give me a minute here, all the blood is busy draining from my brain as I try to describe her. You get the idea.

"I don't know if I grabbed your girl's ass."

"What do you mean, you don't know?"

"Is this your girl?"

Let me explain. In my business I've learned that the fastest way to get to the heart of the matter at hand is to skip all the unnecessary pleasantries and polite conversation and dive right in. If your client is squiring a fine-looking woman, a good way to do this is to simply grab her ass.

# No Paperwork Needed...

My business? I collect past due loans. My name is Trench, and my partner is Kent. I have a quasi-work arrangement with Larry. Folks who've watched too many old gangster movies would tend to call Larry a loan shark. I resent that term. I'll tell you who the real sharks are—folks like the on-line auction sites charging you a fee to share your treasures with the world and then hitting you up for three percent should you manage to unload the crap. Then, the same group under a different name charges you another three percent just to send you your own money your crap sold for. Three percent for their computer's three milliseconds of time. That works out to be about 1.5 million percent per year. And yet, Larry is labeled a crook, a loan shark.

Actually, Larry has achieved the Holy Grail the computer industry has been trying to reach for years—a completely paperless office.

Why do I work for Larry? Several years back I was lusting after a girl named Anne. I had this great idea of putting a few dollars' deposit on a new car, test-driving it for the weekend, hopefully getting a few stains on the backseat Friday night, and then turning the car in on Saturday and getting my money back. The only hitch in the plan was that I didn't have any money in the first place. That's when Larry stepped in: "Sure kid, here's five hundred dollars, no problem—but I better see you in three days with seven hundred and fifty dollars. No, you don't need to sign a thing."

All went well until I wrecked the car, and the only stains to be found anywhere were type O on the front seat—and I was still in the hospital on the day the loan was due. Later that same day, I had a visit from a Mr. Kemmer. He suggested I work something out with Larry in short order, or I should count on an extended stay.

# No Paperwork Needed...

What was worked out was simple. I was to become a collector for the overdue loans among the college crowd. For every five dollars I brought in, two would be deducted from my loan. I wasn't smart enough at the time to notice that my ongoing interest vastly exceeded any gain I might make at that rate. Nevertheless, that's how I got started with Larry.

After working the college crowd for a while, I moved up to shady business owners, various local political minions, lawyers, bankers, and other societal bottom-feeders. As Larry moved up to bigger and better arrangements, so did I. Soon I was collecting from two hundred, five hundred grand clients.

And that is what I was doing at the moment.

"Well, is this your girl?" The guy's name was Gerald Rickson. What a distinguished name for a jerk who was into Larry for over seven hundred grand.

Now, seven hundred grand is big money. This brings me to my second job, occupation, or vocation—whatever. For the last two years, I've also been allied with the US Treasury. I'm not too proud of that. Nobody knows about my second job, not Larry, Kent, or even my mother. She's not happy about my being one of those loan shark thugs, but it would kill her to find that I work for the government.

The feds caught me using my collection skills for Larry shortly after moving to the bigger clients. And one more time, my occupation was determined by making a deal. I was to report the various transactions to help the Treasury with IRS issues.

# No Paperwork Needed...

Gerald's punch moved my jaw south a ways, but I could still talk a bit.

"Larry wants you to know that you are three days late, that your interest has doubled, and that it's going to be easier for you to write a check while you still have both hands."

Before you start thinking I'm a real bad guy, you must understand that neither myself or Kent ever hurt anyone. Much. No, our job is to find the clients, try to start them on the path to righteousness and set things up to make the task of the enforcers a bit more convenient should the client stray. We never really know what happens to those few who never pay up, and even if we did want to know, most times they seem to be pretty hard to find.

Larry simply wanted his money and his interest. After all, this guy had been using the money for six days at this point. What Larry didn't know was that the Treasury wanted to know what Gerald was doing with the money. They strongly suspected it was being used as short-term investment capital that was returning huge profits, and the IRS wanted their share of the scam. They could have cared less about the illegal loans, interest rates, or the collection methods—that was Justice's problem.

Kent's job was pretty straightforward—he was there to keep me from being punched, kicked, hit over the head, bitten, etc. He didn't know about my second job, and was lousy at his.

"I could care less what Larry wants. Tell him to go and—"

I stopped him right there. "Larry isn't the least bit interested in what you have to say. He's only interested in what you do, and that better be handing him a shit pot full of money by the end of the day. Now I'm going to forget that you slugged me and tell Larry that the message has been delivered. And, by the way, yes, I did grab this young lady's ass—any man in his right mind would have."

This time I stepped aside, and thus Gerald didn't connect with his second punch. But I did indeed connect with mine—a right to the stomach as hard as I could. Gerald bent over, gasped, and dropped to his knees, breaking his fall with his hands.

"You see, your hands can be used for more than signing checks—you might want to keep them." With that, Kent and I walked out the door.

All in all, it was a pretty typical contact. I was sure that Larry would see his money—he does most every time. I do remember one time, however, when the client got the better of Larry. This fellow walked in one day and wanted two hundred grand for just a couple of days. Larry asked a few questions and sized him up as being OK.

As it turned out, this guy was a walking corpse. He literally had just days to live with an extremely aggressive cancer. He took the money, bought a used airplane of all things, and made his last landing of the day into the side of a mountain.

It bothered Larry for weeks that he ended up on the short end of the stick. No one had ever fooled him like that before. Larry could smell cancer; he could hear leaking heart valves. No one ever got past him. I often thought he would have made an excellent NFL team doctor.

Speaking of Larry, one shouldn't be so critical of him. If you can for just a moment set aside the possible outcomes of his business, he isn't  that bad a guy. He runs a straightforward and successful operation. No fine print here; as a matter of fact, no print at all. No scams or various conditions may apply. Nope, he gives you the money, and you agree to pay him back a fair bit more than he gave you. What could be more clear?

And every so often, a clean client would come through. Like the guy who needed one hundred grand to close a fast and completely legitimate business transaction that due to his skills and understanding of the subject matter would realize a twofold or threefold profit in a few days, and after fulfilling his obligation to Larry, would leave a tidy profit remaining.

But not very often. Most times it was more like the young man who walked in and wanted ten grand. You could spot right off that he was a community leader of the future. Baseball cap on backward, baggy gym shorts whose crotch fell well below his knees, and enough rings stuck here and there that he looked like a chain-link fence. No doubt about it, this was a kid who was going places.

He said he was totally in love with his girlfriend and wanted to show her a dream weekend of total excess.

"How are you going to pay this back, along with the interest?" Larry asked.

"Simple," the kid said. "My mom will be mailing me the check for next semester's tuition in a few days. I'm just going to cash it and not bother to register for school. Pretty cool, huh?"

But this was only half the story. It wasn't his girlfriend whom he was in love with, but rather, his girlfriend's mother. Shortly thereafter, the girlfriend caught him discussing the merits of higher education while poking the hell out of her mother in the master bedroom. She screamed out all manner of things, including that she was going to tell his mother what he was planning on doing with the tuition check, and true to her word, she did.

I met with the boy and suggested strongly that he face Larry along with a bunch of cash. He did contact Larry, and suggested that he, Larry, contact his mother for all the money and a bit of an extra bonus, and let her know that if she didn't pay, he, the boy, would come to great harm. Larry did just that and received all his money. Everyone was happy, with the exception of Larry, the boy's mother, the girlfriend, and the girlfriend's mother. The boy was happy until a couple of the enforcers caught him one night in a parking lot. They took him to the back of his car, opened the trunk, stuck his arm in the trunk and proceeded to slam the trunk lid forcefully enough that it latched with his arm still inside. The enforcers then calmly got in their car and drove away. It was nothing more than a simple matter of principle.

# No Paperwork Needed...

## Chapter One

I wasn't done with Gerald. The Treasury wanted to know if he still had access to the money, which he did. My next task was to get this information to them without Larry, Kent, or anyone, knowing I was doing so.

As Kent and I approached my car, I felt a hard blow to the head. You always read that one sees stars. I didn't see shit. Sometime later I was aware of Kent trading off between shaking me and slapping my face.

Apparently, Gerald had followed us outside, and when he got the chance, he let me have it over the head with a damn rock he picked up. Once again, Kent had fallen down on his job. I found out later that Kent hadn't been behind me. Inspired by my speech that any normal man would have grabbed the ass of the girl in the very short yellow sundress, he had gone back inside to see if he could grab the ass of the girl in the very short yellow sundress.

To sum up, Kent didn't succeed in grabbing the ass, I did get knocked out, and Gerald was nowhere to be seen. This was getting personal.

After Kent got me stable enough to walk a straight line, we jumped in my car and headed for Larry's place to fill him in. I was also hoping I could drop Kent there so I could leave alone and contact the Treasury.

My contact in the Treasury was a Mrs. Forester. She had all the charm of, well, a Treasury agent. She was never pleased with the amount or the quality of the information I delivered to her, and I knew it wasn't going to be any different this time. I drove to my drab, tiny, and completely depressing apartment and placed a call to my contact.

# No Paperwork Needed...

Forester answered the phone. "What did you find out?"

"Gerald still has access to or use of the money."

"And?"

"And what? Gerald still has access to or use of the money."

"You took a full day to find him, and then spent the afternoon with him, and that is all you found out?"

"No, I found out that rocks are hard, that you can get punched for grabbing the ass of a girl in a very short yellow sundress, and that Kent is as piss-poor as ever at his job."

"Listen, we want to know exactly what Gerald is using that money for. Find out and find out fast!"

With that the phone clicked dead.

My head was still hurting, and I lay down after taking a few aspirin to try to get a bit of rest. When I nodded off, I had this pleasant dream about a parking lot filled with girls in very short yellow sundresses.

The sun in my eyes and the drool running down my cheek signaled the start of a new day. As far as Larry was concerned, I was done with Gerald and was ready for my next assignment—someone named Phil Treadwood, a doctor who had been probing his female patients with one too many instruments and had used money borrowed from Larry to finally calm them down.

# No Paperwork Needed...

But according to Treasury, I was far from done with Gerald. If I understood correctly, I was to find one man in a city of over one million, not knowing who he really was, where he lived or worked—and after a previous meeting that went less than smoothly, I was supposed to ask him to politely tell me what he intended to do with the borrowed seven hundred grand. Oh yeah, and please don't tell Larry about this little meeting.

Sure.

How I would get the info and yet hide the fact from Larry that I did so could be figured out later. First I had to find Gerald.

The thing to try first was obvious. Return to the location of the last meeting. I didn't expect to find him there because I knew that he knew that I knew how to find him there the first time. I knew because of Mack. Mack was one of Larry's sniffers.

Mack, one of several guys who for a fifty-dollar bill would suggest Larry if they encountered someone asking around about a fast, no-questions-asked, no-paperwork-needed loan. Mack had told Larry that he had put Gerald onto him. Mack's suggestion of Larry had taken place at the Ramrod Bar way out on West 120th.

I parked close to where I'd parked the night before, and as I walked to the door, I noticed a so-so sized rock off to the side. I wondered if that was the rock with my name on it.

The place was about a third full. It would be much faster to ask around about a girl in a very short yellow sundress than a sharp dresser named Gerald. If I made a hit, then I could bring Gerald into the conversation. So I started making the rounds.

"No."

"No."

"No."

"Yeah—she was with some decked-out guy talking to two other guys, and all of a sudden, the guy with the girl popped one of the other guys a good one right on the chin—say, you look a lot like that guy!"

"Really? Had you been talking to him before that or happen to hear anything he might have said?"

"No, but he was talking to Tom a bit earlier—have you asked Tom?"

"I don't know Tom—if he's here, point him out."

Tom was there. "He's the guy third from the end of the bar," he said, pointing to his right. I hadn't yet questioned Tom, so I headed that direction.

"Thanks for the help."

"Say, mister, Tom can get pretty mean when he's drunk, and he passed drunk hours ago."

I walked up to Tom's side and asked, "Is your name Tom?"

He turned toward me and inquired, "Who the fuck are you?" I slowly turned around and then quickly did a pirouette, which placed me behind him with my left arm around his neck and my right hand not so gently squeezing his balls.

Anyone watching would have given me a 9.5 for that move, but Tom may have outdone me. Through all of this, he didn't drop a single pretzel or spill any beer.

"Tom," I whispered in his ear, "I need to ask you a simple question, so let me tell you how this is going to work. If I think you are lying to me, I'm going to choke you. If I think you're being rude to me, I'm going to crush your balls—understand?"

"Yes, but fuck yourself anyway!"

"Tom, I think that was rude," I said as I clamped tighter on his balls. "Do I need to explain the rules again?"

He was busy trying to inhale as he gasped while also trying to exhale with a moan, but somewhere in there, I thought I had heard a no.

"Did you talk with a well-dressed guy last night who was with a girl in a yellow sundress?"

"Yeah, but it was a very short yellow sundress," he corrected me.

"Fine—now please tell me what you talked about and tell me everything he said."

"OK, but I may not remember all of it; I was a lot drunker last night." I wasn't sure how that could even be possible.

Tom got started, and I only interrupted him a few times. I now had a few leads. It was frustrating to know that things like where Gerald lived or worked were most likely known

# No Paperwork Needed...

by Larry through the loan process, but way too many questions would arise if I asked Larry himself.

"Do you remember anything else?" He said no and told me he had stopped talking to Gerald because Linda had walked in.

"Who is Linda, and what does she have to do with this?"

"You don't know Linda? Everyone knows Linda. She's the redhead with the giant tits. We play this game each night—I ask her if we could step outside and take her tits for a walk, and she tells me to fuck off—it's fun."

"Sounds like it." I turned to leave.

As I drove off, I replayed the conversation with Tom. A few things didn't seem to add up. Who knows, I may have to visit Tom again, and perhaps there is a chance I might bump into this Linda person. But that would have to wait.

\* \* \*

It was time to pick up Kent and give the good doctor a visit.

Another thing Kent was supposed to do was try to track down the clients so I would know where I could catch them for a pep talk. In truth, he was as bad at this as he was at keeping me from being hit over the head.

Upon arriving at Larry's, I spoke with Kent. "Did you find a time and place that I can have speaks with Dr. Treadwood?"

"No."

# No Paperwork Needed...

Larry had two inviolate rules. One, never talk to a client at the client's home. Two, never talk to a client at his place of business or work. Something about not embarrassing the client. This from a guy who would arrange to have your legs broken without a second thought. Go figure.

"Larry, Kent doesn't have a lead on Treadwood. Can we break rule two?" Larry said he would call Treadwood's office and see if there was a time he would be absolutely alone. If he could find one, I could indeed talk to him there.

Larry called. The doctor was free and alone, so he gave me the address, and we were off.

When Kent and I walked into Treadwood's office, the first thing I saw was the ever-reassuring sign that Dr. Phil Treadwood was licensed to practice medicine. I hope one day to find a physician with a sign that says he's licensed to *perform* medicine. I hammered the little silver bell on the counter, and out came Dr. Phil Treadwood.

I knew there was no way I had hidden my double take. Standing before me was the frailest-looking, meekest-appearing individual I truly believe I had ever seen in my life. Kent was definitely not going to be needed.

"Are you the Dr. Phil Treadwood who has been...?"

"Well, yes," he said.

"What kind of doctor are you?" I asked.

"Well, yes—but I'm not that bad a person."

# No Paperwork Needed...

"No. No, I'm not asking about your character; I pretty much have that figured out. I mean, what is your specialty?"

"Well, yes. I specialize in nose and throat treatment."

"Nose and throat? From what I understand, you are missing to the south by a mile!"

"Well, yes."

"Seriously, how do you get from examining some lady's throat to, how do I say this, fucking them?"

"Well, yes. You see, when I examine their throat, I first dip the tongue depressor in a highly functional and fast relaxant. A few minutes later, they are completely at ease. Actually, most women seem to enjoy things."

"And yet, you borrowed five hundred grand from Larry—which he now very much wants back, by the way, along with the interest—which you used to keep a few of them at bay because they figured out what was going on."

"Well, yes. Now and then a lady will come to and wonder why her throat exam had taken the better part of an hour. And a few of those women figure things out. That's when things get a bit ugly."

"Enough. I don't want to know any more. What you need to know is that you better show up at Larry's within the next day or two with a bunch of money or there'll be a few guys making an appointment with you, and they really will be just practicing a bit of medicine. Understand?"

"Well, yes. But I can't come by this afternoon, as I've two more examinations to give."

# No Paperwork Needed...

I shook my head and left.

As I was walking out, a redhead with large breasts was walking in.

"Is your name Linda?"

"What?" she said.

"Never mind."

Having completed my meeting with the doctor, it was time to drop off Kent and follow up on the few leads I had received from Tom.

Tom had mentioned that he had seen Gerald either coming or going from Ramrod's parking lot a few times. Each time Gerald was either getting in or out of a fancy sports car, always with dealer plates.

Was Gerald a car dealer? Perhaps part of a car delivery service. Or part of an auto theft organization. The dealer plates were perfect for this. They were never checked by the police, as they weren't associated with a particular car, but rather with a car dealer. They could be on a BMW in the morning and a Lincoln that same afternoon.

There were only thirty-five or so high-end dealerships and exotic auto outlets in town, and I had all day.

After combing the phone book, I had written down thirty-eight addresses. Armed with my portable navigator, I was off.

At each place I stopped and asked, "Do you have a sharp-dressing guy—I think his name is Gerald—working here or working for the place? I bumped into his car the other day and was told he might work here. I sure would like to settle up with him."

Luck was with me. It was about the seventeenth stop when the answer was, "Yes and no, the prick."

Pay dirt!

# No Paperwork Needed...

**Chapter Two**

"Yes *and* no?" I enquired.

"Yes, he used to work here. We found out that he was checking out a high-end car and using it to play Mr. Big Shot with the ladies when he had said he was demonstrating the car to a potential buyer. The boss canned him yesterday."

"Do you know where he lives?" I asked.

"It's funny you should ask. A couple of us went by the address he listed on his employee sheet, and it doesn't exist, the prick. Bottom line, it turns out we don't know much about him at all."

"Just out of curiosity, why do keep calling him a prick?"

"Because I have a buyer for the last car he checked out, and he has yet to return it. That's why we went out to his house."

"What kind of car is it?"

"A Turbo S Porsche—yellow convertible—a stunning car. By the way, are you thinking about a new car?" Once a car salesman, always a car salesman.

What could working for an exotic car dealership have to do with borrowing seven hundred grand and not paying it back? Exotic cars cost a lot of money, but why would he be buying cars, if indeed he was? It wasn't his dealership; he wouldn't be buying hot cars and selling them from the lot.

# No Paperwork Needed...

At any rate I was back to nowhere. I now knew where he used to work. I knew his given address didn't exist, and I knew he still owed the money, but mostly I knew if I didn't make some progress soon, neither Larry or the Treasury was going to be too happy with me.

And speaking of Larry, I needed to check in, as Kent had called and said Larry had another client I was to visit.

I pulled up in front of Larry's, parked, and walked in.

Kent was sitting in the outer office. "Larry in his office?" I asked.

"Yes—careful, he doesn't seem to be too happy."

*What's new*, I thought. "Hi, Larry, what's up?"

"You need to visit a fellow and do it fast. One of my sniffers caught wind of the fact that the guy just purchased tickets for Milan, and he's into me for three-hundred and seventy-five thousand."

"All right, what's the name, and does Kent have any starting points?"

"William or Bill Jennings, and you'll have to talk to Kent."

"Anything else?"

"Yeah, what have you found out about Gerald?"

"Just that he no longer works where he used to work and that he lives at a place that doesn't exist."

"Great—and the doctor?"

# No Paperwork Needed...

"I take it that means he hasn't shown up. He told me he had a couple more examinations this afternoon, so he wouldn't be coming by today. I'm sure he will be in tomorrow. I have nothing else on him, but you needn't worry."

"How long does it take to do a couple of examinations anyway?"

"Depends, I guess."

"You're a hell of a lot of help—go find Jennings."

Kent, big surprise, had no idea where we might connect with Jennings at the moment.

He suggested we start with contacting Mick, the sniffer who had put Larry on to the fact that Jennings had tickets for Milan. Mick's hangout was a sports bar and grill called Score. A cute name with a number of innuendos—sports, sex, drugs, etc. And the place lived up to all of them.

This was as good as anything I could think of, so we were off to Score. See what I mean.

As we drove out, for about the thousandth time, I thought about Larry's inviolate rules on never attempting to contact a client at home or work. It just seemed so illogical to me. But truth be known, the few times that Larry had given us this information about a client, the client was never in either place.

The clients, while not usually rocket scientists, were smart enough to not hang around home or office when they were behind in their payments.

# No Paperwork Needed...

We parked beside what Kent thought might be Mick's pickup. Luck was with us; it was Mick's pickup, and he was inside the bar.

He was busy trying to convince an extremely heavy, middle-aged woman that she should leave with him for an evening of delights. If she said yes, he was going to need that pickup.

"Hi, Mick."

"Hey, what's up, guys?"

"Just a couple of questions. You were the one who put Jennings on to Larry for some cash, correct?"

"Sure."

"Then you called Larry and told him Jennings had tickets for Milan. Please tell me you didn't know about the Milan thing when you set Jennings up with Larry."

"No, of course not. I found out about three days later."

"How did you find out?"

"The usual. He was here shooting off his mouth to some other guys I know about how he had come by a bunch of money and was going to leave this shit hole and go to Milan and enjoy Southern Italy. He said he was never coming back."

"Well, setting aside the fact that Milan is in Northern Italy, why Italy?"

"I have no idea—maybe he likes spaghetti."

"Is there any chance you know what day he's leaving? What airline?"

"The airline, no, but I would guess Thursday, because he said he was coming by here about noon on Thursday to get his passport."

"Since when did the Score become a federal passport office?"

"Come on, Trench, you know this place. Someone here knows someone else who can fix you up with just about anything you want. The passport work will not be done here, but this is where the money and passport will change hands."

"Thanks, Mick. I'll tell Larry to drop a fifty on you. By the way, I keep hearing about tickets, plural, not ticket. Do you know if someone is going with him?"

"No."

"OK."

As we headed for the car, I told Kent I wanted to stop by my place. I had an idea that might help. At my place I picked up my old passport and once again sighed at the fact that it didn't contain one single foreign country stamp, world traveler that I am. I needed to stop sighing so much.

At the airport we made a quick check of all the carriers that had routine flights to Milan. Just three.

I asked Kent to wait and walked up to the first counter. I tried to get the attention of an agent who looked like she still had one shred of interest in her job.

# No Paperwork Needed...

"Miss, I have a friend named William Jennings who has a flight to Milan on Thursday; at least I think it's Thursday. He left his passport at our office, and try as I may, I cannot find him." With this, I quickly flashed my old passport.

"I don't know if he's using your airline or not, but if so, I would like to leave his passport here for when he checks in."

"Oh my. He will certainly need his passport. Let me check."

After a few moments, I was told they didn't have anyone named William Jennings booked for the Thursday flight to Milan.

"I also checked that same flight for every day starting as of today through the next two weeks. Sorry, no Mr. Jennings."

Of course he could be using an assumed name, but anyone dumb enough to borrow three-hundred and seventy-five grand from Larry and assume he could get away with not paying it back wasn't a deep thinker.

At the second airline counter of the three, my little song and dance worked to perfection. If we didn't find Jennings any sooner, we simply needed to be here two hours before departure on Thursday—American Airlines. The agent didn't give a second's thought to the fact that I didn't hand over the passport.

I asked Kent to see if he could locate Jennings any sooner, but we at least had a plan.

# No Paperwork Needed...

I dropped Kent off at Larry's so he could get his own car and headed home. I was back to Gerald in my mind. I wanted to sit back, relax, and replay my conversation with Tom in my mind's eye. It's surprising what you can sometimes pick up doing this. Things that didn't perhaps click or make sense during the first part of the conversation, because at the time you had yet to hear the last part of the conversation, can come clear after the fact, because you have access to the entire conversation in your mind.

Rethinking conversations brought to mind the time Larry sent me to have speaks with a Mr. John Gibbons. This led to an overheard conversation that was pretty clear right off the bat. John had borrowed one thousand from Larry and had failed to repay on time.

It's the small loans that pissed off Larry the most.

"You can get your hands on a thousand or two by simply clubbing a few little old ladies and grabbing their purses, for Christ's sake," Larry had said. "There's no reason for the small loans not to repay."

In any case, I found Gibbons at his usual hangout and sat down at a table by the pay phone, which he was using at the time.

He was excitedly recounting his morning to someone.

—"That bitch Donna is never going to fuck around on me again. I stopped by her apartment this morning, you know, the one in the four hundred block of Fairlane Avenue, walked in and grabbed her by the neck, drug her into the bedroom, beat the shit out of her, fucked her one last time, and then slit her throat from ear to ear. She's lying there in the middle of her fucking blood-soaked bed. Nope, she's never going to fuck around on me again—"

This little outburst was overflowing with clues. Thinking it over, it seemed to me that Gibbons had probably gone over to his girlfriend's house on Fairlane, beat the shit out of her, raped her, and then slit her throat and left her bleeding on the bed.

All in all, Larry was going to have to eat his thousand plus interest, as this had escalated beyond our involvement. This was now a matter for the law.

That, however, had its own problems. I couldn't simply give the police a call—

"Hello, this is Trench. I was trying to collect a thousand dollars plus interest from a Mr. John Gibbons for Larry, the friendly loan shark, I guess you could say, or let John know he would soon be walking on his hands, when I overheard him telling someone he had raped and then slit his girlfriend's throat from ear to ear. She is in some apartment on the four hundred block of Fairlane Avenue."

—there were bound to be a few questions.

No, this was best handled with a drop-off. I called Kent, picked him up, along with a couple of long nylon tie straps, some tape, and a piece of cardboard, and then returned. We walked in, discreetly clubbed Gibbons unconscious from behind, then hauled him out to the car, where we placed one tie strip on his hands, a second on his feet, and wrapped a couple loops of duct tape around his mouth and head for good measure. We started our search for an empty police car. It didn't take long to find one. We tossed him in the backseat—one thing Kent was good at was breaking into cars—and hung a small sign around his neck that read, "I just killed my girlfriend." It's as simple as that.

But that was the past. Gerald was the now.

Rethinking Tom's conversation revealed that I was no longer looking for Gerald. I was looking for a yellow Porsche, and not just any Porsche, a Turbo S Porsche convertible. At over two hundred grand a pop, you just didn't see one on every street corner. Find the Porsche, find Gerald.

I phoned Kent and asked him to put the word out to all sniffers, enforcers, and all the joints we had at least a reasonable relationship with, that we were anxious to find a yellow Porsche Turbo S. Anyone's tip that put me in the same parking lot as the Porsche was worth a crisp hundred dollar bill.

I still couldn't put Gerald, the Porsche, and the seven hundred grand together. I could indeed put together Gerald, the Porsche, and the salesman's statement that Gerald was using checked-out cars to impress the ladies. Remember the very short yellow sundress?

I phoned Forester at the Treasury and filled her in with the latest. As always, she was less than impressed. This time I didn't blame her. I was getting nowhere and could only hope someone would spot the Porsche.

The best I could do was drive around the rest of the day hitting all the dives to see if I could spot the Porsche myself. I did this with no luck, as I did again the next day.

But on Thursday I connected with Kent, as we had a date at the American Airlines counter with Mr. William Jennings.

# No Paperwork Needed...

# No Paperwork Needed...

**Chapter Three**

After I picked up Kent, I drove over and picked up Mick.

"Kent, any ideas on how to play this out?"

Kent, who, as I've mentioned, is a piss-poor bodyguard, now and then can come up with a pretty clever approach to a problem.

"Yeah, let's sneak up from behind and club him."

I guess this wasn't one of those "now and then" times.

"You do remember we are going to be in an airline terminal most likely surrounded by hundreds of people?"

"Oh, right—let me rethink this."

Unless I disturbed him, that would be the last I heard from him for a while.

"We need to get him to take his ticket out where we can see it," I said. "Without his ticket he isn't going anywhere. I have an idea. Just stay with me. If you get the chance, grab his ticket, and I'll take it from there."

We parked in the closest available spot, which was in a lot that was itself a short flight away from the terminal, and the three of us boarded the tram. The reason Mick was along, of course, was that neither Kent or myself had ever seen Mr. Jennings.

Entering the terminal we made our way to the American Airlines counter area. We spread out a bit and waited for Mick to point out our man. About twenty-five minutes later, Mick gave me the signal and pointed to an average-built guy wearing an absolutely beautiful, perfectly fitted suit.

It came to mind that he no longer had the full three hundred and seventy-five grand.

I walked over to him and more or less positioned myself so he had to stop.

"Excuse me, but are you on the flight to Milan?"

"Yes. Why?"

"Good. You know, I think there's a problem. They have us going to gate C-23, but my ticket and the boarding pass I just received read gate D-23. Would you mind telling me what gate is printed on your ticket?"

And just like that, as if by magic, his ticket disappeared from his inside suit breast pocket and appeared in front of his face so he could read the gate number. But before he could, like magic again, his ticket disappeared from his hand and reappeared in Kent's pocket.

"Hey! What the hell gives—give me my ticket back!"

I smiled. "Sorry, Mr. Jennings, if I did that, you could fly away, and Larry wouldn't like that."

It was like letting the air out of a balloon. It wouldn't be missing the mark by much to say that he shrank before our eyes. His perfectly fit suit all of a sudden seemed a bit askew. He stood motionless for a few minutes, and then his eyes started to water.

# No Paperwork Needed...

"I...I just wanted to start a new life," he finally said. "I can't make my problems go away, so I thought I would go away from them."

"Well, Bill, it doesn't look like that's going to happen. I don't know about your new life, but if you want to preserve a bit more of your current one, I would suggest you see Larry, give him all the money you have left, and work out some arrangements for what you still would owe."

It was one of the few times I felt a bit sorry for a guy. I was about twenty feet away when I turned and walked back. He was still standing there looking like he had no intention of ever moving.

"Listen. Tell Larry I think you are good for it and that you are one of a few who should be allowed to slide a bit."

It was about a month later I heard he did find Larry right away, handed him the money short by an airline ticket and a nice suit, and made arrangements for the balance, which he did indeed honor on time. This time everyone truly was happy. I heard Larry even passed on a few good words, which led to a nice job for Mr. Jennings. If only they could all end that well.

\* \* \*

Three days had gone by and not a peep from anyone about the yellow Porsche. It was time for a team meeting at Larry's. Once about every two weeks or so, we all gathered at Larry's—me, Kent, and the enforcers for a short meeting.

Our current enforcers, Don and Jack, had been with Larry for a couple of years. These were the guys who were sent

# No Paperwork Needed...

to the clients who didn't respond to my visit. Larry made the loans, I collected the ones not paid on time, and the enforcers stepped in if the clients ignored my instructions. Both Don and Jack were pleasant enough fellows, but had no hesitancy whatsoever to crack open someone's skull, break an arm or two, shoot a hole through a foot, or provide any other physical reminder they felt was needed to help remind the client of his obligation. To the best of my knowledge, they had never killed anyone in the line of their duties. This was partially due to Larry's inviolate rule not to do so. However, one thing was sure: A client never, and I mean *never*, wanted to be visited by them twice.

We discussed the various loans that were still out, the ones that were OK, the clients who had been contacted, and if they hadn't been contacted, Larry discussed our next step. Lastly, any new assignments.

"Gerald is still at the top of the list," Larry said. "Do we want to try for another contact or send the enforcers?"

"Seven hundred grand is a real bite," I said. "Let me try another contact."

Of course, what no one knew was that if the enforcers got to Gerald before I did, then I couldn't get to the Treasury. Not good at all.

"Do you think he might listen this time?" Larry asked.

"It sure can't hurt to try."

"OK, I'll give you one more week."

"Fine. By the way, did Dr. Treadwood show up?"

# No Paperwork Needed...

"Yes. What a meek, well-mannered little fellow. He stopped in, squared his entire account. We had a nice little chat. He didn't even blink at the extra charge for being late."

"Did he happen to mention where he came by what must have been close to five hundred and fifty grand?"

"I didn't ask because I don't care. I just wanted it paid."

He rarely asked what a loan was for or how the client was going to find the money to pay it back; he truly didn't want to know. And he truly didn't care. That was the client's business; getting the loan paid back with interest was Larry's business.

"He did, however, mention that some middle-aged lady enjoyed her nose and throat exam so much that she put him on a huge retainer and paid in advance. Does that make any sense to you? I mean, how many times does a person need a throat exam?"

"Who knows, it's a strange world. But I'll give you a tip. If you are ever around him, and he pulls out a tongue depressor, run."

"What's that mean?"

"Nothing. Any new clients gone astray?"

"Yeah. A Mrs. Susan Homer. She's late on twenty-five thousand. Kent has a couple of ideas on locating her. I had him follow her for a while after she picked up the loan."

Larry made this arrangement with Kent if he didn't feel one hundred percent about the loan.

# No Paperwork Needed...

Now, here was something different. Maybe one out of ninety to a hundred times, the client I had to visit was female. Larry did a surprising number of female loans, but their record of fulfilling the terms of repayment was stellar compared to the guys.

"I only have one inviolate rule," Larry said. "Don't screw around and somehow get involved with her, at least not until the loan has been collected."

Truth be told, I had no idea how many inviolate rules Larry had. There seemed to be one or two new ones with every client.

"You got it? You can fuck her blind for all I care; just don't get emotionally involved."

"I got it," I said and left to catch up with Kent.

"OK, what's the story with our lady Susan?"

"I think she wanted the money to pay someone to rough up her husband—seems as if he has been cheating on her," Kent said.

"Twenty-five thousand? Christ, Kent, she could hire a taxidermist to stuff and mount him for that much. There must be more to it than that."

"Don't know. Ask her. You know women, they're happy to tell a complete stranger how many times their husband moaned the last time he climaxed—if they were there, I mean."

"Funny. Where do I find her?"

# No Paperwork Needed...

Kent said when he followed her on and off for a while after the loan, she had stopped by the new medical center downtown on Eighth Street a few times.

"Fine," I said. "Let's give it a try."

We stopped off to grab a couple of cheeseburgers and soft drinks and drove on over to the medical center, parking as close to the main doors as we could. After several hours and having taken a couple of turns napping, Kent tapped me on the shoulder.

"Here she comes."

We jumped out and ran to the front doors, entered, and caught up with her about halfway across the lobby.

"Susan, my name is Trench, and Larry asked me to have a little visit with you."

"Oh, you mean Larry the, oh my, the loan, ah, guy."

"It's OK, you can say shark. You are late in paying your loan back, and that never makes Larry happy. Thus this visit. I'm afraid we'll need to know a bit more about the loan, how much money is left, what you are going to do with it, but most importantly when you plan on paying it back. I don't like to threaten women, but a loan is a loan, and if you don't make and keep arrangements to pay it back soon, some other guys nowhere near as nice as me are going to make you wish you had."

Kent was right about women—explain she did.

"I know I'm late, but it's not all my fault—the clinic is running behind."

# No Paperwork Needed...

With that she poured out the entire story.

"I found out my husband was cheating on me. Not just once, mind you, but every chance he got. He was with complete strangers, neighbors, even a women I thought was a good friend. But there was this one woman he seemed to prefer. It was obvious to me what he saw in her, and I'm going to fix that. So I decided to punish him. It took a while running around to various bars, but I found a man who said he could fix it so my husband would be bedridden and thus not able to leave the house for a while. He wanted six thousand dollars."

"You borrowed twenty-five thousand. What's the other nineteen for?"

"Oh, that's why I'm late and here at the medical clinic. It's what I'm going to fix. You see, the woman he was spending the most time with has large breasts, is stacked, as I believe you men like to say. If I'm going to punish him and see to it that he's home for some time, I also want to say I'm sorry and give him what he must like. That's why I'm here—I'm getting breast augmentation surgery. My left one was always a bit smaller than the right, so I'm going to get them enlarged, plus equaled in size. The clinic has finished all the preliminary work, and my operation is scheduled for later this afternoon. My husband is scheduled for his punishment this evening. We should both get home from our individual hospitals at about the same time. The surgery is nineteen thousand— isn't that simply dreadful?"

I'm going to admit it right up front—I tend to look at things a bit differently than most folks. The thing that hit me first about all this was the price of the surgery. Nineteen thousand. That made no sense. She has two tits, an even number. So why nineteen thousand? Shouldn't it be

# No Paperwork Needed...

eighteen thousand, or maybe twenty thousand? The odd number just doesn't seem right to me. Why would one tit be more than the other? Maybe it was because they were different sizes. That perhaps does make sense. No matter, I felt I had an explanation, and this put my mind a bit more at ease.

"Now wait a minute. You're telling me you're pissed enough that you're going to basically have him crippled, and yet, to say you are sorry and to make him happy, you're going to have your tits stuffed."

"Well, it only seems fair."

"OK. OK. I'm going to tell Larry you're in the hospital, but unless you want basically the same treatment you've arranged for your husband, the minute you can stand upright without your new tits falling off, you better show yourself at Larry's and get something worked out. By the way, how are you going to get the money to repay, if I may ask?"

"Easy. Through insurance. I'm going to burn my husband's new Jaguar to the ground. He's not going to need it."

I was starting to see things from the husband's viewpoint. I think I would want to spend some time away from Susan myself.

It's indeed true—almost every crime or real bad decision revolves around the bed, the buck, or the bottle.

\* \* \*

# No Paperwork Needed...

Several days drifted by with no word whatsoever from the small army of guys who were watching out for the yellow Porsche.

I was at the apartment wondering what to try next. Something had to break soon. That turned out to an understatement. The phone rang.

"Hello."

"Trench, this is Larry. Can you meet me at St. John's Hospital? Kent's been shot."

"What?"

"Sorry, I don't know much more than that—just meet me there."

I arrived at the hospital as fast as my old car would get me there. I did need a new car. Larry was in the lobby.

"He's just out of surgery. The doc says he should be coming around in short order, and we can visit him in the recovery room."

"What happened? Where? When?" All I knew was the *who*.

"One of the sniffers phoned me and said he had found a yellow Porsche parked at that Mexican restaurant all the way out on Links Road. I passed this on to Kent. I guess he tried to call you, but you didn't answer, so he drove out alone, thinking if it was the right car, he could at least stick a tracking bug under a fender."

OK, here's another of my quirks. I detest all this modern electronic tracking, monitoring, and surveillance crap. Did

# No Paperwork Needed...

Broderick Crawford have a GPS tracker in Highway Patrol? No. And he always caught his man. Did Marshall Dillon have a two-way radio on his horse? He did not, and yet, he too always got his man. Did Superman have— never mind, bad example. I hated the damned highway patrol officers who sat behind a giant billboard eating doughnuts waiting for a little black box to tell them someone was traveling eighty-five in a sixty-five mph zone. It was simply not fair. Not to mention, time and time again it's been shown that speeding tickets are a matter of revenue, not safety.

"Did he find the car?"

"I don't know anything else; we'll just have to wait to talk to Kent."

It was a couple of hours later that Kent came around. One bullet had lodged in his right upper leg, and a second had pierced his left shoulder. In and out with little actual damage. This guy had been very, very lucky, according to the doctor. That is, of course, if you set aside the fact of his being shot in the first place.

"Kent, do you feel well enough to talk a bit?" Larry asked. "Trench is here too. The doc says you're going to be just fine."

"I don't feel anything," Kent said. "Must have me on some good stuff."

"Kent, it's Trench. Was it Gerald?"

"Yes, he caught me in the process of putting a bug under his front fender. He yelled and I slowly stood up and turned around. He was holding the gun on me. He bent

# No Paperwork Needed...

down and removed the bug from the front fender, stood back up, and without a word, put two slugs in me."

"The doc says 'through you,' but that's a detail. Don't worry. We'll find the bastard if it takes forever."

"It shouldn't take long at all. The bug under the front fender was just for backup. I had already finished putting one under the rear bumper long before he showed up."

With that, Kent sort of smiled and drifted back off.

# No Paperwork Needed...

## Chapter Four

Upon leaving the hospital, it was back to the office to pick up one of the GPS transponder receiving units. It was pretty simple. The unit Kent attached under the bumper of Gerald's Porsche constantly determined the location of the car on the planet earth to within a couple of feet. This data was then transmitted on a specific frequency that changed constantly, based upon an entered code. The unit I was going to carry would change receiving frequencies lockstep with the transmission frequencies. My unit would take the received location data and feed a navigation unit that would tell me step by step, turn by turn, how to drive directly to the Porsche. It was a no-brainer. It was also completely unfair, in my mind.

"Continue straight for one and a quarter miles," my navigator said. A bit later I heard "turn left in three hundred feet on West Lincoln."

On and on it went, until I heard, "Your destination," meaning the yellow Porsche, "is on the left."

Sure enough, there it was. I took note of the location so we could set up a watch detail. The fellows who would be called in this time were the enforcers. Gerald had crossed a line when he shot Kent. Larry had to remind Don and Jack of his no-killing inviolate rule.

And watch they did, for three full days. Gerald never showed, and the car never moved. We watched for another two days and then tossed in the towel. Gerald had either figured out the car had been tagged prior to the tag he saw Kent put in place, or simply decided that the car was just too hot. After all, he must have known that the owning dealership had reported it as stolen by now.

# No Paperwork Needed...

Our hope had been to catch Gerald with the car, but he had obviously abandoned the vehicle. We would soon contact the dealership and tell them we had just found the car and give them the address where it could be located. But first a couple guys from the office would search the car high and low for anything that could possibly give us a few more tips on finding Gerald. They were good at this, and little escaped their notice.

When the guys were done—this had taken several hours—we called the dealership.

We were back to step one; we didn't have the car to follow, and we didn't have Gerald. I was anxious to hear what may have been found in the car.

"Trench, the car was clean," said Phil. He was one of two guys Larry used for this kind of work, and he had combed the car. "We didn't find so much as a scrap of paper—nothing."

"Well, there goes that," I said.

"We did, however, find a valet parking stub."

"I thought you just said you didn't find as much as a scrap of paper."

"Yeah, I guess it would be more accurate to say we found an imprint from a valet parking stub. As you know, it's been pretty humid lately, and the driver must have dropped a valet stub down between the seats at some point. It was pressed up against the side of the passenger seat, and with the moisture in the air, it left an imprint of the ink on the skirt of the seat. He cleaned out the car well enough to find and remove the stub, but the ink imprint was still there. Very faint, but if you read it in a mirror, you could see that the stub was for the Pheasant Rise Country Club—the date puts it at seven days ago."

"Thanks. I don't know how you guys do it, but thanks."

So, we were back to one hint. It was time to visit the Pheasant Rise Country Club.

I drove south of the city and then east toward the prairie. Several miles out a sign for the Pheasant Rise Country Club pointed south again. Just a mile or so later, I crested a small hill, and below me spread out this stunning valley. And in the middle was the club.

As I got closer, I could see that everything I had ever heard about the place was an understatement; the grounds and buildings were spectacular. There was little doubt—here was a playground for the very well-to-do.

As I looked around, one of my first concerns was where I was going to park the car. It just didn't fit in with the array of exotic and expensive cars already here. For a moment I considered driving around the main lodge and parking in back by the trash Dumpsters. Anyone who frequented this place would have dismissed it, as if someone else had simply thrown the car away.

But around back of the building would have meant a half-hour walk to get back to the front. Finally, I just thought *to hell with it,* and parked close to the main doors.

On the way in, I was stopped by a young man who ran up to tell me I couldn't park my car where I had left it. He offered to park my car for me.

"Do you offer to park all cars?" I asked.

# No Paperwork Needed...

"Yes, it's part of the club's services. Free valet parking. Almost everyone uses it."

"Have you ever parked a yellow Porsche?"

"Several of them. One is a beautiful Turbo S convertible."

"That would be the one I'm interested in. Do you know the guy?"

"Just from parking his car now and then. A real jerk; he never offers a tip."

"Does he come here often? How many times do you think you've seen the yellow Porsche?"

"I've only seen the Porsche a few times. But he's here pretty often. He keeps showing up in different cars—always exotic, expensive cars."

"Thanks. As for my car, please leave it right where it is. I'm here on police business," I lied.

With that I walked in. The lobby was enormous. I headed for this circular bar complex whose center was a repeating array of small waterfalls and fireplaces. Stunning.

The barman walked over and asked me what I was having.

"A classic highball and a few answers."

He gave me a cautious look and asked, "A few answers about what?"

"First the drink, and then I ask the questions."

# No Paperwork Needed...

He returned with the drink, and I handed him a fifty and told him to keep the change.

The look changed from cautious to "happy to help."

"The kid out front tells me he's parked a yellow Porsche for a well-dressed guy a few times. Any idea who the owner might be?"

"I have no idea who the owner is, but the driver is a Mr. Gerald Rickson."

"Do you have any idea where he lives? What he does for a living? Anything you know about him would help."

"Who did you say you were again?"

"I didn't. But I could use another fifty-dollar highball."

"Oh, sure."

He returned with the drink and the "happy to help" look once again.

"I've no idea what he does for a living. I would guess nothing; he seems to be absolutely loaded. I've never seen him in the same suit twice, and they all look like tailor-made perfectly fitted suits.

"As for where he lives, you're asking the wrong person. Try talking to Kim; she's the club's exercise coach. Everyone knows she's left here with Gerald a few times—his house or hers, I don't know. Sorry, don't know much else."

"Where do I find Kim?"

# No Paperwork Needed...

"Go up to the third floor and take the glass skywalk to the west. It's marked as the workout area. I think she's on duty now."

Following the instructions, I soon arrived outside the door of the workout area and stepped in. Three middle-aged guys were working on various machines, one and all looking absolutely miserable doing so. A shapely young lady had her back to me and was talking with one of the guys.

"Kim?" I said.

"Yes," she said as she turned around.

She wasn't wearing the short yellow sundress, but everything else, and I do mean everything else, was there. The ultra-black raven hair, the deepest green eyes—it was indeed the girl who was with Gerald that first night at the Ramrod Bar. It's always a bit frustrating when little things come back to haunt you. I now felt a bit embarrassed at the pinching-the-ass episode.

"You!" she said.

So much for her possibly not recognizing me.

"Yes. First, let me apologize for last time. Second, I would like to ask a few questions. Before you say, 'no', you need to know your friend Gerald has been a bad boy, including shooting my partner twice."

The look on Kim's face went from furious to deep concern. "He shot someone?"

"Yes, my partner. Twice."

# No Paperwork Needed...

"Come into my office."

"When was the last time you saw Gerald?"

"It's been a bit over a week. We, uh, aren't seeing each other anymore."

"Why?"

"He got a bit rough with me a couple of times. I felt things were heading down a path I wasn't going to have anything to do with."

"Good for you. Do you know where he lives? Or any idea what he does? He owes my boss a large amount of money, and we've been the better part of three weeks trying to make contact with him. And now there's the shooting."

"Yes, I know. Some seven hundred thousand dollars."

"Do you know what he's doing with the money?"

"I have no idea. The only reason I know the amount is  he told me time and time again that he only needed a little bit more—again, I have no idea what for."

"OK, how about where he lives?"

"Again, no. He's never talked about or taken me to any house or apartment. From his conversations, I was left with the feeling that he was never in the same place for more than a couple of days."

"Do you know when he may show up here next?"

# No Paperwork Needed...

"Well, he doesn't come by as often since I called it quits. But he has been by a couple of times, so I would guess he might show up again."

"The bartender downstairs is going to phone me if he does. Would you be willing to do the same?"

"He shot your friend?"

"Yes."

"Sure. I'll call you if I see him again."

All I could do was start waiting again.

# No Paperwork Needed...

**Chapter Five**

Arriving at my apartment, I played a phone message from Larry. He wanted me to stop by and pick up the info on a new client.

"Hi, Larry. What's up?"

"I have a potential new loan—a large one. A Mrs. Ester Perkins. If you can believe this, she's a nuclear physicist, of all things."

"No disrespect, but what the hell is a nuclear physicist doing with a place like this?"

"The same as everyone else, she wants some money. It seems she's close to publishing a paper on some research, but needs funds to purchase an expensive piece of equipment for some final data collection. She is told that she will be funded by the NSF—that's National Science Foundation to a knucklehead like you—for the equipment, but not in time to allow her to get the data and publish the paper. Apparently she's worried that someone else will publish first, and I guess this is potential Nobel Prize quality stuff."

"Why would she not just go to a bank? After all, she's a nuclear physicist, not a nightclub hostess."

"I asked that. She said she tried, but the banks, as always, want absolute proof that you don't need the money before they'll lend you the money. They wanted verification from the NSF that they are indeed going to fund the project, and the NSF folks tell her that will take as much time to do this as to actually advance the funds."

"Have you given her the money?"

# No Paperwork Needed...

"Not yet. I hate to admit it, but I'm nervous about this. This lady is sharp. I mean, really sharp. I want to know that everything is on the level. I'm not sure Mrs. Perkins couldn't take me down the garden path and I would never know."

"All right, I'll visit her, but this time you're going to have to let me know where I can find her. She hasn't borrowed the money yet, so I see no reason not to contact her most anyplace."

He gave me all the information he had, and I told him I would get ahold of her later in the day.

"Imagine, me, helping out the NSF," Larry said.

*If he wants to think of it that way, so be it*, I thought.

"Anything else you want me to look into?"

"Yeah," Larry said. "You remember the fellow a few weeks ago that we had such a good time joking about his name?"

"You must mean Karch Mulroney. What about him?"

"I gave him three weeks on his loan—three weeks are gone."

"I'll need a few hints. Remember, I don't have access to Kent. How is Kent, by the way? I've not been able to get over to the hospital for a couple of days. I hope to go this afternoon."

"He's doing just fine. Should be out in another day or two. Ready for work a couple of days after that. You know I don't like doing this, but his address is 2202 Lamont, and he works at Sparkie's Electrical Shop."

It sounded like an interesting day: first the hospital, then the physicist, then the electric shop.

\* \* \*

"Hi, Trench." Kent greeted me as I stepped into the hospital room. "How are you?"

"More to the point," I said, "How are you?"

"Doc says I should get out no later than tomorrow, maybe even later this afternoon. They probably want to be rid of me."

"Larry says you should be moving around again in a few more days. Hope so. I sure miss having you around, even if you are of absolutely no help."

"Funny. You know that without me, you would be lost."

For all my complaining, he was right. Kent had saved my butt way more times than he had slipped up, but I would never admit that to him.

"Hey, did you notice the paper yesterday?" Kent asked. "Seems as if someone's new Jaguar burnt to the ground. I guess Susan followed through."

"You know, Kent, that lady was a bit scary."

"What do you have on tap for today?" Kent asked.

# No Paperwork Needed...

"Well, I have to talk to a nuclear physicist about a loan she wants and then visit our old buddy Karch Mulroney at his workplace."

"Man, oh man. That's going from one end of the spectrum to the other. A physicist on one end and Karch on the other. What was the great idea Karch wanted the money for? Never mind, I remember. He had invented a microprocessor-controlled fishing reel. It would monitor the number, pattern, and frequency of tugs on the fishing line or something like that and make the decision of when to set the hook and quickly reel it in. What a dope. When you ask him about the loan, ask him if he found someone stupid enough to buy his idea."

"Will do. You get some rest now and give me a call when they spring you. I'll pick you up. OK, I'm off to speak to our lady physicist."

I called Dr. Perkins—Ester—and asked if it would be OK to drop by and ask a few more questions about the loan she wanted from Larry. She said right now would be just fine; she was in a hurry for the loan.

It took a while to find her office. Everywhere you turned, the view was like a section of the NASA launch control center. How could anyone possibly know what all this equipment was for?

Finally. "Dr. Perkins?"

"Yes. Hello, come on in."

"Hi. As I mentioned on the phone, my name is Trench. I'm a partner, more or less, of Larry's."

"Yes."

# No Paperwork Needed...

"Well, he's a bit nervous about this potential loan and wanted me to get a bit more information."

"He has nothing to be nervous about, but go ahead. What can I tell you?"

"Surely you understand this is a bit abnormal. I can assure you we have never before been asked to essentially be a front man for the NSF. That stands for the National Science Foundation, but I bet you knew that."

"Yes, I knew that. It's very simple. There is a Dr. Kenneth Macintyre who is hot on my heels in my area of research. No matter what I discover or resolve, it seems as if he is only a day or two behind. I've grown to suspect that someone here is passing information to him."

"I didn't know you professor intellectual types went for that kind of stuff."

"Don't kid yourself. Academic integrity is one of the great all-time contradictions of terms. At any rate, I'm just a few days of data collection away from being able to publish, and to do that, I need a specific piece of equipment. My old data collection system completely failed. Thus the money. The NSF is indeed giving me a grant to purchase the equipment, but by the time that happens, I'm afraid Macintyre will publish first, using all my work. Damn it, I'm simply not going to let that happen. I assure you that your Mr. Larry will get paid; a person in my position cannot open herself up to the scandal that would occur if I didn't. I don't mean to sound like a prima donna, but this publishing could indeed have Pulitzer Prize implications, not just for me, but for several people."

After a few moments, she asked, "Why is he so worried?"

# No Paperwork Needed...

"He wouldn't like my confiding this, but he's concerned that you're sharp enough to pull a quick one, and he would never know until it was too late."

She laughed. "Well, tell him thanks, but no, nothing funny is going on. I just want to protect some twelve years of work."

"Fine. I'll drop by the office and tell him the loan is OK by me. If he agrees, he'll call you and let you know that you can pick up the money, all two hundred and forty-five thousands of it, in an hour or so. But let me give you a tip. If you can't pay back the amount on the terms and timeline you agree to, you better be Johnny-on-the-spot with a good reason. Our collections department works a bit differently than the local banks."

I let Larry know I thought the physicist was OK in my book and then headed for Sparkie's Electrical Shop.

I did my best not to grin when I asked for Mr. Karch Mulroney. I had no idea why I found that name so funny. My problem, I guess.

Karch walked out, and to my surprise greeted me with a great big hello.

"I meant to get over to you guys yesterday but got a bit behind in work. I was going to stop by later today."

I had heard this over the years so many times that it no longer registered with me.

"Sure," I said. "Were you coming by to pay up, ask for more time, or simply visit?"

# No Paperwork Needed...

"Well, not to pay up, but to let you know that I'll definitely be able to pay up soon, along with any interest that may be due."

"And just how will you be able to pay up?" I asked.

"I sold my fishing reel design to a small Japanese firm for 3.4million dollars. The contracts and an advance are being sent to me overnight. As you can imagine, I'm really happy."

He was happy? I couldn't wait to shove this little tidbit in Kent's face after all his comments.

"OK," I said, "If you're on the level, just wait until tomorrow and bring over a bunch of money and details on the 'whens' about paying the rest."

I walked out thinking about $3.4 million for a microprocessor-controlled fishing reel. What in the hell was this world coming to? What was next, a computer-controlled paintbrush?

All in all, it was a great day. The lady physicist had made a believer out of me, Kent was doing well, and Karch was tickled pink.

Everything had gone so well that I had almost forgotten about Gerald. Almost.

Absolutely nothing happened for a couple of days. It took Kent one day longer to get released than he thought, and I picked him up from the hospital as promised.

"Hi," he said.

"Three point four million," I said.

# No Paperwork Needed...

"Three point four million what?"

"Dollars. That's how much that dope Karch was paid by a bunch of stupid industrialists for his newfangled fishing reel. Remember, you asked me to tell you."

He sat back in the seat and didn't say another word until I got him home.

Again, another couple of days went by free of any action. And then the office received a tip on Gerald.

Unbeknownst to me, both Kim and the bartender at the Pheasant Rise Country Club had tried to call me with the information that Gerald had returned to the club. Failing to connect, they both had called the second number on the list. This was the number for Jack, the head enforcer. Jack gathered up Don, his right-hand man. These were two fellows you simply didn't want to mess with. And they were on their way to visit Gerald.

The enforcers had been told to bring Gerald in, no ifs, ands, or buts. Do as you will, but make sure he could still talk.

What the enforcers didn't know was that Gerald wasn't at the club alone. More importantly, they didn't know they were walking into a trap.

When Jack and Don showed up, Gerald and company were ready. The long and short of it was that Gerald, his pals, and the two enforcers who went to the club simply disappeared. No fighting, no guns, no rough stuff at all. Everyone disappeared, along with the enforcer's car and whatever car or cars Gerald's group had used.

# No Paperwork Needed...

Jack had left a note for Larry before they headed out to the club; otherwise, we may never have known this all had taken place.

After a couple of hours, Larry gave me a call to see if either of the enforcers had contacted me.

"No. I didn't know any of this was taking place. Have you sent anyone else out to the club?"

"No. I thought I would drop by and pick you up and head over there."

I didn't respond for a few minutes. Larry never, and I mean never, left the office for work reasons.

"Are you sure you want to go? I think Kent is well enough to head out with me," I told Larry.

"We can stop and get Kent, but I want to go. Something is wrong."

The first person I questioned upon arriving at the club was the bartender.

"You saw Gerald and called one of the numbers on the list," I said.

"Yeah, the first number didn't answer, so I called the second one and told the fellow who answered that Gerald was at the club. About twenty minutes later, two fellows showed up and asked for Gerald. I told them he was upstairs. They went up and just a few minutes later walked back down with Gerald. They left via the main doors. That's all I know. Is something wrong?"

"Yeah, something is wrong, but I don't know what."

# No Paperwork Needed...

Larry, Kent, and myself took a small table in the corner where we could more or less be alone.

"Do you guys have any ideas?" I asked.

"This was planned," Larry said. "You know Jack and Dan; it would have taken several guys and a well-executed plan to get the best of them."

"That's for damn sure," Kent chimed in.

"This was planned," Larry repeated. "Gerald wanted the two of you to show up but got the enforcers instead. We won't know much more until we find Jack and Dan."

"That is if we find them," I said.

"What do you mean—if?" Kent asked.

"Look, we have no idea what makes this guy tick. He shot you, Kent, for Christ's sake. Suppose he not only plans on never repaying the loan, but he's also arranging things so no one is left to pester him about it?"

"You mean taking us all out? You've got to be kidding."

"Once again, Kent, he shot you. And now both Jack and Don are not to be found. He may just be working toward closing your business forever, Larry."

Larry summed up the situation with a loud "Fuck! So where are we with this?"

"We're absolutely goddamned nowhere, is where we are. Gerald is never going to show up here again. The only

# No Paperwork Needed...

thing we know is what kind of car Jack and Don drove here."

"OK," Larry said. "Put the word out for everyone to watch for it—tell them we'll take good care of anyone who leads us to the car."

With that we left for the office. Larry dropped both Kent and me at my place. I wanted to start at square one with the Gerald situation and discuss it with Kent.

**Chapter Six**

Several beers and a couple of hours later, we were exactly where we started—nowhere.

I took Kent home, stopped by one of the local greasy spoons, and grabbed a bite, then went home. Things were indeed not going well, and it was also way past time to call that witch at the Treasury. To hell with it. I would call tomorrow. Maybe.

The phone rang. "Hello."

"Trench, it's Larry."

He sounded depressed. For all of his threats and misdeeds, he truly was a concerned guy when it came to his staff.

"What can I do for you, Larry?"

"I'm going to take a bit of time off. With Kent getting shot and now Jack and Don missing, I need to get away from this for a while."

"OK, but who's going to run things—are you sure you want to do this?"

"Yes. And you are."

"Time out, Larry. I'm not ready for that, and you know it."

"You're better prepared to take over for a while than anyone else. And you damned well know that I consider you my number two man. No objections, it's you."

# No Paperwork Needed...

"I'm not sure I feel OK with this, but if you say so. How do I get ahold of you for the big decisions?"

"You don't. You don't get it, do you? All decisions, big or small, are yours. I need to get completely away."

"Somehow I feel you may change your mind a bit if I make a big loan and it goes south."

"I've had a few go south, haven't I?"

"A few."

"So, what's the difference? Do whatever you feel you need to do. I'll get back to you when I can face this again."

With that, he was gone. And I mean gone. I was soon to find out that repeated calls to his home would go unanswered. I truly was on my own for the time being.

I called Kent and asked him to come by my apartment as soon as possible.

"Kent, have you spoken with Larry since he dropped us off this morning?"

"No."

"OK. Well, he called me about an hour ago and dropped a bomb in my lap. He's going to drop out for a while and as of this moment, he wants me to take complete control. All decisions, all collections, everything."

"You're kidding. You know damn well you aren't up to that. I just can't see you telling the enforcers to casually drop by someone's place and break their legs. That's not you."

"Well, Larry thinks it is. No matter what, that's the deal. We need to make some plans, and we need to do it now."

"Fine, what's first?" Kent asked.

"Gerald. Gerald will always be first until we have the son of a bitch. The only reason we'll do anything else in the meantime is because the only thing we can do about Gerald at the moment is wait."

"Fine. Do we still have everyone we can think of looking out for the car that Jack and Don drove out to the country club?"

"Yes."

"Are we on top of everything else?" Kent asked.

"I think so. Susan, as you pointed out to me, has torched her crippled husband's car and told Larry that the insurance check should arrive in just a few days, and that she would be in and pay up. Karch, remember, the guy you called a dope, did indeed get his advance and stopped by and paid in full. He is now waiting for the balance of his 3.4 million dollars, the dope."

"All right, all right, maybe he wasn't such a dope after all," Kent said.

"Ester, our lady physicist, has ordered her equipment. She called Larry and told him she had received the first piece of grant paperwork from the NSF stating she was going to receive the money. Boy, that lady has Larry

# No Paperwork Needed...

spooked. Larry had me drive over and get copies of the paperwork—he wasn't going to just take her word for it."

"Is that everything?" Kent asked.

"Yep. Did Larry mention anything to you about any new clients in the last day or so?"

"He did. He was going to talk to two people tomorrow. I guess that's for you to do now."

"OK, I'll talk with them, but remember, we drop everything if we get a lead on Gerald."

The next morning I went to the office and waited for the first client.

An hour or so later, a nicely dressed young man came in and introduced himself as a Mr. Eric Lane. I was instantly relieved, as you could tell from his manners and dress that he wasn't one of those damned college kids.

"Hello, Mr. Lane. My name is Trench. I'm filling in for Larry. May I ask what you do?"

"I'm a college student—third year."

"Really? Well, what can I do for you?"

"I need to borrow some money, a lot of money, and I need to get it fast, or I'm going to miss out on a great opportunity."

"And what is this great opportunity?"

"I want to open a late-night men's entertainment club."

# No Paperwork Needed...

"Entertainment club?"

"Oh hell, all right, a whorehouse."

"Pardon?"

"You know, a place where a man can purchase some, ah, comfort and warmth."

"OK, so you did say whorehouse. Well, now I know why you didn't attempt to acquire the funding via the more traditional channels. Listen, kid, things work a bit differently here. If you don't repay on schedule, you don't simply receive kindly notices in the mail that start out with an apology that if your payment has already been sent, please disregard. No, here the message is hand delivered by one of our staff, who starts the discussion by breaking some part of your body. Is that clear enough?"

"Yes, but that won't be a problem. My family is rich, and I'm just a week or so away from receiving my yearly stipend check from my grandfather's side of the family. But we have found the perfect location, and I have seven girls who are all ready to go. I don't see any reason to miss out on any income."

"May I ask where and how you found your seven girls?"

"At school; they're all college girls. Real cute too."

"Why in the hell would a bunch of college girls want to get mixed up with this? How do you even get around to asking a girl if she would like to be a whore for you?"

"Oh, that's the easy part. It only takes about four or five dates. I find a real cute, well-built girl and ask her for a date. Most times they say yes. By the second date, they are enjoying a little bit of pot with me. The next time we go out, after a bit of pot, most of them are curious to try a little coke. Then in no time, it's some meth. After a short while, they're begging me for some more blow or meth or whatever else is their drug of choice. I say, sure, but you have to do some work for me."

I just sat there for a few minutes. The asshole was proud of this.

Larry only had one inviolate rule; you never based your loan decision on what the client was going to do with the money. The decision was based only on the client's ability to pay back the loan. I had only been sitting in the boss's chair for about an hour, and I was going to break his rule.

"Listen, Mr. Lane. I'm not going to lend you the money. But I am going to give you a good piece of advice. If I or anyone else in this organization catches wind of your turning one more girl on to drugs, I'm going to see to it that you involuntarily take a massive overdose. Do you understand what I'm saying?"

"Sure, but your bluster means nothing to me. You aren't the only game in town. I'll find the money."

"Get your ass out of here while you can still walk."

Sadly, I knew he was right—he would find the money.

"Kent," I screamed. "If you're out there, come on in."

A minute or so later, Kent walked in. "Yes," he said.

"Did you hear that last clown? After all the shit I've seen and heard, I still get a new one now and then. I hope the little prick's dick falls off—then he won't need his or anyone else's whorehouse. What I want to know is when the next guy is due in for a loan; you said there were two."

"Yep, two, and the second one is waiting in the outer office."

"All right, send him in."

"Will do, but it's a her."

She was a plain Jane, average eighteen to twenty-two-year-old woman. She introduced herself as Ms. Debbie Dodd.

"Hello, Debbie. You're not a college student, are you?"

"Well, yes. I'm majoring in pharmacology."

*These goddamned college students*, I thought. Why the hell couldn't I get a simple, straightforward ax murderer or something?

"OK, Debbie, what can I do for you?"

"I want to beat the rush and get a high-quality marijuana production going. As you probably know, it has already been legalized in two states, and even the US president says he has bigger fish to fry than to mess with federal marijuana laws. Besides, I know a fair bit about this with my major, and my partner is a botany major. This just all comes together too perfectly!"

"I'm left with the impression that this has been thought out fairly well. How would you pay the loan back? It seems like to me that it'll take a long time, if ever, to get sales to the point that you can honor the loan."

# No Paperwork Needed...

"We've already looked into advanced pre-production sales at significant discounts. I was able to demonstrate our proposed quality by letting distributors sample a bit of grass we grew in my uncle's basement. I know that wasn't legal, but if we wait for everything to be legal, we'll be too late."

"You must have a cool uncle."

"Kind of. We have to watch him like a hawk. He smokes the crop about as fast as we can grow it."

"OK. How much do you want? Do you understand that you aren't dealing with the local credit union here? We'll come to an agreement on the amount, the interest, and the schedule or time for repayment. Very unpleasant things can happen if you don't adhere to the schedule. Do you understand what I'm saying, I mean, really understand?"

"Yep. If I thought I had a chance in hell of getting a job when I graduated, I wouldn't be doing this. Besides, I have a ton of student loans. I'm familiar with the concept of a life-ruining loan."

She had a good point there. The federal student loan program was the penultimate loan operation in Larry's eyes. He had commented many times that the Holy Grail of efficiency was to run his loan business with as much efficiency and ruthlessness as the student loan program. Broken legs, arms, or extensive beatings simply didn't hold a candle to the lifelong pain the student loan program could inflict on an individual.

She wanted thirty thousand for lights, pumps, misters, trays, and on and on. We agreed on a payment schedule, and I told her to drop by the next day and pick up the cash.

I called Kent back in. "Is that the last client for the day?"

"Yes."

"All right, then we're done. Let's call it a day and go grab a beer."

"You don't want to do that. Just got a call—Jack and Don's car was spotted at the old rail yards."

\* \* \*

We stopped by and picked up one of the guys we use to search cars, apartments, and so forth, and then drove directly to the yards.

Parked between two small sheds, we found the car. No sign of Jack or Don.

While the car was being searched, I asked Kent to search the old roundhouse, and I entered one of the locomotive houses. Neither Don or Jack was to be found, but as in most abandoned enclosed buildings, the presence of man was abundantly obvious. The floors were littered from one end to the other with beer and whiskey bottles, uncountable cigarette butts, and many different colors of used condoms. Mankind at his best.

About five minutes later, Kent ran in. He looked as if he had had the shit scared out of him.

"Fuck, Trench, you aren't going to believe this!" And then he puked.

# No Paperwork Needed...

"What?"

"Just come with me," he said after several minutes.

We entered the roundhouse.

As my eyes adjusted to the light, I could understand Kent's state.

"Jack is over there. And over there. Both he and Don are all over the fucking place!" Kent said.

He was right. I've never seen such a goddamned mess. This wasn't a kidnapping, not even just a murder. This was a message. You had to admire Gerald's communication skills. The scene screamed, "Back off."

There was absolutely nothing we could do. We usually had the enforcers clean up various messes. But this was an incredible mess, and the enforcers were the mess!

After standing there looking like a couple of idiots for a while, we finally came to our senses well enough to walk to the car and get the hell out of there.

We drove back to the office in silence.

"What in the hell are we going to do?" I asked Kent.

"The three of them have got to be thoroughly disposed of, and fast."

"Three?"

"Jack, Don, and the car."

"How? Who the hell do we call?"

# No Paperwork Needed...

"You remember that guy Tom you squeezed for some info at the Ramrod Bar?"

"Yeah, what a temper. What about him?"

"Mack, one of the sniffers out there, told me a few days ago that Tom was looking for some high-paying work and didn't care too much what it was."

"OK. We'll have to play this one carefully, but get him in here and I'll try to feel him out."

# No Paperwork Needed...

## Chapter Seven

"Tom, do you remember me?"

"Of course I remember you. My nuts hurt for days."

"I understand you may be looking for some fast, down and dirty, high-paying work."

"If the cash is right for the job, yes."

"Do you have a record?"

"No."

"OK, thanks for coming in."

"Wait a minute. Wait a minute. No, I don't have a record, but that's only because I'm pretty fast on my feet. When I think things are getting a bit too hot, I move on. I don't know what you want, but there isn't much I haven't done."

"All right, let me get right to the point. We have two bodies and one car to hide forever. Is that in your skill set?"

"Holy shit! Are you serious? That puts me in a bit deeper than I've ever been before, but for the right money, and I mean a shit pot full of money, I think I could handle that. I turned down a job like that a month or so ago up in Wyoming; that's where I was last. There are some independent sons of bitches there. You wouldn't believe some of the things I was asked."

"Never been there. How long were you there?"

"Long enough. I'd been part of enough jobs that I felt it was time to leave. Weird place. There are more guns in the state than people. They just made this handgun the size of a small cannon the state gun. Someone told me that a few years back the rattlesnake was made the state reptile. I understand that progress is being made on making Trojans the state condom. Yeah, they're pretty independent. But no matter what, it was time to go. Winter was setting in, and it gets so cold in the high country. You would look out the window in the morning and judge the sweaters and coats you needed by counting the number of dogs stuck to your hubcaps."

"Is anyone from Wyoming, or anywhere else for that matter, looking for you?"

"No. That's enough questions. What does this job pay?"

"There are a few things you need to know. Mainly, the bodies aren't in one piece. They're spread all over an old rail yard building."

"No problem. That'll make it easier to pick them up. Again, what's it paying?"

I was beginning to think that maybe Tom was indeed the man for the job.

"Twenty grand. One half up front and the other half when I look the place over and am pleased. What do you say?"

"Give me the ten grand."

"One last thing, this has got to happen fast, very fast."

"So, stop talking and give me the ten grand. Where are they?"

# No Paperwork Needed...

"Down at the old rail yard. The car is between two smaller sheds, and the bodies, or pieces of bodies, are in the roundhouse."

"Get that second ten grand ready."

And with that, he was gone.

Come the next morning, I simply couldn't put it off any longer.

"Treasury Department, Agent Foster speaking."

"Hello, it's Trench."

"Well, well. Where the hell have you been? Look here, asshole, I'm starting to lose confidence in you, not that I had much to start with. Even you must have found out something by now."

"Listen, let me set you straight. We now have two dead, dismembered men, as well as another man who has been shot, all to Gerald's credit. If you don't get off my back, I'm going to sneak this to the Justice Department, and they are going to ream you out for keeping this at the Treasury level."

Even Mrs. Forester could see the truth in that.

"OK, OK. Do you know anything? What's your next step?"

"I don't have a next step. Until someone on my side happens to see him, he is simply gone. He will never show up at any of the spots we've connected with him in the past. I don't even know if he's still in town, although I would guess he is, simply because if he were planning on disappearing into the sunset, why the hell would he have

# No Paperwork Needed...

offed Larry's two enforcers? Nobody wants this guy as badly as we do. Hell, we even cleaned up the mess so the cops wouldn't get involved."

I immediately wondered if we had indeed cleaned up the mess. Tom hadn't yet claimed his second ten grand.

"This could take some time. I'll call you the minute I have something, but I believe Gerald has graduated from tax evasion and moved on to the Justice level."

With that I hung up. If she did pass this on to Justice, then I would no longer have any hold over her, and she would be right back to pestering the shit out of me about any taxes that might be due from our clients who came out on top of things.

It was frustrating that our only chance of seeing Gerald again was one of simple blind luck if and when one of us just happened to bump into him.

I sat at my desk wondering if there was anything I could do to help in any area, and I kept coming up with absolutely nothing.

About that time Ken yelled out that Tom had just walked in. This should be good.

"Hi, Trench," Tom shouted. "I've completed your job—you got that second ten thousand ready?"

"Yes, but remember, I need to look the scene over to see if we are safe on this."

"Let's go then. I want my ten grand."

# No Paperwork Needed...

We drove out to the rail yard. I had asked Kent to come along. The three of us entered the roundhouse with flashlights.

After walking around for about fifteen minutes, I asked Kent if things looked OK to him.

"Yeah, it looks fine. I don't see any, ah, remains or anything."

"What did you do with the bodies?" I asked Tom.

"Every piece or part I could find went into the car. The car was crushed, and then the block of sheet metal was dropped over the side toward the middle of the dam reservoir lake. Nothing will ever be found."

"What do you think?" I asked Kent.

"Sounds good to me."

We headed back to the office, and I handed Tom ten thousand dollars.

"Tom, you did well. Would you consider filling the role of an enforcer for us? At least for a while."

"Sure, if the pay is good. But you need to know that this last task, disposing of a few bodies as I just did for you, is as far as I'll ever go outside the law."

"Fine. You'll not be asked to cross that line."

I asked him to always be close to the phone.

"You may not be called for days, and other times you may be called several times a day. Just be ready."

# No Paperwork Needed...

As the next several days passed, I was getting more and more despondent about our ability to ever catch up with Gerald again.

Day after day was the same thing. No new clients, no clients currently past due on payments, and not a word about Gerald.

Then one morning I walked into the office, and before I could turn around and sit at my desk, I heard, "Hello, Trench."

It was Gerald! Of all the goddamned things. All of us had been looking high and low for the asshole, and out of nowhere, there he sat, in my office.

I sat down slowly, and casually slid open my left-hand middle desk drawer. And just as slowly withdrew the handgun from the drawer and placed it on the top of my desk, not letting go.

I personally don't think much of guns. I couldn't have told you what kind it was to save my life. I had always felt that most guys into guns subconsciously viewed them as penis extensions.

But now and then, one had to overlook one's biases . This was one of those times that my penis alone wasn't going to be of much help. And the extension just might.

"Don't move," I said. Man, right out of the movies. "I'm going to call Kent. I just know he would love to talk to you."

"Kent's not home," Gerald said.

# No Paperwork Needed...

"How do you know he's not home?"

"Do I look stupid or something? Do you think I would show up here prior to making some kind of arrangement that would guarantee I walk out safe and sound? We have Kent. Of course, I can't tell you where, but I can tell you he's fine and will be released if I return intact in a reasonable amount of time. If not, well, you got to see some of the boys' handiwork at the rail yard."

I stared at him for a few minutes. "You do know Larry is never going to give up on you, right? It's now beyond the money, although he does want that back. At this point, disappearing you is at the top of his bucket list. What the hell are you doing here anyway?"

"I need to borrow a little more money."

"Are you fucking kidding me? Did I hear you right?"

"You heard right. It looks as if my plan is going to take a bit more money, and I couldn't think of a better place to get it than right here."

"There is no way either Larry or I will be giving you any more money. You just don't get it, do you? Larry wants you dead, and the sooner the better. Larry has never asked the guys to eliminate anyone before; that puts you in selective company. No money."

"Kent is going to be sorry to hear that."

I'm too embarrassed to go into the details of the discussion, but in the end, Gerald walked out the door with yet more of our money. But I did have his word that he would explain everything in a few weeks. We both knew his word was worthless. I was also told I'd better call off all the dogs.

I had no idea when I might hear from Larry, but it wasn't too hard to imagine part of the conversation when I did.

—"Did you ever get any of our money back from the asshole Gerald? Even more important, did the enforcers punch his ticket?"

"Well, no, but I did lend him an additional two hundred and fifty thousand."—

The reply would be as far away from "Good job" as a statement can get.

I had to stop daydreaming and get back to the issue at hand. Gerald, after receiving his money, told me he would be calling with the location where I could find Kent.

"He will be in one piece," he had said.

I called Tom and asked him to get to the office right away so we could be ready to leave when we received Gerald's call.

When Tom arrived, I did my best to explain what had happened.

"Tell me again the part about giving him an additional two hundred and fifty grand?"

"I had no choice. He made it perfectly clear that if he didn't return, Kent was a dead man. Further, if he did return but didn't have the money, Kent might as well be dead."

# No Paperwork Needed...

"How do you know he isn't going to kill Kent anyway?"

"I don't. But what other choice did I have? Besides, think about this for a minute. Kent has been under close guard since Gerald arranged to have him picked up. Kent may not always be on top of things, but he doesn't miss much either. He may well have overheard some little item that could be of great value to us."

"Yeah, if we see him alive again. I'm new to you guys; maybe you do know what you're doing."

I had no idea if we knew what we were doing, but Gerald did indeed call about two hours later and told us where we could pick up Kent.

"He's tied to a section of track in the roundhouse at the rail yard. I know you know the place." With that he laughed and hung up.

We drove to the rail yard. I was terrified as to what we might find. I couldn't think of a single reason why Gerald would chose to leave Kent alive; all I could do was hope.

Kent was indeed in the roundhouse. Not a mark on him, but madder than hell. We all walked back to the car slowly without much being said. Kent was going to blow a gasket when he found out we were now two hundred and fifty grand deeper into Gerald. He was going to have to wait for a while before hearing that.

Back at the office, I asked him a few questions.

"Did you hear anything that might give us a clue as to where Gerald can be found or what he plans on doing with the one million dollars?" I asked Kent.

# No Paperwork Needed...

"What do you mean one million dollars? I thought it was seven hundred and fifty thousand plus some interest, not one million."

"Shit," I said under my breath. "It's a long story; I'll fill you in later. But back to my question, did you hear anything that might help?"

"I heard a lot of things, but none if it made any sense to me."

"What do you mean?"

"I think they were speaking Russian."

"Russian?"

"Yes. Gerald was speaking Russian as well before he left to come see you. As a matter of fact, Russian, if it was Russian, was the only thing I heard from anyone from the moment they grabbed me until they took off, leaving me there alone, tied up. It sure sounded like Russian, but no matter what it was, they all understood it very well. They were speaking very fast."

*OK*, I thought, *let's assume Russian*. Was Gerald's first language English, or was it Russian? As I replayed our few conversations in my mind's eye, it dawned on me, as crazy as it sounds, that he had absolutely no accent, none at all.

"Russian," I said. "Do you remember any of the words or sounds? Perhaps some word they were using again and again?"

"I think I remember what a few of them sounded like. One I heard several times sounded like *atomnails droysfa*. Another was *ogin kresna boombaa*."

"Do we know anyone who speaks Russian, I mean other than Gerald?"

"Not that I know of, but I could play with Babblefish."

"What the hell is a Babblefish?"

Kent sighed. "Babblefish is a translation website. You can type in a phrase in any language and then ask it to translate it into any other language. You can even ask it to pronounce, that is, speak, the translated phrase."

"Fine, give it a try. We have nothing else to try. I'm calling it a day. If this crazy idea yields anything, give me a call at home."

Early the next morning, the phone rang, having been dialed by a breathless Kent.

"I got it. Damn it, I got it. And you aren't going to believe it! I gave up trying to type in the Russian phrases that sounded like what I heard, mainly because I've no idea how you would spell what I heard, or thought what I had heard, in Russian. So, I started typing in English phrases and asked for them to be translated into Russian and then pressed the Speak button to see what it sounded like. I tried things that would seem to go with a nice guy like Gerald. Things like guns, drugs, killing, stealing, murder, torture, terrorism, extortion, and on and on. Early this morning I started again, and after a while I typed in 'bomb'. When translated it was a weird word that sounded just like *boombaa*! After that, it went pretty fast. My *atomnails droysfa* is Russian for 'atomic device,' and my *ogin kresna boombaa* means 'very dirty bomb.' What do you think of that?"

I sat in stunned silence. After several minutes I told Kent to get over to my place as fast as possible. No matter what, this was now so completely out of our hands. The big boys absolutely had to be brought in.

When Kent arrived, we went over and over our every interaction with Gerald from the beginning. It all ended at the same point. This had to be bumped up to Justice, the FBI, CIA, whatever. We could kiss our one million dollars good-bye and most likely our freedom as well, as I was sure our part in this, when revealed, would put us in some federal prison for some time. This wasn't the movies where you can destroy a few buildings, kill six people, and then simply walk off into the sunset because one of the guys you killed was number one on the FBI list. It just didn't work like that in the real world.

My first call had to be to Mrs. Forester, the sweetheart of the Treasury.

"Treasury, Agent Forester speaking."

"It's Trench."

"Swell. What do you have for me?"

"Nothing for you, but I want to know how to pass the Gerald mess on up the ladder. It is now way beyond Treasury. It is CIA, Homeland Security, or whatever, and—"

She cut me off with, "Aren't you being a bit melodramatic? I'm not letting this go until we know the potential tax ramifications of all the money."

# No Paperwork Needed...

"Listen. Will you just shut up and listen? And don't, I repeat, don't, cut me off again. I want to know how we can move this up and yet not get hung out to dry because of our part in this. Surely you must remember that loan sharking is illegal, and now we have a shooting and two violent murders mixed up in the deal as well. The good guys are simply not going to just overlook this."

"Why so excited? The murders had already taken place the last time we spoke, and it seemed as if you still wanted to try to get your money back without exposing the entire mess."

"Because as of the last time we talked, the bad guys hadn't yet used phrases or words like 'atomic device' and 'dirty bomb.' I think Gerald is some pissed-off natural Russian and has decided to take out some major U.S. aggression on his own. I think the money he got from Larry, and now me, is part of the funds he is going to use to purchase a small nuclear device."

You could hear the gears turning.

"OK. You're right; it's time to let this go. The best I can do is pass most of this on up the line with the explanation that the only reason I know about it is that you called in blind and ended up getting me when you were asking about whom you should contact with this. If and when it comes back to me, I'll do my best to convince them you knew of the risks of contacting the proper authorities, but felt it was the only thing to do. If they buy it, they may cut you a bit of slack. If you ever tell them I knew anything about this beforehand, well, I'll see to it that you get buried so deep, you'll never see sunshine again. Fair enough?"

# No Paperwork Needed...

"Fair enough," I said. "So what should I do?"

"Nothing. Trust me; you'll be contacted by someone very soon."

She hung up, and that was that. Perhaps given a day or two to calm down, I could get back to the good old normal loan business. A few cut-off hands and a broken leg now and then would be a walk in the park compared to the Gerald business.

# No Paperwork Needed...

**Chapter Eight**

It was a beautiful afternoon, and Jeffery Holmes was enjoying it to the fullest as he was tooling around in his magnificent 1967 sky-blue Austin Healey 3000 Mark III. With the top down, the gorgeous white interior was in full view. The car was absolute perfection and had been Jeffery's nineteenth birthday present from his father. It had cost a bit over fifty thousand, but this was nothing more than pocket change to his father. Mr. Holmes was among the city's elite in terms of power and wealth. Anything his son hinted at, his father provided. Jeffery simply didn't understand the concept of not getting something he wanted. It had never happened during his first nineteen years of life, why should it start happening now? Jeffery had everything that could be imagined in the realm of material goods. When it came to personal traits, however, the list of lacking characteristics was as large as his list of material belongings. Honesty, dedication, integrity, and compassion were a few traits on the long list of character shortcomings.

As he drove around, it came to his mind that he was currently skipping another class. He couldn't remember which class it was, but he was pretty sure he had some class at this hour. Oh well. But he had attended a class that morning, and it was during the class that he saw the thing he wanted next. He would later find out that her name was Angela Cornell.

Angela was a cute and bouncy medium-height blonde. She came from a middle-class family that was struggling with the cost of her tuition, but her family was dedicated to putting her through college. She would be the first in the family. Her world was as far away as could be imagined from Jeffery's.

# No Paperwork Needed...

Without her knowing it, Jeffery had decided to bring Angela into his world, at least for a couple of nights.

He made a mental note to be sure to attend the morning class the next time it met and to be early enough to worm his way into a seat next to hers. The next morning, as with all things, he got his way and spent the class sitting by her, looking her over from top to bottom, time and time again. This was prime stuff. At the end of class, as she started to rise, he tapped her on the shoulder, said his name was Jeffery, and, as if it were his prerogative to do so, asked her if she wanted to go with him to the movies on Friday night. He hadn't yet bothered to ask her name. He wasn't sure how to respond when she politely said 'no', and turned and walked away.

No. No? What the hell did she mean, no?

It was time to talk to Tony. Jeffery and Tony were destined to be best of friends. Ask anyone who would be the most worthless young man around, and right after Jeffery, Tony Clark would instantly come to mind. These were two peas in a small pod. Tony's father was also one of the very well-to-do—not on the same level as Mr. Homes, but indeed in a financial position to get his way in any issue presented to him. Tony, like Jeffery, had never experienced no.

Jeffery and Tony were second-year students at the local campus of the state university. Jeffery's father had the power, influence, and money to obtain enrollment for his son at any school in the country, but Jeffery had said no to leaving town. Why would he want to leave the utopia he experienced right at home? It was only because of a fair bit of intervention and pledges offered by his father that Jeffery was allowed to be a second-year student. Any

# No Paperwork Needed...

other student performing as Jeffery had during his first year would have been long gone.

The more he thought about the rejection, the madder he got. Nobody had ever told him no, at least about anything he had wanted. Who the hell did she think she was telling him no? After she left the classroom, he asked around and found out her name. Angela was going to learn that she, like everyone else, didn't tell him no.

He headed for Tony's, and by the time he arrived he was just about as mad thinking about this as when she had rejected him earlier that morning. He was going to teach her a little respect, and he knew he could count on Tony to help.

Tony was downstairs in the home theater room playing Gears of War. It had been a good morning for him, as he had enjoyed butchering more than fifty opposing troops in the time it took to drink one beer.

"Hi, Jeff, what's up?"

"Not much. I wasn't sure you would be home. Don't you have a class about this time of day?"

"Yeah, I think so, but man, I'm so hot with the game today that I just couldn't quit."

"I need your help. I asked a girl this morning if she would go out with me Friday night, and she said no."

"You're shitting me, dude. She told you 'no'?"

"Yeah. But that's not going to be the end of it. I need to figure out a way to get her alone and set her straight."

# No Paperwork Needed...

"Who was it?"

"You don't know her, but her name is Angela Cornell. She's in my morning English class. I haven't been to the class for weeks, and I don't remember seeing her before yesterday when I saw her for the first time and then again today, but she is one hot chick."

"Sure, I'll help. We can both ask around and find out more about her. Where she lives, what other classes she's taking, any clubs she belongs to, and things like that. It shouldn't take long to find a time and place where you can get her alone."

And it didn't. A few days later, Jeffery and Tony were waiting outside the athletic center's pool doors. It was early evening, but all the light had left the sky. At around eight-thirty, Angela came through the door.

The plan was to grab her and rush her to the small but plush camping van his dad used now and then to go fishing. They would drive out to the country and explain to Angela that one simply didn't say no to Mr. Jeffery Holmes. They wouldn't hurt her, but they were indeed going to scare the shit out of her.

"Hi, Angela," Jeffery said.

"Hello."

"I would like to talk to you. I've got my car right over here. Maybe we could go get a Coke or something?"

"No, I'm sorry, but I can't go."

Fuck! She had told him no again! Jeffery looked around, and seeing no one else, he grabbed Angela's arm and yelled for Tony. Tony ran to them and grabbed her other arm.

"Quick, let's take her to the van," Jeffery yelled.

Angela's screams and Jeffery's yelling went unheard, masked by the exuberant cheering taking place for the swim meet inside. A few minutes later, all three were in the van, and Jeffery was heading west out to the old water treatment plant, a dark and abandoned structure.

What was to be nothing but a scare ended up as a multiple rape and a brutal beating. Angela would never be the cute young lady she was again. Just before the final blows that rendered her unconscious, Jeffery yelled into her ear that if she ever mentioned a word of this to the police, he and Tony wouldn't only kill her but would also kill her parents. He opened the van's side door and kicked her so violently in the side that she rolled out of the van onto the ground. He looked down at her naked and bleeding body and grinned.

"I bet you'll never tell me no again," he said as he moved to the driver's seat. Jeffery and Tony gave each other high fives as they drove off, leaving Angela in the dark. Jeffery knew nothing would ever come of this. His dad wouldn't let it. Besides, how many times had his father mentioned that "boys will be boys?"

# No Paperwork Needed...

## Chapter Nine

A few days later, I had indeed more or less forgotten about Gerald and the first seven hundred thousand dollars. The last two hundred and fifty thousand I gave to Gerald might be a bit more problematic to explain to Larry when he surfaced. But all in all, I was in a good mood and looked forward to a new client. I didn't have to wait too long.

She was a slightly overweight, middle-aged woman, and while still pretty, must have been a knockout when a bit younger. She introduced herself thusly...

"Eat this."

"Pardon?"

"Eat this. At least take a couple of bites. I bet you like it."

Her eyes were wide with anticipation and excitement.

"You aren't trying to poison me, are you?"

"Of course not, silly. Please try it."

*What the hell*, I thought, *how bad can it be?*

I took a small bite and then a much larger bite. The pastry was about as far away from bad as it could get. It was hard to describe. At once it was sweet, creamy, fruity, flaky, aromatic—in short, fantastic.

"That was better than sex!"

# No Paperwork Needed...

She winked and said, "Perhaps someday we can test that out, but in the meantime, I need money so I can open a bakery for my pastry. My name is Jean Reynolds."

When were the women of the world going to learn that they can't get everything they want by simply insinuating that they would be willing to share their favors in exchange? It may work on some men, but not me.

"How much money do you need? We have a lot."

She laughed.

"Seriously," I asked, "why don't you get the money from normal sources? We can be a bit unpleasant to deal with if things don't go as planned."

"Because all I have to my name is the recipe for the pastry you just tasted. The banks won't even talk to me."

"Then I have to ask you how you think you're going to pay us back plus the interest?"

"The same way half of the small businesses in the country get funded. Once I start making money, all of my greedy relatives will come out of the woodwork and offer to buy in for an outlandish share of the profits."

Here was a lady who knew how the world worked. I cannot remember the last time I felt so confident with a loan. We worked out the amount and the repayment details. I told her she could drop by tomorrow and pick up the money. I mentioned I only had one more request.

"When you pick up the money, can you bring a couple more of those pastries?"

# No Paperwork Needed...

She smiled and left.

The remainder of the day was without incident.

The following morning I was contacted by a new client. I told him to come on over and we could talk.

About an hour later, this guy right out of a 1940s western movie walked in the door.

"Name's Cody Rider."

Looking at his hat, bandanna, tight jeans, snap-button shirt, leather belt with the four- by-six-inch buckle, and lastly, the pointed boots, I couldn't help but ask, "Is that your real name?"

"Yep. And it worked out real swell. I'm a rodeo cowboy. Bull rider, to be exact."

"But you are rather new to it, correct?"

"Yep, how did you know?"

"Well, the lack of a crooked arm or bent neck, and walking without a limp were some clues. What can I do for you?"

"I lost my entire rig in an accident last week on my way to Spearfish and not being able to afford it, I had no insurance. I need the money for a new pickup, trailer, and horse. Some guy at a bar on the edge of town said to contact a guy named Larry, so I called."

"If you can't afford insurance on a truck and trailer, how the hell are you going to pay us back?"

# No Paperwork Needed...

With that he handed me a small stack of papers and explained what some of them meant. This guy was well on his way points wise to both a ton of winnings and a national championship.

"Don't you guys have a sponsor for things like this?"

"Yep, I did. But the regional manager for my sponsoring company told me that all the money had just stopped after he walked into my bedroom and watched his naked wife jump out of my bed."

"Well, yes. That will do it," I said. "If I lend you the money, you're sure you're going to be able to pay it back?"

"Listen, mister. This is my last hurrah. All I know how to do is ride horses and bulls. I'll either win the national championship or die trying. Either I win the money to pay you back, or I end up in bad enough shape that there isn't much more you can do to me that will matter."

As I thought about this, a few things came to mind. First, there was the total enigma of why anyone would risk life and limb to be considered the world's best at a totally useless skill. You need a lot more than bull rider to list in the skill set section of your résumé to get a job. Second, this guy had no idea what all we could do, and indeed, some of it might matter.

"Do you think you can win enough?"

"Yep, I do. But even if I don't, I could resell the truck, trailer, and horse. Some feller will pay me a ton more than I paid just because I was the one who owned it last."

"How much do you need?

# No Paperwork Needed...

"I figure about two hundred and seventeen thousand."

"All right. Here are the terms."

He agreed and said he would sign the papers.

"What papers?" I said. "Come by tomorrow and you'll get your money."

* * *

I went home and using a jar of marinara sauce, two broken-up, leftover hamburger patties, a can of mushroom bits and pieces, and a half of a sleeve of angel hair, made myself a huge plate of spaghetti. It made me think of Jennings and his aborted trip to Milan. He just wanted to get away. Two beers later, while musing over the last weeks and days, my mind bumped into Linda. Try as I might, it wouldn't go any further. Why was I fantasying over a lady I hadn't ever met, let alone seen? Deep down I full well knew why—it was the beer, red hair, and big tits.

Moments later I was on the phone.

"Tom, tell me about Linda."

"Sure, she is one fancy lady. There isn't a guy down at the Ramrod who hasn't tried to hook up with her. If someone has succeeded, I don't know about it. She is absolutely beautiful with that long red hair. And of course, there is the matter of those tits. I'll be happy to introduce you, but don't get your hopes up. When do you want to meet her?"

"Will she be there tonight?"

# No Paperwork Needed...

"Maybe, you never know. You just have to try."

"OK. I want to try tonight."

"Fine. Meet me there at seven. I don't see you making any progress with her, but if you do, you need to be thinking about a long-term relationship."

"What long-term? I just want to meet her and see if we can share an evening or two."

"It's going to take a full evening just for each tit all by itself. Let alone getting to the promised land."

"Cute. See you at seven."

By seven enough of my liquid courage had dissipated that I was wondering if this was such a good idea. Nevertheless, I drove over to the Ramrod.

Tom was already there.

"Is she here?" I asked.

"Not that I can see. Sit down and have a drink. If she's coming, she'll be here shortly."

"No thanks on the drink. Too many drinks are why I'm here in the first place."

I ordered a cup of coffee and sat there sipping and just looking around. About fifteen minutes later, she walked in, long red hair bouncing from side to side. Tom was right; she was simply beautiful.

She walked directly over to Tom and said, "Hi, how are you tonight?"

# No Paperwork Needed...

"Great," Tom said. "Say, I would like you to meet a friend of mine, also my boss. Trench, this is Linda. Linda, this is Trench."

"Hello, Trench. Happy to meet you."

"Hi. Same here. I don't mean to stare, but that is a beautiful dress."

"Thanks. I own a small dress shop. It allows me to try out a lot of different dresses. Silly, but fun."

"I don't see why it's silly. I see a lot of guys sporting around in some extremely sharp suits. If I could even dream of affording some suits like that, I would be trying a different one every night. Have you seen the commercial on cable that pictures a football player in uniform that they slowly clean up and undress and then piece by piece place him in a magnificent shirt, tie, suit, watch, and shoes? The end result is nothing short of spellbinding. I would kill for a suit like that."

"Yes, I have. And I agree. In fact, I think clothes can make a bigger change in a man than in a woman."

"Is your dress shop close by?"

"Fairly close. That's why after I finally get the shop closed for the day, usually around six-thirty or so, I drop by here for a drink to wind down. I usually exchange a few barbs with this old grouch here," she said, pointing to Tom. "What do you do for a living?"

This is where most women I meet smile and tell me it was (*was* being past tense) nice to meet me, followed by a good night. I've never found a nice way to tell them that I collect overdue loans for a loan shark and have to arrange for some rough stuff now and then.

"Well, it's a bit difficult to explain, and if I try, then I'll never be able to do what I want to do right now."

"And what's that?"

"Would you accept an invitation to dinner sometime later this week? Not the invitation sometime later this week— the invitation now, the dinner sometime later this week. Damn, you know what I mean."

"Yes."

"Great, you'll meet me for dinner?"

"No, I meant yes that I knew what you meant. But yes again, I would be delighted to join you for dinner."

"Well, my work is done here," Tom finally chimed in. "Good night." He got up and left.

"Trench," Linda said, "I know what you do."

I'm sure my face instantly passed red and went directly to vermillion.

"How?" I stammered. "Tom agreed to introduce us, but he never said anything about having told you what I did."

"He didn't. I asked Mick a few weeks ago. I had seen you in here a few times deeply involved in conversation with Mick, so one night I asked him."

"Are you OK with what you heard or found out?"

# No Paperwork Needed...

"First, never, never underestimate a woman's ability to find out anything she wants to know about some guy. Second, according to Mick, when push comes to shove, you do take care of those who deserve it. His comment was that anything you hand out is far less than the person deserved. I'm OK with that. Besides, you just lent a pile of money to a friend of mine who wants to open a pastry bakery. She's a good lady. You did well."

I'm constantly surprised at what a small world we live in. After a bit more small talk, we agreed upon a date and time. I apologized for my car up front and told her I would pick her up the following Friday. I left. I was close to my apartment when I realized I was singing out loud to the radio, for Christ's sake.

When I entered the apartment, I had a phone message from Tom: "I just don't believe it, I just don't goddamn believe it." Then he had hung up.

I slept the night through as if I didn't have a care in the world. The next morning I was in the office a bit early. Shortly thereafter, Kent arrived and brought a small package to me.

"This was on the front desk. It has your name on it."

I opened the package and pulled out a scrap of paper on which was written, "Thank you so much for helping me get started. I hope everything is going well for you, but if not, use the contents. It will help smooth things out."

I pulled a bag of what had to be weed out of the box.

"Call me," Debbie wrote.

# No Paperwork Needed...

Later that morning I received a call from Ester, the physicist.

"Hello, Trench, it's Ester Perkins."

"Hello."

"I was just called by the department head. He tells me that the university has received the funds for my grant from the NSF. The equipment has already been paid for with the funds your, ah, organization advanced. So I need to find a way to prove to administration that I've already advanced the funds and paid for the equipment because of timeliness issues and thus the funds should now be released to me as a reimbursement. When that is completed, I'll send you the money. This should all happen in short order."

"How long is short order?" I asked.

"Short order for a university is about four weeks."

"All right, I'll keep the lid on things for that long, but if there are any delays, you must contact me immediately. By the way, did the equipment help with your data collection or whatever you were doing?"

"Yes. I'm playing with temperature, voltage, frequency, and a couple of other factors that I keep to myself, all in an attempt to control the speed of light. We need to log seven different values simultaneously in an attempt to prove a theory I developed a few years ago. Very, very exciting stuff. I'll contact you with any delays."

I was thinking that I had a difficult time programming my DVR as I told her congratulations. I expected to hear from her again soon.

# No Paperwork Needed...

The schedule for the remainder of the day was light, so I thought I would indeed give Debbie a call—thank her for the pot and see how she was doing.

"Hello, Debbie, it's Trench."

"Hi. Did you get my present?"

"Sure did, thanks."

"That's not any of the new crop. Just a bit left over from my uncle's basement, one of the few bud clusters that he hadn't already smoked. I'm glad you called, as it gives me a chance to bring you up to date. I know you guys don't care how things are going, you just want to be repaid at the time and with the amount agreed upon, but I still wanted to reassure you that everything is indeed on track. We have made a down payment on an old commercial greenhouse complex that grew various plants for wholesale distribution to nurseries. Can there be a better place to hide some pot than in plain sight? We've cleaned out every building to the point where they're spotless. We've equipped several of the greenhouses with humidity, temperature, and light-control systems. But at this time, you could search high and low and not find as much as one marijuana seed. We are completely ready for the day when it will be legal to plant and grow."

"It sure sounds as if you're on top of things. You've got to love the politicians, the hypocritical bastards."

"How's that?"

"Well, after thirty-five years of wasting time and money in an attempt to curb the dreaded threat of marijuana, all of a sudden it dawns on them, the amount of revenue they

# No Paperwork Needed...

are missing out on via taxes, and poof, all of a sudden, it's not so bad after all. A good half of them in their youth would have smoked pickled cucumbers if they thought they could get a buzz out of it. Don't mean to jump on a soapbox, but hypocrisy bugs the shit out me. So, are you telling me you think you're on track with fulfilling your loan obligations to us? I don't think I need to remind you that things can get unpleasant fast with defaults."

"No, you don't need to remind me. With our advanced discounted sales, we are already close to the needed payback amounts. Several more of our potential distributors have bought in after seeing our new facilities. Things should be just fine."

"I sure hope so. You are a fairly unique client."

"And how's that?"

"You're one of the first damned college kids I didn't want to choke to death on sight. Take care and keep track of the date."

I asked Kent to come in.

"I think we had just one more client this afternoon. Have you heard from her?"

"She's waiting out front."

"Great. Send her in. What was the name again?"

"A Mrs. Mary Ellen Winestone."

"Mary Ellen Winestone. What a gentle, melodic name. What does she want—enough money to open a poodle massage center?"

# No Paperwork Needed...

"Not quite. She wants to frame her gardener and needs some seed money. But maybe she owns a poodle."

"All right, send her in."

She was tall, thin, and dressed as if eloquence were her standard.

"Hello. My name is Trench. And you are?"

"Mary Ellen. Mary Ellen Winestone."

"Please, sit down. What may I do for you?"

"I would like to borrow about fifty thousand, but do it in such a way that absolutely no one knows."

"OK. The guy who owns this place would probably hand you the money based solely on your appearance, but I have to be a bit more careful. Can you tell me what you're going to do with the money?"

"Sure. I want to frame my gardener for theft."

"Why?"

"So he'll go to prison."

"Why do you want to send him to prison?"

"Because someone needs to send him to prison."

"Why should anyone want to send him to prison?"

"Because he deserves it."

# No Paperwork Needed...

"Hold on. We aren't getting anywhere here. Why would you, or anyone, want to send him to prison? What did he do to you to justify this?"

"Well, I found out he's been screwing Anne, the service maid."

"So? If I may ask, what's that to you?"

"For the past six years, we've been involved in a discreet affair. He had pledged his full devotion to me. As soon as we took care of John, we were going to be married."

"Who's John?"

"Why, my husband, of course."

*Of course*, I thought. *Who the hell else would an adulterous woman and her gardener want to get rid of?*

"Please don't tell me any more about you and your husband; what's your gardener's name anyway?"

"Phillip."

"OK, I don't want to hear any more about Phillip's and your disposal plans. You mentioned a maid and a gardener. Are you rich or something?"

"Yes. I'm filthy rich. Or at least my husband is. It was to be all mine when John was out of the picture. By the way, that's how I'll pay you back. I'll be happy to pay you fourfold if you'll help me with this."

"Can you put this all together for me? Let's pretend for a second I've just handed you fifty thousand dollars. Step by step, what are you going to do?"

# No Paperwork Needed...

"First, I'm going to continue sharing my bed with Phillip so he thinks all is well. Then I'm going to plant the fifty thousand in Phillip's quarters in the servant's quarters out back and then call the police and report I've been robbed. I'll suggest that to eliminate any doubts that any of my staff are involved, all quarters should be searched, as well as all my rooms. The staff will instantly agree because they know they're innocent. Soon, the money will be found in Phillip's room, and that will be the start of his journey to prison. You can see why I can't ask my husband for the money; I just know he would ask what it was for. After the money is returned to me, I'll use it to arrange for my husband's disappearance. His holdings will then transfer to me, and I'll then pay you some two hundred thousand. You didn't think my losing Phillip was going to derail my plans for John, did you?"

"You realize you just laid out plans to arrange to have one man falsely imprisoned and another murdered?"

"So?"

Well, there isn't much one can say to that response. "Bring me something that shows in spades that your hubby is crawling with money, and we'll go from there."

Without a word she rose and walked out. This was one cold lady. I had to force myself to look at this as a businessman. Mary was going to do hubby in independently of my involvement. Knowing all about it, she was going to have him disappear, as she put it. She would do exactly the same if I knew nothing about it. And I sure as hell wasn't going to get involved in trying to stop it. None of it would be my doing. My end of it was to loan her fifty thousand and to receive two hundred thousand.

# No Paperwork Needed...

Who would question that as anything but a good business deal?

I checked the calendar for the hundredth time—damn, it was still only Wednesday. Would Friday never come?

# No Paperwork Needed...

## Chapter Ten

Doug Winters pressed the cappuccino button on his DeLonghi Gran Dama 6700 Espresso Machine after using the built-in cup-warming feature. He loved his excellent coffee in the mornings. Always two cups. He remained fascinated by the machine, watching and listening to it instantly heat the water, grind the beans for the type of coffee he had selected, listening to it press the fresh ground beans into a small puck, and then force the steam through the puck. The aroma was so intense and perfect. It was, of course, a very expense machine, but he gave it no thought; he certainly could afford this pleasure. In this he was mistaken, as he was to find out before he had finished his second cup.

He answered the phone. "Doug Winters speaking."

"Hello, Mr. Winters, this is Randall Evers calling from the Ridge Line Bank and Trust. How are you this morning?"

"Fine. May I ask the reason for your call?"

"Of course. I regret to inform you that we have received a tendered check of yours that we'll not be able to honor due to insufficient funds. Because of your longtime standing with our bank, I'm happy to hold the check until this afternoon to give you time to make the necessary deposit. Actually, Mr. Winters, we are currently holding several checks, and your account balance will not cover any of them."

"I don't understand. Your bank is where we maintain our general business fund account. The bookkeepers see to it that the operational balance never drops below ten thousand dollars. Are you sure you have the correct account?"

# No Paperwork Needed...

"I'm quite sure. Your balance is now standing at seventeen dollars and thirty-three cents."

"I'm sorry, but that is simply not possible. And I know we haven't issued any large checks for several days."

"Were you aware of the $10,000 cash withdrawal yesterday afternoon?"

"What? What withdrawal? Who signed for the withdrawal?"

"Your partner, Mr. Downey. According to our records, he is the only person other than you allowed to withdraw from the account."

"I know nothing about this. I'll contact Roy, Mr. Downey, and see what's going on. What amount needs to be deposited to cover the outstanding checks you have received?"

"Please hold a minute, and I'll get that number."

Doug tried to think of a reason why Roy would have withdrawn such a large sum of money, leaving the account essentially empty. He drew a blank.

"Mr. Winters, I have that number. If you could please stop by and deposit a minimum of one thousand dollars, we can honor all current checks. Of course, I have no idea what may be presented tomorrow."

"OK. Please withdraw the one thousand dollars from our capital funds account and deposit it into the general business fund account. I'll stop by a bit later and sign any needed transfer papers."

# No Paperwork Needed...

"I'm sorry, Mr. Winters, but I've already looked into the capital fund account as a possible solution, and I must inform you that the account has been drawn to zero and closed, as per Mr. Downey's instructions."

"That's not possible! There was over four hundred thousand in that account that we were getting ready to use for a warehouse expansion project."

"I'm sorry, but the account is indeed empty and closed."

"OK, then honor the checks, and I'll get down as soon as possible and sign any needed short-term loan papers."

"Again, I must say I'm sorry. Your current obligations to the bank are at the full credit line limit; we simply cannot advance any further funds."

"I've done business with your bank for over twelve years. You do whatever you think is the right fucking thing to do." Doug hung up the phone.

*What in the hell was Roy doing?*

Doug tried to phone Roy at the office. Doug and Roy were partners in a small but flourishing wholesale supply business. They had been friends throughout college and had early on recognized that the secret to wholesaling was automation and computer control—anything that allowed for fewer employees and higher yet faster volume of sales. They had steadily grown year after year and would have been considered a success in anyone's book.

Not getting an answer at the office, Doug tried the plant, then Roy's house and finally the club that both he and Roy had been members of for years.

# No Paperwork Needed...

At the club he did get an answer.

"Hey, this is Doug. Is Roy there?"

"Hi, Doug. No, he isn't here. As a matter of fact, he hasn't been in for several days."

Something was wrong. Roy, unlike Doug, never missed his daily workout at the club. Indeed, something was wrong. Doug spent the remainder of the morning making other calls and driving to several locations in an attempt to locate Roy. Arriving back home, he processed everything he had learned and could no longer deny the fact that both Roy and all of the company's funds were long gone.

# No Paperwork Needed...

## Chapter Eleven

It was late enough in the afternoon that I told Kent to take off; I would lock up the office and call it a day.

As I was heading down the front steps, I noticed two black suits and white shirts walking lockstep up the sidewalk. They looked like two IBM field reps from the sixties. But I knew better.

"Mr. Trench Richards?" one of them questioned.

"Maybe. Who's asking?"

"I'm Agent Hall, and this is Agent Coats. We're here on a matter of national security."

"Oh. Well then, yes, I'm Trench Richards. How can I help you?"

"You can start out by not saying another word and getting in that car," he said, pointing to a light-tan Chevy parked at the curb.

We all walked to the car, and Agent Hall, or maybe it was Agent Coats, opened the back door. I got in and the door closed. One of them slid in behind the wheel, and we were off. I was nervous enough that I couldn't remember who was whom.

"Where are we going?" I asked.

Complete silence.

About twenty minutes later, we turned into an alley and then parked behind a large government-appearing building. I would find out later it was city hall.

# No Paperwork Needed...

The door was opened, and I was asked to follow them. We walked in, took some stairs down two levels, and entered a small room devoid of any furnishing except a small table, four chairs, one tape recorder, and a notepad.

One of them turned on the recorder and said, "Please take a chair. From this moment on, every word that is said by us or you will be recorded."

"Nothing is going to be recorded because until you guys tell me exactly who you are and what is going on, nothing is going to be said."

"We are agents of the CIA attached to the Division of Homeland Security." With that they each removed and displayed a flashy gold badge.

"Are those badges real?" I asked.

"Of course they're real! Why do you ask that?"

"Because it's now 4:45 in the afternoon, and if you are true civil servants, you would have already long since gone home."

"Don't get cute. Do you have any idea how much trouble you're in?"

"No. But I suspect you're going to tell me. And you haven't answered my second question; you haven't told me what this is about."

"You know damned well what it's about. A Mrs. Forester from Treasury called us. She reported that you had called her with some story about someone you suspect is a

# No Paperwork Needed...

Russian terrorist being hell-bent on using a nuclear bomb on this country. Does any of this ring any bells?"

My fantasy that all this didn't have anything to do with me vanished.

"You are going to start at the very beginning and tell us every single detail, understand?"

"No, I'll not start at the beginning and tell you every detail, because a bunch of it's self-incriminating and has nothing to do with the issue at hand."

"We'll determine what is self-incriminating."

"No. No, you won't. And I'm not going to start at the beginning. I'll start at the end and work backward, stopping prior to anything that would be imprudent to say."

"Mr. Richards, you just don't get it, do you? We'll make up the rules here. But for the moment, OK, get started."

"A friend of mine overheard a couple of guys speaking in Russian. He played around on his computer with something called Babblefish and figured out they had been saying things like 'atomic device' and 'dirty bomb.' We put two and two together—that is, Russian and bomb—and decided we'd better call someone. End of story."

"Not quite. Let's try this again."

And that started a marathon session of questions and answers, the end result of which was their knowing every single thing from the moment Gerald walked into the office asking for the first seven hundred thousand dollars.

# No Paperwork Needed...

"That wasn't so hard, was it?"

"Are you guys about done? I have a date Friday night."

"So, this is only Wednesday."

"I know."

"We'll need to speak to this Larry and Kent."

I hadn't told them about Tom and his body disposal task.

"Give us addresses, phone numbers, and anything else that will help us find these two as fast as possible, and then you can go. But take note, we are far from being done with you. You need to know that your part in all this is going to lead to some serious consequences. We'll be in touch. Don't try to leave town. If you do, when you are found, and you will be found, you will instantly be detained."

I gave them the information they had asked for, and they, without another word, delivered me back to the office.

I gave Kent a heads-up call and left for the day.

Early Thursday morning, I was back at the office. I went over the outstanding loans in my mind's eye and determined nothing needed immediate attention. It was about 10:30 when I noticed Kent hadn't yet arrived. I wondered where he was, and then it dawned on me—I knew full well where he was. Ten to one he was enjoying a conversation with the CIA. The only thing I could do was wait.

# No Paperwork Needed...

An hour or so later, Susan followed her brand-new tits into the office.

"What do you think?" she asked.

"Excellent. If I ever need any bodywork done, I'll call you and get the doctor's name. I assume you are here to cover your loan?"

"Yes, and the interest. The insurance check for the Jaguar arrived yesterday."

"Good," I said. She paid in full and that was that. Another loan closed.

I couldn't help but ask, "How is your husband doing?"

"Not so well. I should have purchased the $4,000 work-over. There is some question as to whether he will ever walk again."

"Good-bye, Susan."

"Bye, and thanks."

A few hours later, Kent walked in. He looked as if he'd been ridden hard and put away wet.

"I assume you were talking with the agents?"

"Yes. For about four hours."

"How did it go?"

"OK, I guess. They had a Russian translator present, and they asked me time and time again to try to mimic various things I may have heard while tied up in the roundhouse.

# No Paperwork Needed...

Every so often I would say something, and then the translator would repeat many phrases in Russian until he said something that truly did sound familiar. I would tell him that I thought I did hear that, and he would make a note. He never told me what he had said."

"So you think they got some ideas?"

"Yeah. A few times after he would write something down, he would show it to the two agents, and they would seem to get rather excited."

"You think we might be OK for a while?"

"Yes, but Tom is in deep shit."

"Tom? When I called you last night, I told you to not say a word about Tom, no matter what."

"And I didn't. But it seems they've been hitting all the joints we frequent and thus stumbled onto Tom. Apparently, they scared the shit out of him, and he responded with something like, 'I didn't kill them, I was just paid to dispose of the bodies.'"

"Oh shit, Kent. That's it then, there's no doubt we'll be doing some time for this. I didn't sign up for this kind of stuff. Bottom line, I was to tell a few people they should repay their loans or else. That's all."

"I know. But what kind of upset me was that the agents referred to us as a couple of clowns. Said we needed to keep absolutely quiet and hidden to the best of our ability and let them, the professionals, do their job. When all was finished and done, they would in turn deal with us. He did say, however, that any help they ask for and got would be remembered. Keep in mind, the only so-so things we

# No Paperwork Needed...

have done are to make some illegal loans and arrange to have a couple of bodies disposed of—we didn't kill anybody."

*Maybe Kent was right*, I thought. *Perhaps we can come out of this more or less OK after all.*

"Kent, I have a headache. I'm going to go home and try to convince myself this will all turn out OK and think about my date tomorrow night."

Friday had finally arrived. I spent most of the day sighing and feeling sorry for myself. I did need to stop sighing so much.

I spent an inordinate amount of time trying to get myself looking as good as I could. I had to conclude that this had more or less failed. My clothes were plain indeed. That's what happens when you use the janitor at J.C. Penney as your fashion consultant. I would need to apologize for the clothes.

But at last, it was time to pick up Linda. I walked out and got in the car. Here was another thing I would need to apologize for. For Christ's sake, my job, my appearance, my car, and if it got to that, my apartment. Would the apologizing ever end?

I pulled up in front of Linda's place and parked. I threw a bit of trash lying on the passenger's seat in back and tried to dust the seat off. She answered the doorbell on the second ring and said, "Hello, Trench, come in, please."

She looked stunning. The dress was tight, short, low-cut, slit up the side, everything a dress should be.

# No Paperwork Needed...

"What a beautiful dress. I'm sorry I don't have a suit that would come close to matching."

"You look fine. Shall we go? I'm famished."

I walked her to the car, opened the door, and watched her slide in. This was just not right. It was akin to placing a diamond necklace in an oilcan. At least I didn't sigh out loud.

I again commented on how nice she looked as I drove to the Lagoon, a seafood restaurant holding our reservations. Once at our table, I ordered some recommended white wine, and then there was nothing left to do but talk.

"Is that dress from your dress shop?"

"Yes, it's part of a new line I started carrying about two months ago. It sells well."

"I can see why. You look fantastic in it."

"Thank you. Do you come here often?"

"No. I asked around a bit for a recommendation of a nice restaurant where a fellow could take a first date that wouldn't instantly squelch the hope of a second date. I was told about this place, so I called and made reservations. If seafood isn't your thing, they have beef and poultry as well."

"Seafood is great. Shrimp, crab, lobster, what's not to love?"

We studied the menus for a while and then placed our order.

# No Paperwork Needed...

"How did you get started with your dress shop?"

"After a couple years of college, I got a job in a rather large dress shop in my hometown. About a year later, I was promoted to head salesclerk, and not too long after that, to part-time manager. As manager I had more time to talk to the customers and get their feeling on what they did and didn't like about the store—what they thought of the clothing lines, etc. This is kind of embarrassing, but while doing this, I was asked several times where I found my personal dresses—that I looked so nice and, well, sexy, in the dresses I chose. I started to keep some notes on all this, and one day it just hit me. Why don't I do this for myself instead of making all this money for someone else? So I quit, moved here, and started the shop. It was lean at first, but with all due modesty, nowadays I'm doing very well. And what about you? I'm pretty sure you didn't aspire to be in the unsecured loan business throughout your youth."

Unsecured loan business. What a nice way to say "loan shark."

"No, of course not. I got into a bit of trouble with some money I shouldn't have borrowed, and well, one thing led to another, and here I am. It all started with this car I said I was going to buy and—"

"Trench, what color are my eyes?"

I looked up to see, and she had her hand over her eyes. I didn't even get the chance to open my mouth and most assuredly stick my foot in it.

"Never mind," she said. "Do you realize you have spent the entire evening thus far staring at my breasts?"

# No Paperwork Needed...

"Oh God. Was it that obvious? I'm truly sorry."

"Would it help if I opened my blouse so you could see them and we could get on with other things?"

"Here? At the table?"

"No, you idiot. And I was trying to make a point. What would you think if after we sat down, I put my head under the table and stared at your crotch all night?"

"Point taken. Again, I'm truly sorry. I did want this to go well."

"It's going fine. Here comes our dinner."

So, it was some crab for me, lobster for her, wine for both, and I did my level best, so to speak, to look straight forward for the remainder of our dinner.

After dinner and a Goldschlager cinnamon schnapps liqueur each, we took our leave. On the way to her house, we didn't have much to say, but upon arrival she hesitantly asked if I would like to come in for a last drink.

"What works best to help assure a second date? Coming in or leaving?"

She smiled. "Let's have that nightcap on the next date."

I walked her to the door and floated back to my car. You would have thought I was in junior high or even worse, a goddamned college kid.

# No Paperwork Needed...

## Chapter Twelve

Setting aside being shot at, it was a quiet weekend.

It all started about midday on Saturday. Kent called and told me to get my ass over to the office.

"Why? It's Saturday."

"Because I just received a call, the message of which was that I was a dead man."

"That's all? You're a dead man?"

"Isn't that enough?"

"No, I mean, was that the entire message?"

"Yes. But I'm scared shitless. Remember, I'm the one who's already taken two slugs. I want to talk to you about this. I guess, even more importantly, I don't want to be alone right now."

"No problem. Let me pick you up in about twenty minutes."

I drove over to Kent's, pulled in front, parked, and honked the horn. Kent came out and got in the car. Before I could put the car in gear and pull away, the rear window disappeared.

I looked at Kent.

"Did we just get shot at?" Kent didn't have to answer. The shattering of my side-door window answered the question.

# No Paperwork Needed...

We both jumped out of the car and dropped to the ground. I crawled around to Kent's side. The shots were coming from my side.

"I see him!" I yelled. "Toss me your penis extens—"

"What?"

"Gun, gun! Toss me your gun!"

Now, as it happens, perhaps I don't like guns because I'm hands down the single worst marksman in the world. I have no idea how many bullets the gun held, but I know I fired every goddamned one of them. And after that, I have no idea how many times the pistol went "click."

"Enough already," Kent said. "You ran out of bullets twenty clicks ago. But before you did, I'm sure I heard a scream."

Sure enough, we were no longer being shot at, and all seemed to be quiet behind the hedge across the street. Ever so slowly we moved from behind the car and did our best to see what had happened. After several minutes we cautiously walked across the street, and there, behind the hedge, with a brand-new third eye, lay the shooter. You talk about being deader than a doornail. This guy had to have been gone before he ever hit the ground.

"That's gross!" Kent said, "You couldn't have hit him more dead center in the head if someone had taken a tape measure and marked an 'X' for you. I wonder if this guy had any idea how bad his luck was, for you to hit him in the first place."

"Thanks. We need to get the agents over here and right now. Don't touch a thing."

# No Paperwork Needed...

We walked back across the street and into Kent's apartment. I pulled Agent Hall's card from my wallet and dialed the number.

"Agent Hall speaking."

"Hall, this is Trench Richards."

"Go on."

"Kent and I were just shot at."

"Did either of you get hit?"

"No, but we and my car were shot at several times. I fired back in self-protection, and, well, whoever was shooting at us is dead."

"Great. You realize we might have been able to get some information out of him?"

"Believe me, I didn't hit him on purpose. I was simply pointing the gun across the street and pulling the trigger as fast as I could."

"Where are you?"

"At Kent's."

"Don't move. We'll be right over." He hung up.

Shortly, Agent Hall's car pulled up to the curb. Hall had brought Agent Coats along.

The four of us walked back across the street. The shooter was exactly as he had fallen. Agent Coats took a look at the bullet hole, looked at me, looked at the bullet hole again, and finally fixed his gaze on me.

"Agent Hall said you told him you were just pointing and randomly firing across the street in self-protection. How do you explain this shot? That bullet hole is in the exact center of his head. It's like he has a third eye."

"All the bullets had to land somewhere," I shrugged and said.

The agents walked back to my car and looked it over. They then looked at the bullet holes in the front of Kent's house. Even to the most inexperienced investigator, it would have been obvious that the car was indeed here and in the line of fire; it did indeed receive its bullet holes here.

Agent Hall reached up and brushed a couple of little square pieces of tempered glass off my jacket.

"No doubt you were in the car when the window shattered. The shooter had to have fired first. For you to have shot first, you would have had to roll your window down. If it had been down when the shooter fired, it wouldn't have been broken. I'm going to log this as self-defense. After the lab guys show up and photograph the car, you, Kent, and your car are free to go."

About an hour later, the scene was all printed, dusted, photographed, and cleaned up. The body had been bagged, and everyone had taken off. Except for several holes in Kent's house, it was like it never happened.

Kent and I stood by my car for a while and then headed for the office. Once again this had been a setup from the start. I would be willing to bet that a second shooter had been at my place.

Strangely, my car looked none the worse with the two missing windows and array of bullet holes. I did need to get a new car.

We had only been at the office for about thirty minutes when the phone rang.

"Hello."

"You miserable son of a bitch, you killed one of my men."

"You killed two of mine," I fired back quickly. It was Gerald.

"You were lucky this time—you and Kent, your dimwit helper. Next time that will not be the case. Actually, I'm kind of glad you didn't get shot, because I personally want to see you suffer much more than that. You'll regret until the day you die that you got the CIA involved in this. That day is close at hand."

How in the hell did this guy know the CIA was involved, and even knowing that, how did he know I was the one who started it?

"It is you whose days are numbered, my asshole friend. In the meantime why don't you go and fuck yourself." I slammed down the receiver with much more bravado than I felt.

"Kent, let's get out of here. I'll see you on Monday."

Sunday was a relaxing day. No one shot at me, for a starter. How bad could a day be if you can avoid that?

# No Paperwork Needed...

**Chapter Thirteen**

I walked into the office around 8:30 on Monday morning. The moment I closed the door, I heard, "Trench, is that you?"

I stopped dead in my tracks—it was Larry! I tried to replay in my mind's eye the explanation for the additional two hundred and fifty thousand I gave to Gerald, but simply drew a blank.

"Larry, are you back to stay?"

"I guess so. I didn't mean to leave you alone with this so long, but I really needed to get away. Sit down and tell me what's been going on."

"Do you want details or an overview?"

"Start with the high points for now."

"There are no high points. First off, both Jack and Don are dead."

"What?"

"They were called out to the country club. It was a setup, and they were hauled to the old rail yard, and Gerald's men cut them to pieces."

"Christ. How did they get killed?"

"I just told you, they were cut to pieces. Literally."

"I didn't hear anything like that in the news."

# No Paperwork Needed...

"I hired a new enforcer named Tom, and he cleaned up the mess, so the police never found out. But the CIA knows about it."

"What?"

"I had to call the federal people in, which ended up being the CIA, because while Kent was being held to assure Gerald's safety, Kent overheard what sounded like a Russian terrorist plot to explode a nuclear device somewhere in the country."

"What?"

"Would you stop saying, 'What,' for Christ's sake? At any rate, we absolutely had to report that to the feds. We are in a bit of trouble with this, because close to one million dollars that I believe Gerald is going to use to purchase the device came from us."

"What one million dollars? I thought he was into us for seven hundred thousand."

"Well, he was until I gave him another two hundred and fifty thousand."

To his credit, he didn't say, "What?"

"And why on God's earth did you give him additional money?"

"Because he was holding Kent and promised to parse him up like Jack and Don if I didn't. And I believed him. Then just this past weekend, Kent and I were ambushed, and I got off a lucky shot and killed one of Gerald's men who was trying to shoot us."

# No Paperwork Needed...

Larry sat silent for a while. Finally...

"Is that all?"

"I think so. If anything else comes to mind, I'll let you know."

"Christ almighty, I was only gone for three weeks!"

"Yeah. Who would have guessed it?"

"So, where are we? What do we do or perhaps, not do?"

"The CIA guys cautioned me to continue on just as we have been doing. I guess that means to continue with the loan business as well. I mean, after all, when they're trying to prevent what may be a terrorist plot of immense proportions, stopping a couple small-time loan sharks is far down on their list. Not to mention, we are bleeding money. We need to collect on some current loans and make some clean new ones."

I was glad to be back to making first contacts with past-due clients. The loan-making decisions were best handled by Larry, and he was back.

I heard the front door open. At this hour it had to be either Tom or Kent. I walked out of Larry's office to find Tom sitting at his desk.

"Tom, come on in and meet Larry. He's the owner and boss of this outfit."

We walked into Larry's office. "Larry, this is Tom. Tom, meet Larry."

The two shook hands.

# No Paperwork Needed...

"I hired Tom to fill in as a part-time enforcer. His first job was to clean up the Jack and Don mess. That was when I still had hopes of getting our loan back and wanted to conceal it from the police."

I left Larry's office so he and Tom could feel each other out a bit. It sounded as if things were going to be fine between the two.

When Tom came out of the office, I called him to my desk.

"Tom, I need you to run a collection. Northwest of town on Clarkson Road about three miles out, you'll find a large auto salvage yard. The guy who runs it is named Mickey Tollard. He's a repeat customer and has always paid up, but he was due in here a few days ago, and I've not heard anything. He's an avid early car collector and borrows money from time to time to attend auctions and estate sales. He repays with his car sales business. The reason he comes to us for funds from time to time is that not all of the cars he sells are his to sell. But that isn't any of our business. Run out there and pick up the sixty-five thousand plus twenty-percent hit. Let me know if you have any problems and don't get too rough. He's good for it."

No sooner had Tom left than a nervous-looking younger man walked into the office.

"Can I help you?" I asked.

"Forgive me, but is this the place where you can make arrangements to borrow some money, more or less no questions asked?"

# No Paperwork Needed...

"A few questions, perhaps. My name is Trench. Come on in and sit down. Excuse me a minute."

I walked into Larry's office.

"Larry, I think we have a potential new client. Should I send him in?"

"No, I'd rather not. Go ahead and take care of it. I'm still doing my best to swallow everything you just told me. As a matter of fact, even though I'm back, I still want you to handle most everything. But at least I'll be here for any questions."

"OK."

I wasn't sure what that was all about, but I had indeed dumped about twenty pounds of shit into his five-pound bag. I walked back to the center office and invited what might be a new client into my office.

"Come on in and take a chair. As I said, the name is Trench, and you are?"

"Jeff Lancing."

"OK, what can I do for you, Jeff?"

"I need fifty thousand so I can get my daughter back."

"Tell you what. Just so I don't have to ask you a bunch of questions, why don't you start at the beginning and tell me what is going on? There has to be a dark side to this, or you'd be getting your money somewhere else."

"My ex-wife is a complete sociopath, and she has my six-year-old daughter. We were divorced about eighte months ago, and the court awarded her Debra and denied me any visitation privileges. This is my last option—I want to hire a kidnapper to get Debra back."

"We are pretty open-minded here, Jeff, but enabling child kidnapping is a bit of a stretch."

"But the fellow at the bar—by the way, he said to tell you it was Ryan who sent me—told me that basically the rules were any amount, for any reason, and that anything could happen if it's not paid back."

"More or less true, but even we loan shark assholes aren't too high on kidnapping, especially if it's a kid."

I hadn't used the word *kidnapping* for some time. An interesting word. If you put the grabs on a forty-five-year-old wife, it was still kidnapping.

"OK, please listen. The real crime here is that my ex has Debra. I don't remember how many times we were in court, and every time it was the same damn thing—the child is in a better environment when with the mother. In this case nothing could be further from the truth. My ex is a perfect sociopath. Do you know what a perfect sociopath is?"

"No, I guess I don't."

"A perfect sociopath is one who performs and responds so appropriately that absolutely no one can tell she is a sociopath. You could question her for days and never get a hint that deep down she has absolutely no empathy or concern for anything. She could set a dog on fire, sit there, and watch it burn, and never blink an eye. I'm telling you with all my heart, my daughter is at extreme risk."

# No Paperwork Needed...

"Forgive me for asking this, but why should I believe this? For that matter, given what you've said, is there any reason for me not to wonder if perhaps *you* are a perfect sociopath? But before we go any further, I need to tell you that first, I'm going to need a shit pot full of proof that you are on the level with this, and second, I need an ironclad plan for the repayment of the loan. You seem to be fond of the word *sociopath*. This isn't the bank. If you don't meet the terms of repayment, you are going to find a couple of sociopaths on your doorstep. Understand?"

"Yes, and here is some proof."

He reached in his back pocket and tossed an envelope on the desk.

"Please don't ask me how I obtained some of this. But if I'm willing to borrow money from, well, criminals and use that to hire a kidnapper, it shouldn't be such a leap to accept the fact that I was willing to do what I did to get these papers."

Inside were medical records from three different hospitals, all located in different states. The pictures told it all. One was a picture of a small hand with a three-inch nail sticking through the center. One depicted a small foot with two unimaginably smashed toes. Lastly, a picture of a tiny little bottom showing a pattern of circular burn marks. No question, a hot electric stove.

"Trench, do you believe a six-year-old can have that much bad luck? I have no idea what else has happened since this all took place. This stuff wasn't available for the court sessions, but it wouldn't have made a bit of difference. My ex could sit on the witness stand and convince Jesus that he was an atheist. She is truly frightening to watch."

"These all have different names."

"Goddamn it, open your eyes! Sure, the names are different; even an idiot would know to change the names, but look at the physical description, the comments. The report on the burns even mentions the disfigured toes."

"Listen, this still doesn't add up. If a child with injuries like this shows up at a hospital, the physicians would have the department of family services—DFS is what they used to call it—on this like a duck on a June bug. The same thing goes for school; a child showing up with these wounds would get reported to some social organization so fast, the parents or parent wouldn't know what hit them. The only reason I know anything about this is due to a client named Frank from a few years back. He had apparently used a belt to lash his junior high son on the butt for something he had done, and the gym teacher noticed the marks the next day at school. Some social organization was on him instantly, and before it was over and the kid was back home, Frank was in here borrowing fourteen thousand to pay for the legal help."

"That is the reason that each report is from a different state. Debra was never allowed to go back to the same school after she was injured. Karen, my ex-wife, would move to a different state and keep her out of school until things were well healed. As far as a hospital not reporting, I can only once again try to describe my ex. She could so quickly come up with a logical story and tell it with such unflinching conviction that all those around would eat it up hook, line, and sinker. I hope you never get to see her in action, but that's what it would take to truly understand.

"OK, OK. But we have to cover step two. How are you going to pay this back?"

"I'm power of attorney on a trust that is only valid if Debra has been legally placed in my custody. My parents set this up so I could care for Debra. The various terms are to prevent me from doing something like I'm trying to do right now. The trust has more than enough to pay you back."

"Did I miss something? Kidnapping Debra doesn't constitute your being the legal guardian."

"No, but—and I admit this is the tricky part—after I get Debra in my hands, my ex is going to stop at nothing to get her back. I've been told many times that if I ever try to take Debra, she will kill me. With her, that is a simple statement of fact. I'll have to be careful, but without a doubt I'll be able to record or document her attempt to get Debra back. When that's presented in a courtroom, she will be imprisoned, and I'll be granted custody of Debra."

I said nothing for several minutes. Finally...

"You do understand that there are about a thousand things that could go wrong with this plan?"

"Yes, but I can think of nothing else. You would never understand what I'm really up against."

I thought of all the crazy things we had advanced money for—the good, the bad, the depraved. This was a time when just maybe, helping out was the right thing to do.

"OK, you get the money. We'll have to work out the terms, but you don't get a cent until you've arranged for everything, if you know what I mean."

# No Paperwork Needed...

By everything, what I meant was the kidnapper.

"I know what you mean. How do I find a kidnapper?"

"How the hell did you find me? Go back and carefully start asking questions. When you have someone lined up, have Ryan give me a call. Then you can have the money."

Jeff had reached my doorway when I stopped him.

"Jeff, most times around here the only thing we care about is getting the money back, but I do hope this works for you."

Without saying another word, he disappeared through the door.

A few months ago, a situation like Jeff's would have had me calling my psychiatrist for an appointment. You can only listen to just so much of this before it starts to take its toll. But I no longer did that. After an uncountable number of sessions—her bills being one of the reasons I still had my piece-of-shit car—I finally found the relief I needed in a defective fortune cookie. Really. I had dined out at a Chinese place one night, and when the bill and cookie arrived, I opened the cookie, only to find it had no fortune. I thought about that for a second and had all my answers. Don't ever expect or count on anything. Don't expect normal actions, don't expect common human behavior. Don't even count on getting a fortune in your goddamned cookie.

A couple of hours later, Tom called.

"Trench, it's Tom."

# No Paperwork Needed...

"Hi—did you get the money?"

"No. Mickey tells me he was going to pay you with money he should have received by now for a couple of cars he sold to a guy. Do you want me to ask again using a bit of pain?"

"Hold off a minute. How real is the money that Mickey says is due him?"

"Hang on."

After a slight delay, Tom was back on the line.

"Mickey says it's dead real, and furthermore the guy owing Mickey is past due, and lastly, Mickey is convinced the guy has the money."

"Put Mickey on the line."

"Hi, Trench—honest, the guy, Jason, owes me money. I was going to use some of it to pay you."

"Some of it?"

"Well, yes. He owes me a hundred and ten grand."

"OK, Mickey, here are your options. I can tell Tom to break a couple of your fingers for being late, or I can have Tom collect your money, and we keep the original sixty-five thousand plus the twenty percent hit plus an additional twenty grand service fee. The remainder will be returned to you. What do you say?"

"You mean other than, 'fuck you!'—I thought we were friends."

# No Paperwork Needed...

"Come on, Mickey—there are no friends in this business, you know that."

"Go get your fucking money and bring the balance to me. I'm going to need my fingers so I can greet you from here on."

"Mickey, like they say in the movies, it's just business. Put Tom back on the line."

"So?" Tom said.

"Get all the information from Mickey. Go find this Jason guy that's into Mickey and collect his one hundred and ten large. If you can, collect one hundred and thirty. Whatever, put ninety-eight thousand in your pocket and deliver the remainder to Mickey."

"OK. How serious are you about this?"

"Do whatever you need to do. Don't leave without the money."

Tom entered the office a few hours later. He was sporting a few cuts and bruises. It looked as if he had tried to dye his tan jacket red.

"I take it things didn't go smoothly with Jason. Smooth or not, did you collect?"

"Yes," he said, handing me what counted out to be ninety-eight thousand. "I took thirty-two thousand to Mickey."

"So you got the one hundred and thirty thousand. Good. What did Mickey say?"

# No Paperwork Needed...

"Thanks for collecting the twenty grand fee instead of tapping him for it, but you are still supposed to go and fuck yourself. I think you hurt his feelings."

"What happened to Jason? You look like shit."

"The minute I mentioned Mickey's money, the bastard sucker punched me. I've been hit harder, but I think it was a horse that did it up in Wyoming. It went downhill from there. After about five minutes of trading blows, I finally managed to get him down and twist his arm like a pretzel. I heard the bone snap. I thought that would be it, but the bastard jumped back up and lit into me again. After a couple more rounds, I disabled his other arm. I cleverly mentioned that now he was going to have to pay cash because I knew he was unable to write a check. The fucker just smiled and from where he was lying on the floor, kicked me in the balls. After I straightened up from that, I jumped up and landed full force on his right leg. I heard that snap too. He finally said 'enough.' The cash was in a small desk drawer."

I handed five thousand back to Tom. "Here, put this in your pocket—you earned it. And run over to this address and have Mark take a look at a couple of those cuts. You may need a few stitches."

* * *

Mark was the seedy version of the town doctor. He was knowledgeable from the medical point of view, but was severely lacking in the bedside manner department. A patient was never overweight in Mark's world; he or she was fat. His diet advice? Stop eating so fucking much. This aspect of his personality had simply destroyed his business. The irony was that most of his remaining patients listened when the medical advice came from

# No Paperwork Needed...

Mark. "You're fucking going to die soon" seemed to make a bigger impact than "Continuing with your health patterns may lead to less than satisfactory outcomes." He was a no-insurance, cash-and-carry, one-stop medicine man.

He would stitch you up because you were bleeding to death, not because you may be left with a scar. He was the practical man's physician. If your X-ray showed a deficiency that required a procedure, he would give you two options—carry out the procedure (cash only) or for fifteen bucks he would fix the X-ray with a Magic Marker and tell you to forget about it.

We weren't a completely heartless bunch of assholes. Many times after the enforcers reported in and discussed the motivational techniques they had used on the client, we would arrange for Mark to make a house call. Mark had become somewhat of an expert at repairing broken extremities.

I found out later that all of Tom's cuts weren't of the bleeding-to-death kind, but Tom prevailed from the vanity point of view, and for a hundred bucks on the spot, Mark did the needlework.

The remainder of the day was as quiet as could be. I must have been in the john when Larry left. He hadn't said a word; he just left.

The rest of the week was without incident, as it drew closer and closer to Friday and my second date with Linda.

On Friday, I had two things I wanted to do. One was to get a different car. It was turning out that Linda was understanding, but riding in a car with no side or back window might be crossing some kind of line.

# No Paperwork Needed...

I had needed a new car for a long time anyway. It wasn't finances that were holding me back. I used every bill I had to pay as an excuse why I didn't get a new car. The fact of the matter was that I was simply cheap. Larry had been paying me very well for the past several years, and I was deep into stocks, bonds, CDs, multiple accounts, and so forth. Truth be told, I was well-to-do primarily because I never spent a cent unless I needed to. The shitty apartment, the lack of decent clothes, the car, all of it could be solved in one afternoon and a few checks that would have little impact on my account.

Today I was going to write one of those checks. I took off and promised myself I wouldn't return until I was in a decent car. But what kind? After stopping at several dealerships and used lots, I ended up writing a check for a used 2003 Lincoln Aviator SUV kind of thing. It looked very nice and was filled with things beyond my imagination. Heated seats, no less. Eating a few burritos had taken care of that in my old car.

Item two on the list was to stop by the health club for a workout and a steam. I wanted to look and feel my best that night. My workouts left a lot to be desired. More than once I had wondered if the process of getting undressed and into my sweats and the reverse at the end of the session didn't tax my energy more than the actual workout. But nonetheless, I put on the sweats and started my walk. Round and round you go. I walked by this shapely woman lying on her back arching her pelvic area up and then down. About the seventh pass, it entered my mind that I could recommend an exercise that involved the two of us that would be much more pleasurable. If I were involved, it would also be a short workout session. *God, I must be horny.* Maybe, just maybe, tonight might help a bit with that.

# No Paperwork Needed...

When the time was right, I did my best to dress fairly well and walked out to my new car. Damn, it was nice. I should have traded in that old heap of mine long before. If I had done so before the two missing windows, I might have gotten a hundred bucks trade-in instead of "If you buy this car, we'll not charge you for having yours disposed of."

I pulled up to Linda's place and parked, killed the engine, and walked to the door. I hadn't planned for the evening, at least the early part.

She answered the door and invited me in for a quick drink before we left. Once again, she was looking fantastic in a slinky red dress.

She pointed to a chair and asked what I would like to drink.

"Whatever you have or are going to have will be just fine."

"I'm making a Long Island Iced Tea. I'll make two."

I watched her make the drinks. I don't know what all goes into a Long Island Iced Tea, but she poured from bottle after bottle. About the only thing I didn't see her pour in was some iced tea. She handed me a glass, we did a short toast to the evening, I took a sip. It was good.

We chatted about our weeks a bit, she with a lot more candor than I.

She asked me what I had in mind for the evening. I told her that I had more or less dictated our first date, so it was her turn; I was up for most anything.

After discussing various food and entertainment likes and dislikes, we settled on a barbecue joint and a movie, a comedy, if possible.

We walked out the door, and shortly she asked where I had parked. She couldn't see my car.

"Oh, I have a new one. It's right there in front."

I opened the door, and she sat down.

I walked to the other side, jumped in, started up, and we were off. After a few miles, she commented on how much nicer this was than my old car. And she hadn't even seen the old car after the window removals and sheet metal ventilation.

The food was spicy, and the movie was funny. What more could you want? We headed back to her place, and as she mentioned on the first date, I was invited in for a last drink.

As we entered her house, she pointed to the couch and started work on two more Long Island Iced Teas. She brought them over, handed me one, and sat on the couch beside me.

"Cheers," she said. "Some music?"

"That would be great." I suppose I should mention that I'm a huge music fan. I have a large and varied collection of music, and my pride and joy was a fantastic high-fidelity system. All tube type and very old, but the absolute top of the line in its day. The sound was so rich and mellow, you could get lost in the music. I didn't have a favorite type of music, but I did indeed have a type I detested. Rap, they call it. It would be much better characterized by simply appending the letter C on the front of the word.

She inserted a CD containing various selections of J.S. Bach. I recognized the first cut as "Partita No. 3."

After a bit she leaned over and placed her head on my shoulder. It was perfect. A great drink, beautiful music, a wonderful woman, and the night. After a couple hours of soft music, I said I had better go.

At the door I gave her a quick kiss and turned to leave.

"Be sure to call again," she said.

"Nothing in the world could stop me," I said and headed for the car.

It was Saturday once again. I couldn't help but think it would have to be better than the last one. In this, like most things, I was wrong.

It all started about eight-thirty in the morning. I was still in bed thinking about the night before with Linda. The phone rang and that was that.

"Hello."

"Trench, it's Agent Hall."

Great, only eight-thirty, and the day was off to a shitty start.

"Meet me at Kent's in one hour. We are going to make a move on Gerald today."

# No Paperwork Needed...

"What do you mean a move on—" But the phone had gone dead.

I was at Kent's in slightly under an hour. I walked in; Hall, Coats, and Kent were all present.

Hall instantly took charge of the gathering.

"Trench, as Kent already knows, we picked up some phrases Kent thought he had heard being mentioned while Gerald's men were holding him. Our Russian translator has worked extensively with this, and applying them to the local environment, scheduled events, news releases, etc., we have what we think may be the first step in Gerald's plan of action. We are going to stake it out and watch. If we get lucky and are positive he is in possession of the weapon, we'll grab it and him. If not, all we can do is watch."

"Watch what, where?" I asked.

"We think we have picked up a date, and a location. The date is today, and the location is the waterfront docks, one of the marinas. We have been planning this operation for days. It was time to bring you guys in on this."

"Why?" Kent asked, "what can we do? Why do we have to be there?"

One could tell that Kent wasn't real excited about this.

"Because we only have your two descriptions of these guys. We've never seen them."

"Oh."

# No Paperwork Needed...

"We think that the device has either been, or will be, shipped in via a small vessel to the private docks at the Stillwater Marina. This is currently our best guess. If guesses are all we have to go on, we have to act on them."

Neither Kent or I said a thing.

"OK, let's load up. We'll be meeting team members from several different organizations at the site just out of range and deploy from there."

As we were riding in the back of a van to the docks, I quietly asked Kent if he had ever been deployed before in his life. He said he had been fired once, did that count? I gave him a blank look.

"Deployed or employed, get it?"

If someone got shot during this, it needed to be Kent.

We arrived on the scene, exited the van, and began to await instructions.

"As you can see, most other federal agents from the various organizations are already in place. We'll locate just south of that green freight building."

I looked all around. If there were other guys there as part of this situation, I sure couldn't see them.

We took our assigned locations, and Hall handed both Kent and me a pair of binoculars.

"Both of you keep a steady watch. If your eyes get tired, take turns interrupting your watch. I want one of you watching every second. Be forewarned, this could take hours."

What he meant was hours and hours. The twelve-ounce binoculars seemed to grow to about twenty pounds.

Around two o'clock in the afternoon, Kent whispered, "Hey. Hey, here comes that cocksucker who tied me up at the rail yard!"

I didn't know about that, but in the group of about five guys whom Kent was looking at was Gerald.

"It's him, Gerald," I whispered to Hall.

"You guys don't need to whisper," he said, "we are a good six hundred yards away, and besides, I can't hear you over the harbor noise."

"It's Gerald," I said a bit louder.

I heard Agent Hall asking someone if he had any joy over the radio. I found out later he was asking if someone had picked up any signal of radiation emission. The Agent he was talking to must have been a hell of a lot closer to things than we were.

Gerald's group of five was heading toward a sailboat; it looked to be about forty to forty-five feet in length.

"I don't see any of them carrying anything, so concentrate on the boat," Hall said once again into the radio.

Shortly he replied, "Are you sure; you're picking up nothing?"

# No Paperwork Needed...

The answer must have been "Nothing" because Hall let loose with a bitter "Fuck!"

Everyone was told to continue their assignments. Gerald and gang boarded the boat and shortly thereafter cast off. What I didn't know was that the craft was being tracked by both a helicopter and a remote-controlled drone, and lastly being photographed in several different spectrums by a re-tasked satellite. These boys had one big and neat sack of toys.

The sailboat disappeared from sight, but we stood our ground. Some three hours later the boat reappeared and slowly made its way to the dock. Four guys got off the boat and headed for the various cars. Five got on, four got off—someone must have fucked up bad. They drove off and that was that.

I looked at Kent and he looked at me.

"That's it," I said. "That's it, that's all you're going to do? Let them drive away?"

Hall sighed, "What do you want me to do? Everything points to the fact that all they did was go sailing. Well, that and maybe dumping someone over the side. They didn't have the device. We want them, but nowhere near as much as we want the device, and they are the only ones who can take us to it."

"But they just drove away! Aren't you going to follow or something?"

"While they were gone, we placed some small tracking devices on the cars, but it most likely will not lead to anything. These guys aren't your normal five-thousand-dollar loan clients. These guys are for real. Those cars are most likely ditched and replaced every other day or so. Unless we get lucky, we may have to switch to plan B."

"Well, you took enough pictures of all of them. Are you going to need us for plan B?"

"Yes," he said while giving us a disconcerting look.

I didn't like that at all.

Sunday was quiet. I didn't leave the apartment. Nor did I answer the phone, which wasn't that difficult, as it also didn't ring.

On Monday, the first call of the day was from Ester, our first and most likely last physicist. She wanted to stop by a bit later and pay up. I told her to drop by anytime. This was going to make Larry's entire day. He was still spooked by working with such a sharp woman.

I was chatting with Tom when Ester walked in.

"Hi. Glad to see you," I said.

"I'll bet you are. Hello."

"Come on in," I said as I walked to my office.

She dropped an envelope on my desk prior to sitting down.

"There is all your money plus the, what is it you call it, the hit?"

"Thanks," I said, somewhat distracted—I was already counting the money. "All there. Did you have any problems moving things around so you could do this?"

"Not much. The hard bit was the hit; that came out of my own pocket. But I think things will be fine. I added that last round of data collection to my paper, and it's now under peer review—most importantly, it's the first paper covering this subject under peer review. I have no idea if it will go anywhere, but I wasn't going to just stand by and be scooped, especially by someone I'm convinced was getting half his results from my work. By the way, I think I know who is passing on my results, and I'm trying to figure out what to do about it."

"Please don't tell me," I said. "I'm working as hard as I can to get this outfit back to being simple loan sharks, no more, no less."

She smiled. "Good luck."

We shook hands; she walked through the front door and out of my world. I never saw Ester again.

Jean Reynolds, aka the pastry shop lady, called.

"Hello, Ms. Reynolds. What can I do for you?"

I was confident I knew what the call was about—when a client calls in a week or two in advance, it means they already know that they aren't going to meet the payment deadline.

"Mr. Richards, I'm afraid I'll not be able to pay back the loan on time."

# No Paperwork Needed...

Usually when I hear this, I don't say anything for a minute or so. It gives the client time to consider the possibilities.

"What happened to the plan of your greedy relatives buying in when you get going?"

"Nothing. They will buy in. I'm going to have a problem getting going."

"And that problem would be?"

"Every couple of days when the work crew and I arrive, we find that a bunch of their previous work has been damaged or destroyed. We have even had one small fire that the foreman tells me had to have been set on purpose."

"Who would want to impede you?"

"I don't know, but there is another pastry shop two blocks down the street that may not be all that sad if I don't open. Just a thought."

"Have you put up any signs or mentioned in any way that it's a pastry shop you are opening?"

"No, not a word. I wanted to have a surprise grand opening."

"Can you trust your foreman?"

"Yes, I think so. He has been very nice and helpful. He gives me tips all the time on how to do things for a little cost savings."

"OK. Ask him to get you a list of names, numbers, addresses, etc., for everyone who currently is or has been working on the job. Get the list to me, and I'll see if there is anything I can do."

"I'll get it to you as soon as I can. Thank you."

"No problem," I said and hung up.

I shook my head. We normally didn't get involved in the client's issues. Was the pastry really that good? I asked Kent to come into my office.

"Kent, there's a pastry shop some two blocks down the street from where Jean Reynolds is trying to remodel an old neighborhood bakery into a new pastry shop she wants to open. Would you drop by and look into the operation— who owns it, who they employ, etc. We'll later compare what you find with a list of names that Jean will be giving me shortly."

"What's this all about?"

"Someone or several someone's are doing their best to see that Jean never gets open, and it seems that a competing shop might be a place to start asking questions."

"Will do."

"Thanks."

I picked up the phone and placed a call.

\* \* \*

"District police dispatch, Officer Thompson speaking."

"Hello. Is Officer Blondski in?"

"One moment, please."

A few clicks and beeps later, I heard, "Blondski speaking."

"Hello, Don. It's Trench Richards."

We had a love-hate relationship with Officer Don Blondski. Two years back, his younger brother got mixed up in a scam that was being run by some real bad actors. What his brother didn't know was that while he thought he was part of the receiving end of the scam, he himself was one of the marks. One thing led to another, and when the light dawned, he realized that he needed some serious cash, and fast, if he were to escape the situation. So of course, he ended up on our doorstep. Twenty thousand dollars solved that problem but simply created another one. When the time came to pay us, he was considerably short.

That's when he called his brother, Don, the cop, and got him involved. In the best tradition of "you scratch my back, I'll scratch yours," we called the kid's loan paid, and Don agreed to look the other way any time the police got close to us. Even more importantly, he agreed to feed us information that might be germane to our various clients' actions. And that's what I was asking for now.

"Don, do you have anything on a Mrs. Mary Ellen Winestone?"

"Yes, as a matter of fact. Her name came up in a robbery case. Seems as if one of her employees stole a bunch of cash from her home office. We caught the guy essentially red-handed. The cash, to the penny, was stashed in one of the closets in his living quarters. When we tossed the place, one of the guys found it in about ten minutes. The guy was one hell of an actor, though. He said he had never seen the money before with such sincerity, it was almost hard to not believe him."

Anyone with an ounce of decency would have opened his mouth about this time. After all, here was a completely innocent clown who was looking at a handful of years in the big house.

"Don't know anything about it," I said.

"Why are you interested in this anyway?"

"Don, you know the rules. I get to ask questions, and you get to answer them, remember?"

"Yeah. Yeah."

"Thanks, Don, we'll talk to you soon."

"Great," he said and hung up.

Mary Ellen seemed to be on track and was carrying through with her plans. I started to feel sorry for her husband.

Mid-morning, three young men entered the outer office. Kent asked what we could do for them, and they said a guy named Mick had given them this address as a place where they could borrow some money.

"Perhaps," Kent said, "Wait here."

Kent told me what was happening, and I asked him to send them in.

# No Paperwork Needed...

"Hi, we would like to talk to you about borrowing some money. My name is—"

I interrupted him. "You're college students, aren't you?"

"Yes, what difference does that make?"

"We have a lot of trouble with college students. We had to kill the last two."

Their reaction was absolutely delightful!

"OK, now that we are off to a good start, what can I do for you?" I said.

"Well, the three of us are going to graduate at the end of this semester, and despite unending attempts by every one of us, we can't seem to get a job interview, let alone a job. If we're going to make any money, we're going to have to do something on our own. We have a great idea for what may be the next huge thing in software, but we need money to get started."

"How are you going to pay us back? No, let me guess. One of you has a grandfather who's going to give you a shit pot full of money when you graduate. Or you have a trust that opens up after you get a decent career started. No, I know. One of you has an ugly girlfriend, and her parents have told you that you'll be taken care of if you marry the girl. Or something like that, right?"

Most of these goddamned college kids, through no effort of their own, had the world by the tail if they could just be patient enough to wait for it to happen.

"Nothing like that for me," one of them said. The other two chimed in with similar responses.

# No Paperwork Needed...

"All right, before we get to your brilliant idea and how you are going to pay us back, I need to know which one of you will be the responsible person."

"What do you mean?"

"OK, let me ask the question this way. When you guys don't pay us back on time, whose legs do we break?"

"Oh." Their response made my day. I just about handed them the money on the spot. All three of them pointed to someone else and said, "Him."

"So be it," I said. "OK, what is your idea?"

Their answer started with a question. "Do you have any idea how many fat people there are in this country?"

"Not an exact count, no."

Their idea involved a huge server center, wireless scales, and a slick piece of server-based software. They explained in absolute detail. When they were finished, I was ready to invest my own personal money.

"We would like to repay the loan on installments with money we earn as the system grows."

I would need to talk to Larry about this one, but as far as I was concerned, we would be fools not to jump in.

"Leave me your names and numbers. I'll get back to you in a couple of days. For what it's worth, remember I don't make the decisions around here, but I think you have a great idea."

# No Paperwork Needed...

Over the lunch hour, I gave Linda a quick call. Yes, she would like to go out this weekend.

The afternoon was without incident until about three-thirty.

That's when Agent Hall phoned and shoved Gerald Rickson back into my life.

* * *

"Trench, it's Agent Hall."

Right after I sighed, I said, "Yes."

"We have a hit on Gerald. As a matter of fact, we have two hits on Gerald that arrived within thirty minutes of each other. First, we finally got a hint on Gerald's true identity via a combination of photo scanning and facial recognition software. We can't be absolutely positive, but we think he is Nickoli Validencof. There are no records whatsoever of his entry into the United States, so he came in under a different name, God knows what, and then changed his name to Gerald Rickson. And are you sitting down for this? Back home he was the number two man on a nuclear weapons miniaturization team. The story seems to be that he was overly involved with the lead team member's wife, and the entire affair ended ugly. No known reason for his apparent utter hatred for the United States."

"You mentioned two hits."

"Yes. He may have slipped up. A satellite picked up the tracker we placed on his car at the docks. The car—we hope he drove it—is currently in Livermore, California."

"What's in Livermore? I've never been there."

# No Paperwork Needed...

"That's about to change. A car will be picking you up in just a few minutes. Is Kent there?"

"No."

"OK, just you then. When the car gets there, get in. No questions, don't bring a thing, just get in. You'll be taken to a small field nearby and will board a helicopter. Then a short ride to the airport, where you'll meet me and board a G-four. We'll be in Livermore shortly thereafter."

"What's in Livermore?"

"We're hoping to see who Gerald is making contact with or what he's doing. We have a few ideas, and none of them are too pleasant. Is the car there yet?"

"No. What's in Livermore?"

"What?"

"For the fourth time, what the hell is in Livermore?"

"The Lawrence Livermore National Labs. Their web page says something about ensuring the safety, reliability, and security of the US nuclear stockpile. They have a weapons program."

"Oh shit." I was having a hard time thinking that I perhaps had been part of this mess.

The car arrived and as instructed, I got in, and without a word by anyone we were off. The driver obviously wasn't the least bit concerned about the possibility of a speeding ticket. We arrived at the open field just to the north of the street we had traveled, and sure enough, there sat a helicopter with spinning blades. It was ready to go, and the minute we boarded, the pilot took off. It seemed as if just a few minutes went by before we were touching down beside a beautiful jet. We exited the helicopter and climbed the few steps up and into the jet. The engines were already spinning, and as soon as the door closed, we were rolling.

"Take your seat quickly," Hall said, "we've been assigned priority takeoff."

We taxied for a short way, made a right-hand turn, and I was thrown back into my seat. Faster and faster we rolled. Then the nose pointed up at a terrifying angle, the landing gear went clunk, and we were on our way.

In flight, Agent Hall outlined their next best guess as to what was going on, stressing the things I should be watching for and paying attention to.

"This is going to sound like a script from a B-grade movie, but our think tank has put this scenario together from all the hard data we have thus far. We no longer believe that Gerald has purchased a device and thus is having it shipped in. That day at the docks was just what it appeared to be. They simply went sailing and used the opportunity to weed a bad apple from their ranks. We believe that with the help of someone inside the labs, Gerald is going to construct his own device."

"Oh, come on," I said, "We're not talking about building a vacuum cleaner here; you're talking about a nuclear device, a bomb, a big fucking bomb."

"Listen, one of the latest studies by our threat risk group now shows that for an independent person, the difficulty of constructing a device is far less than the difficulty of obtaining the materials. It used to be you could give all the materials to someone and be perfectly safe, because there was no way they could possess the knowledge to turn them into a working device. This day and age, you can find descriptions of nuclear devices on the Internet that provide eighty-five, ninety percent of all the technology and information you would need to succeed. This isn't the nineteen forties anymore."

Every point I raised, Hall countered. In the end he made a believer out of me.

One of the flight officers walked back and told us to prepare for landing and disembarking; Livermore was about twenty minutes out. He was dead on. Twenty minutes later I was walking with Hall toward an ever-popular black SUV.

## Chapter Fourteen

As Hall and I jumped into the SUV, one of the guys up front shouted out that he had a hit. I looked at Hall. He was all smiles as he explained, "A hit in this situation means that a unit in this vehicle has picked up the tracker on the car that we suspect is driven by Gerald. It's in the tracker GPS navigation mode and will tell us how to drive directly to his car."

Maybe we weren't such clowns after all; we had one of these.

As we were driving, I asked Hall if this was plan B.

"No. This is plan C. Perhaps we'll get to skip plan B altogether."

"What was plan B?"

"That was to stake you and Kent out as bait."

"Oh."

Things worked just as Hall explained, and in a short while, we were parked a few blocks away from Gerald's car.

"We stay here," Hall said. "When Gerald moves the car, we follow. But not in this car. If we drive this thing, we might as well hang a huge sign on the side that says 'CIA Inside.'"

Right after we stopped, Hall had arranged for a nondescript car to be delivered to our location. We would use that to follow, if and when Gerald moved.

# No Paperwork Needed...

Hall had just barely finished describing all this when a spotter much closer to Gerald's car radioed and told us that Gerald was in his car, backing out, and on the move.

Hall mentioned that the driver of our car was one of the CIA's best surveillance team members. "He could follow you into your bathroom when you go to take a shit and you would never know he was there."

We followed for many miles. Sometimes it looked like we were getting much closer than we should, and other times we would drop back so far that I had no idea how our driver was keeping track of Gerald. The car we were driving wasn't equipped with one of those GPS navigation tracking devices. I guess if the driver lost him, he could get Gerald's position radioed to him from one of the agents in the SUV that was equipped with the unit.

Then Gerald turned onto Greenville Road, and Hall started to smile. A few miles down the road, Gerald turned again onto East Avenue. Hall's smile widened.

"We were right, the bastard is headed for the labs!" The labs indeed; there they were, off to the right-hand side.

"What now?" I asked.

"Quiet—but first, are you absolutely dead positive that is Gerald?"

"Yes."

I heard Hall radio some instructions. He described Gerald as best he could and gave Gerald's approximate location in terms of the building. He had been talking to another CIA staffer posted on the inside who would do his best to see where Gerald was going inside the building and with whom he was meeting.

We had the information in ten minutes or so. He was meeting with a Ms. Nancy Kundert, head of listed materials security, and they had entered Secured Materials Room C.

Hall radioed someone with the code word, "Troy." That precipitated some ten agents' quietly gathering outside the room. A call was made in an effort to find someone who had the codes and access permission to the room. Hall had been assured there was only one way in or out, so waiting for help with entry wasn't a problem. About twenty minutes later, everything was ready. The lab staff member opened the door, and the agents poured into the materials room within about twenty seconds. Hall and I ran as fast as we could toward the growing crowd. We arrived breathless and panting. The first thing Hall heard was, "Sorry, Hall, but no one's in there."

"What the fuck do you mean no one is in there? I was told by an agent that he saw Gerald and this Nancy person walk in that room! Get me the agent assigned to monitor this area right now!"

Almost immediately a fellow stepped forward. "I was that agent, and I'm telling you I clearly saw the man and women in question walk into that room. I was right here; there was no way I could have made a mistake."

"Did you take your eyes off the door for even a second?"

"Of course, but only for a couple of seconds at a time; I stepped back around the corner when they started to glance in my direction. Then they disappeared. The only place they could have gone that fast would have been through this door into the room."

After an hour or so of searching, Hall called off the entire team. I didn't think they'd ever figure out how the two got out or where they went to get off the grounds. The lady in question must have known something unknown to everyone else, at least unknown to the staff on hand. We were destined to not hear of or see Gerald for better than three weeks. The only good news was a report Hall received four days later that contained the results of an inventory which showed no missing materials. I don't think Hall completely bought it.

The return trip back home took a much more leisurely pace and was very quiet. The outcome had frustrated everyone. I was exhausted and went directly home upon our arrival.

## Chapter Fifteen

The sun was just breaking the horizon, and Elliot Harding was already making his rounds. He had been part of the county roads maintenance team for many years, and once a month it fell upon him to travel the various county roads looking for anything that needed attention. Usually, the things he found were abandoned cars or piles of trash dumped by assholes to avoid landfill fees. Refrigerators, deep freezers, and air-conditioners were popular items illegally dumped to avoid the fees charged to remove and recycle the Freon or other types of refrigerants.

Today, it was something different. Far ahead, it looked as if someone were walking slowly down the middle of the road. As he approached, Elliot realized the someone was a completely naked young woman. He pulled as close as he felt comfortable doing, stopped the truck, and got out.

"Miss. Miss. Are you OK?"

Obviously she wasn't OK, but it was the only thing he could think of to ask. She stopped walking and slowly turned around.

"Good God," he said and ran back to the truck and fetched a full-length rain slick. He walked over and put it around her shoulders and closed it around the front to cover her body. He stood there, taking in her appearance. Her face was streaked with blood, mostly dried, but with several areas still bleeding. She was covered with numerous deep cuts and massive black and blue swellings. Her nose seemed to be pointing one way and her chin another. What a goddamned mess.

"Can you talk?"

# No Paperwork Needed...

She shook her head 'no' and with her hands, made gestures pertaining to writing on a pad or piece of paper. Elliot fetched a pen and a clipboard with a few pieces of paper attached, and handed it to her.

She wrote, "Take me home—1145 East Frontier St."

"Miss, I need to get you to a hospital."

She violently shook her head 'no' and slapped the clipboard several times. With that her eyes rolled back up into her head, and she sagged toward the ground. Elliot caught her halfway down, picked her up, and placed her in the truck. Ignoring her request, he drove as quickly as possible to the nearest hospital emergency room, ran in, and told the staff on hand that he had an injured woman in his truck.

Angela spent the next seven days in the hospital, and of course the police were called in to investigate. Despite unending and thorough questioning, she absolutely refused to answer any questions or explain anything. She would tell her father as soon as they were alone at home.

Upon her hospital release, her father was summoned by the hospitals accounting office. Unfortunately, her father had a family health insurance policy. Because of the policy, he was presented with a bill, and the bill was more than twice the amount that his insurance would cover.

Angela's hospital stay initiated in the emergency room, and had there been no insurance, there would have been no charge. He had no idea how he was going to pay this balance, not to mention the more important thousands of dollars of surgery to come  required in an attempt to restore his daughter's appearance.

# No Paperwork Needed...

Angela had been home a few days when her father told her that the entire affair had to be discussed. In the course of the conversation, he asked her what she wanted. She said she never wanted him to contact the police for fear of her life and his and her mother's. But what she did want was for both boys to be punished for what they had done. They should be made to suffer the same beating and pain she had endured.

Her father was a proud and practical man. He was pleased that his daughter wanted retribution for these monsters. When he found out the names of the boys, he knew justice couldn't be found via the law and the courts. He would have to turn outside the law. He didn't know how one arranged for something like this, but he was sure it involved acquiring even more money. Between the remaining hospital bill and the needed cosmetic surgeries, and now the cost of teaching the boys a lesson, he was going to need a lot.

# No Paperwork Needed...

## Chapter Sixteen

The next morning, I cycled through the clients in my mind's eye and stopped at Harry Reinheart. Was it possible it was time to send out an enforcer again? I still hadn't completely accepted that we had lost Jack and Don. We only had one enforcer at the moment, and that was Tom.

I thought of the first time Harry Reinheart walked into the office. More accurately, waddled into the office. I guessed he weighed in at better than three hundred pounds, and from his overall appearance, was a complete slob. He was a slob's slob. He was wearing a shirt that was stained and food encrusted. His pants were torn and filthy. A half-chewed cigar hung from his mouth. As he approached my desk, the odor hit me first. All in all, a disgusting human being. In some ways, however, this wasn't all his fault. Over the years, I had grown to believe that naming a newborn male child "Harry" was the kiss of death. I truly had never met one who made a positive impression.

And this Harry, thus far in my life, was the worst. What we had here was the poster child for the local "Have you ever seen a Neanderthal?" movement. Harry didn't have a single redeeming characteristic except, he was an absolute wizard at calling the horses at the track.

This might explain the only other feature that stood out about Harry. He was never without a gorgeous piece of arm candy by his side. These women were outstanding. It simply had to be the money from the track; there was no way on God's green earth that it was Harry.

Harry had borrowed from us time and time again when he had a sure thing at the track. He would place a huge bet and way more often than not collect a purse that was overflowing. He would drop by and pay up. We would pick up 20 percent and have had our money out for only a day or so. I could never figure out why he needed to get the stakes from us when he won so often, unless when he lost, he really lost. The only other thing I could think of was that he simply ate it all up.

He had dropped by, and borrowed fifteen thousand and had never come back. After a week went by, I sent Jack and Don out to find him and collect. They found him, and Harry used the four deadly words, "I don't have it." They roughed him up a bit as a reminder and said they would be back in about a week. I sent them out a second time, and Harry said he still didn't have it. After that, he was going to have to learn to smoke his cigar with his left hand. But this was all in the past.

With everything that had taken place over the last several weeks, I had more or less forgotten about Harry. But he was now seriously past due.

I called Tom into the office and brought him up to speed on Harry.

"He doesn't seem to be getting the point," I said. "Look him up. If you don't find him around his place, try the track. He's a short little fucker. If you don't see him, look for some gorgeous woman; Harry will be the blob standing beside her. If he isn't at his place, get him to his place, and then, short of killing him, collect the money."

"You're not busy, why don't you come with me?"

I don't like to be involved in enforcer-based collections, but Tom had a pleading look in his eyes. I assumed he was still on edge over the Mickey-Jason collection.

# No Paperwork Needed...

"OK. But it's your collection."

We drove out to Harry's place. He was in. He said, "Hello" and then sat back in his chair a bit.

"How's your arm doing, Harry?" Tom asked.

"Much better, thanks."

"Harry, you know why we're here. This is the third and final time. Do you know what that means?"

"I have a pretty good idea."

"Harry, you aren't taking this seriously enough."

"Yes, I am, but I still don't have the money. How can I pay you if I don't have the money? I would love to pay you."

"So what are we supposed to do, Harry? I don't enjoy busting people up; well, sometimes I do, but in general, I don't. But you know we can't just walk out the door empty-handed."

Harry yelled for a Doris, whoever Doris was. Doris walked into the room. I once again was completely perplexed how a slob like Harry could convince someone like Doris to hang around. She was one beautiful lady. It couldn't be money—if Harry had that much money, he could have paid us.

Harry grinned. "What would you guys think about letting Doris entertain you from time to time while I scrape up the money?"

I turned to Doris. "What do you think about that, Doris?"

# No Paperwork Needed...

Doris was a bit more to the point than Harry. "I would love to fuck you guys," she said.

Tom and I looked at each other. For a couple of seconds, I think both of us were considering the offer. Finally, I shook my head no, and Tom walked over to Harry.

"Wait, wait," Harry shouted. "I have another idea. Tom, Trench knows I'm good at the track. How about I send all my track winnings directly to you until I've not only paid my loan and hit, but also paid an additional ten thousand for your trouble?"

"I can't make a decision like that," Tom said.

"But I can," I said. "Harry, I'm willing to give this a try, but we'll be watching, and if I ever suspect you aren't passing the winnings on to us, you'll find yourself in intensive care. Do I make myself clear?"

"Yes."

"Tom," I said, and nodded toward Harry. Tom bent down, pulled a small revolver out of his pocket, and quick as a snake, put a hole in Harry's right foot.

"That's to remind you of our deal and to see that you don't go anywhere. Darling Doris here can place your bets." Harry was still screaming when we left.

When we got back to the office, Larry told me I had received a call from Ryan, one of our sniffers. I placed a return call.

"This is Ryan."

# No Paperwork Needed...

"Ryan, it's Trench. You called."

"A Mr. Jeff Lancing mentioned I was to call you when he had secured the services of a...ah...a child return specialist. So, I'm calling. He has such a man."

"Is the guy reliable?"

"He always has been. This isn't the first time he has helped with the return of a child. The only person he knows who's mixed up in the deal as of this moment is Jeff himself. I never spoke with him; I just gave Jeff his name. Jeff tells me everything is worked out. He said he would get the money if I told you things were arranged and OK."

"OK, the next time you see Jeff, tell him to come by my office."

"Trench, it's none of my business, but are you sure you want to get mixed up in this?"

"This one is different. I may be doing the right thing in helping with this. Remember, you know nothing about this."

"About what?" Ryan said and hung up the phone.

**Chapter Seventeen**

Mrs. Mary Ellen Winestone was completely content. She was sitting in the warmth of the midday sun in her massive two-story sunroom. She smiled as she gazed upon her bird of paradise, which was in full bloom. Racing through her mind was the joyous thought of her gardener well on his way to prison. That would teach the rascal not to toy with her affections. Right behind in her mind was the amazement at how easy it was to imagine seemingly endless methods to dispose of her husband. *So many ways*, she thought with intense pleasure. One small caveat; it had to be a method that would leave her completely innocent in the eyes of the law. This certainly ruled out several methods, but she still had several to choose from if carried out correctly.

Sipping her Earl Gray tea, she marveled at how pleasurable just the thought of his death was to her. She could only imagine her intense joy at the completion of the actual task; she knew she wouldn't have to wait long. For one thing, she needed his money to pay off the loan sharks, plus she would never have to beg for money again.

Poison? No. The police had a bad habit of being able to trace that. Those stories in books and movies about some poisons being untraceable were just that, stories.

The ever-popular self-inflicted gunshot? Easy, but her husband had never owned a gun. A pre-planned car accident? Too iffy. Lord knows how many cars one may have to wreck before the fatal crash.

Thinking of cars, however, did plant a seed. What about a garage accident? Her husband was constantly playing with his cars out in his garage. He had a huge car

172

collection, with many exotic marks. He was forever tuning, tweaking his cars. What if one day he was under a car and the hoist failed? This should be a fairly simple matter. Sneak up on him, knock him out, and then position him so that when the hoist was lowered, one of the wheel platforms landed on his head, right on any mark left by the knockout blow. After the body was positioned, raise the hoist, release all the safety locks, and slightly loosen one of the hydraulic fluid pressure line fittings. Some of those old cars were so heavy, they should be able to crush his head flatter than a pancake. There would be hydraulic fluid sprayed all over the place. What a mess, what a glorious mess! *I would have to be extremely careful to avoid any fluid hitting me or my clothing, which should be simple. I could get rid of the clothes just to be sure. He is gone for days on end with his business trips. I wouldn't report him missing for several days. The staff knows I never go out to his garage. Think, Mary; do you see any flaws?*

Two days later, Mary's husband announced that he would be leaving town for a couple of days on business. *Perfect*, Mary thought; her only worry was that he might skip going out to his garage before leaving. Not likely, however, because he liked to choose a different one of his cars for the drive out to the airport when he traveled. He would drive it to the airport, park it in the hanger, and fly his Citation One to the business meeting. The only thing in this world he loved more than his cars was his plane.

She kept a watch for his departure. Sure enough, he made his way to the garage. After a few minutes, she walked to the garage via the sculptured hedges that offered complete coverage from anyone watching from the house. She picked up the heavy piece of angle iron she had hidden in the hedges days earlier. Entering the side door of the garage, with the angle iron behind her back, she spotted her husband. Wonderful! He was facing away from her with his head bent up, looking at the engine of one of his cars from under the hoist.

She walked to within about two feet of him  and swung as hard as she could. There was a soft crack, and he sank to his knees. She quickly tossed a few shop towels under his head, as blood was already starting to flow freely. She dragged him to the proper spot under the hoist and rolled his body so the head wound was pointing straight up. She pressed the Up button on the hoist to raise it a bit, removed the safety down locks, and with an adjustable wrench, loosened the pressure side of the hoist's hydraulic ram cylinder. She had judged correctly and was indeed out of the way of any spraying hydraulic fluid. The hoist came down smooth and steady. When it reached bottom, it was just a bit higher on one side, being held up by about two inches of what was remaining of her husband's head. She had been accurate in her daydreaming.

What a mess! Dark-brown hydraulic fluid everywhere, and bright red blood in a huge puddle on the floor, with some sprayed on the walls. Her position had also shielded her from the spraying blood. She looked everything over one last time and removed the towels—all seemed well. Retracing her path, she returned to her house. Moments later she was once again admiring the bird of paradise and enjoying another cup of Earl Grey tea. She had a most pleasant smile on her face. In about three days, she would start wondering aloud where her husband might be.

# No Paperwork Needed...

## Chapter Eighteen

I didn't make it back to the office until about mid-morning the following day. I walked into the building and headed for Larry's office. Once inside the door, I came to a complete stop. Piled on Larry's desk was the largest stack of money I had ever seen. Larry sat behind the stack, looking out, with a blank expression and an eyes-wide-open stare.

"What the hell is that?" I finally asked.

"Money."

"I know it's money. From where, who?"

"Gerald. Honest to God, Gerald came in with another guy, who held a gun on me and stacked the money on my desk. He said he preferred to kill us, kill all of us, but he answered to a higher-up who wanted to pay us back in full. After he put the money on the desk, he said we were even, and to consider the two men we lost at the rail yard a punishment for contacting the CIA. Then he left."

"This has got to be some kind of trap, a setup. How much is there?"

"He said one million, all in hundreds. That's ten thousand one-hundred-dollar bills."

I was to find out later that the stack, minus the wrappers, would weigh in at twenty-two pounds.

"Are they real?"

"How would I know, but most of the bills don't look new."

# No Paperwork Needed...

"Larry, we are in way over our heads. Why on earth would Gerald just simply want to return the money? Like I said, this has to be some kind of setup. We have to let the CIA know about this, and fast."

"You're right, just having this much cash sitting around is scaring the shit out of me. Call your CIA guy."

I dialed Agent Hall's number. My fingers were shaking so badly, it took me three tries to get it right. I had a deep-down terrified feeling about this. Hall answered.

"Agent Hall speaking."

"Hall, this is Trench."

"You haven't killed another bad guy, have you?"

"No. Listen, this may be serious. About an hour ago, Gerald showed up and stacked one million dollars on Larry's desk. He said we were now even and left."

"Christ! It's got to be a COD hit."

"What's a COD hit?"

"How have you assholes managed to stay alive this long? You guys are playing in a dangerous world and have no idea what the fuck you're doing. A COD hit's just what it sounds like. A cash on delivery hit. I'll bet a nickel Gerald has contracted with some out-of-town talent to drop by your place and kill every goddamned person he can find, and then most likely burn the place to the ground. Thirty minutes after he arrives, it'll be like you and the business never existed. The reason it's cash on delivery is because their payment is already there; that's what the one million

# No Paperwork Needed...

is for. They come and do their work, then pick up the money and leave. The entire transaction is complete.

You need to pick up the money and any needed papers and get the hell out of there as fast as possible. If the money's been there an hour, you're already on borrowed time. When you're somewhere safe, give me a call. And by the way, somewhere safe isn't your apartment, or Kent's apartment, or anything like that. The last thing you do before leaving is to call all guys who aren't there now and tell them to go get lost."

I shoved the money off Larry's desk into two small garbage cans and ran for my car. Larry called Kent while I was doing this and explained what was going on and asked him in turn to call Tom. Then he was right behind me and turned for his car. Where Larry went, I have no idea. I was about five blocks down the street when it dawned on me that I had no idea where I was going. And then I knew. I could think of no other place than Linda's. With the exception of Tom, no one even knew she existed.

I tried to think how I was going to explain all this when I arrived. Plopping one million dollars on her couch was sure to raise a few questions. I parked in her driveway between her car and her house, with just one side of my car visible from the street. I poured the money onto an old blanket I had in the backseat, gathered it up, and headed for her door. She opened on the second ring.

She gave me a strange look and asked, "Was our date tonight? I'm such a mess."

She looked to be anything but a mess. "No, not tonight. I'm here because, well, I couldn't think of anywhere else to go."

# No Paperwork Needed...

"Come in. Come in. What's in the blanket? You going camping?" she asked with a grin. About this time she noticed I wasn't smiling one bit. "What's the matter?"

"It's a long story. May I sit down and perhaps bum a drink?"

"Of course." She quickly made two drinks, handed one to me, and sat down on a chair across the way. "You look like you've seen a ghost. Please tell me what's the matter."

"Linda, you know the business I'm in. What you don't know is that sometimes it can get ugly. And at the moment, it's about as ugly as it gets."

"For God's sake, will you tell me what brings you to my place and what the hell is inside that blanket?"

They say a picture is worth a thousand words; in this case it was closer to a million words. I stood up and dumped the contents of the blanket on the floor in front of her. Her face pulled itself into a grotesque mask of puzzlement, and with the exception of a huge intake of breath, she uttered not a word. I sat back down and waited for the questions.

"What is that? Oh, I know it's money, but from where? Why? How much...It looks like several hundred thousand."

"One million, to be exact. Linda, if I tell you the entire story, can I have your word not a single bit of it will be repeated? Letting anyone know you know anything about any of this could be dangerous to you. So, please, if you don't want to hear the story, now is the time to tell me."

# No Paperwork Needed...

"You walk in here and dump one million dollars on my floor and then expect me to not ask any questions? You must be crazy. I won't utter a word to anyone, but please let me know what the hell is going on."

"Thank you. I was hoping you would, despite the danger, want to hear the story. I'm scared shitless. At the office I'm expected to be the tough guy, but I need someone to talk to, and I'm thinking that maybe someone hearing the entire story from the start might be able to make some sense of it."

"OK, so tell me."

I started with the fact that Larry had lent some seven hundred thousand to a guy named Gerald for what sounded like a high-return business opportunity and ended my monologue some two hours later with, "and so here I am." She hadn't said a word, but she had obviously been paying close attention.

"Let me see if  have this right. Gerald tried to bash your brains in with a rock and later he shot Kent. Then he butchered two of your men. Later he kidnapped Kent and basically extorted another $250,000 from you. Then he sent one of his thugs after you and Kent, and you shot the guy dead. Lastly, he just tried to kill all of you and destroy your business, but you took the payoff money and ran over here. And, while all this was going on, you put the CIA on to him because you think he's a Russian terrorist and he's going set off an atom bomb somewhere in the United States. And you think that maybe I can make some sense of this? Are you out of your mind?"

"I'm beginning to think so, yes."

# No Paperwork Needed...

"Why did he borrow the money from you in the first place? If he later tried to use it as payment to have you killed, he didn't need it in the first place. If he hadn't gotten mixed up with you, he wouldn't have needed to have you killed."

"You asked the number one question: Why did he bother with us in the first place?"

"This is just a guess, but it's the only thing I can think of. Perhaps he needed the money up front as a way to convince someone else with a lot of money that he already had his share of what was needed to carry out his terrorist attack. It's like walking into a bank. If you can prove you already have a ton of money, they're happy to lend you more. Perhaps it was nothing more than bluff money that allowed him to get the real money he needed. And later the million, no longer needed, was used to erase anything to do with you or the loan or hell, even the business."

It made sense; it made perfect sense! Gerald started out with thorough nuclear weapons knowledge and a huge hatred for the United States. What better way to ally with another nutcase than to flash a bunch of money to reinforce the fact that you were dead serious. Once firmly connected to your partner who had the financial backing, Gerald would no longer have any need for the money. Perhaps the only grain of truth in his message to Larry was that he did indeed have someone higher up to answer to.

"Christ! You make it seem so obvious. That has to be it. It explains everything."

"It may explain everything, but it doesn't solve a single one of your problems."

# No Paperwork Needed...

"What do you mean?"

"Do you think Gerald is going to simply go away? He paid a lot of money to have you killed; not only are you still alive, but also now you have the money that was supposed to change that."

She was right, of course. My next step was to call Agent Hall and pass this all on. And to ask him what we should do.

"I hate to ask, but would you mind if I stayed here for a while until I can get something else worked out? I'll call the CIA guys and get their thoughts."

"No, that's fine. In fact, I would like that. But, please, do something with that pile of money. It makes me nervous."

"Let me call Kent. He has a little cabin somewhere in the hills, and he swears no one else alive has any idea about its location or existence. I'm his best friend, and I've never seen it. That might be a good place to hide it."

I called, explained the situation, and made arrangements to meet at a small restaurant we frequented from time to time so I could give him the money to hide at his cabin. He mentioned he had stopped by his place just long enough to pick up some things and that he was on his way to the cabin anyway. We met, transferred the money—it was now in an old suitcase that Linda said was an extra—and he drove off. The money should now be safe and unfindable. Funny how things can get so strange. I had one million dollars, and the thing I wanted to do most was to get rid of it.

I drove back to Linda's. We discussed things a bit longer, and then I called Hall.

# No Paperwork Needed...

"Hall, It's Trench."

"Are you safe? Is everyone safe?"

"I think so. I have no idea where Larry or Tom are. Kent is safe and is hiding with the money."

"Your only hope is that the out-of-town boys turn to Gerald for some compensation and then leave town. And even then, if you think that Gerald has been pissed in the past, I can't imagine what lengths he would go to now to see you dead."

"Listen, I think I finally know what Gerald's involvement with me and Larry was all about. It was simply a way to get some money up front so he could look like a real player as he tried to ally himself with someone who truly had the funds for an operation like this. This allowed him to flash a million or so and thus appear to be someone to be taken seriously. After he had his partner, his million was of no consequence, and thus it was used to fund all of our deaths."

"That seems to track. But knowing that now doesn't help a bit. Either the contracted boys or Gerald and his men are going to stop at nothing to get rid of you, Larry, and all the rest and get their money."

"So what do I do?"

"Is the office still standing?"

"I don't know."

"OK. Stay where you are and give me a number where I can contact you. Tomorrow I'll check out the office and discuss this with the district leader. About the only thing I can think of is to put you all back in the office so you can carry on as usual but place an assault team in your office. Trench, you have to understand, we want to help protect you, but our primary goal is to get our hands on Gerald, and even more importantly, any device, if it has come into existence. I would stand there and watch you get shot a hundred times if it meant I got Gerald and his toy."

"I don't like it. but yes, I understand."

"Stay tight. I'll call tomorrow." Then he hung up.

"Well?" Linda said.

"They're going to stake me out as bait. Would you mind mixing two more drinks, putting on some music, and sitting by my side? Maybe the three together will help me forget this for a while."

The two drinks turned into God knows how many, the music never stopped, and I held her tightly into the wee hours of the morning.

Agent Hall did call the next morning. Linda answered her phone, and I heard her say, "Just a moment, I'll get him."

Once on the line and after saying hello, Hall asked his first question.

"Who was that?"

"Never mind. And don't ask again. You don't need to know. She has absolutely nothing to do with any of this."

"If you say so, but remember, I'm the one who makes up the rules around here. We were by your office—actually in

# No Paperwork Needed...

your office, as the door was busted wide open. Other than the door, nothing seems out of place. I think it's time for all of you to return and go about your business. I'll place a team inside. If the contract hitters show up, we'll take them down. If Gerald and his men show up, it gets a bit more problematic, since the device is still the most important thing. If he has it, but I can't imagine why he would, we'll take him. If we knew that the device hadn't been built yet, which we don't, we would take him. If it exists and he doesn't have it, we have no choice but to let him walk. In that case we need to scare him off and yet try to keep you and everyone else alive."

The next morning I took a chance and stopped by my place for a couple of minutes to grab some fresh clothes and then headed for the office. The rest of the crew wasn't to be found. I knew Kent was at his cabin, but I had no way to contact him. I had no idea where Larry or Tom were at the moment. Agent Hall, true to his word, had the place crawling with agents. They were all serious-looking young men carrying even more serious-looking weapons. Hall walked in shortly thereafter.

"Just ignore them," he said. Much easier said than done, but I did my best.

Mid-morning, Jeff Lancing called. He wanted to come by and bring me up to date and pick up the money. I suggested this was perhaps not a good time, that I was surrounded by people he wouldn't want to meet. I told him to give me a number, and I would call when the time was right.

# No Paperwork Needed...

**Chapter Nineteen**

Hall did his best to keep me calm. Waiting for a group of guys hell-bent on shooting anyone they could find was a significant distraction. Hall kept insisting the team was absolutely prepared to offer the needed protection and take down whichever group of shooters might show up.

The agents were all decked out in dark gray jumpsuit-type uniforms. Just under the outside light windbreaker jacket was a vest that could stop a nine-millimeter round. The vest would stop the bullet, but the fellow wearing the vest would be knocked back and down, very much like being kicked in the chest by a mule. And of course, the vest was completely ineffective should the bullet land in the legs, arms, shoulder, or most tragically, the head. If you were hit in the head, your ticket was instantly punched right then and there.

The agents were armed with AR-15's, nasty little pieces of machinery. Fully automatic, firing up to one hundred and fifty rounds per minute, the standard thirty-round clip could be emptied in twelve seconds. Firing a twenty-two caliber, forty-grain cartridge didn't sound all that dangerous; it was the fact that the bullet could travel as much as three thousand feet per second that made the weapon the death machine it was. Strapped to their waist was a nine-millimeter semiautomatic Berretta with twelve-round clips. Five of these killing machines were stationed here and there in the office. With a total of ten weapons present, no doubt a good time was going to be had by all.

The event unfolded mid-morning. One second was absolute calm, and the next, all hell broke loose. Hall's radio squawked, and he was told that a group of five men were approaching the door. The outside spotter pointed out that every man appeared to be heavily armed. Within seconds of the radio message and Hall telling his men to ready themselves, the door handle and lock assembly disappeared in a flash of dust, wood splinters, and metal fragments. The neat circular hole outlined by the many bullet holes had been completely unnecessary; the door hadn't been locked. Had an office desk been in line with the door, any occupant would have indeed left the party early.

The door swung open, and in poured five men who instantly spread out and lined up with the precision of a practiced drill team. They were each carrying a nine-millimeter UZI automatic pistol, the weapon of choice of terrorists, conspiracy theorists, inept deer hunters, and assholes in general the world around. Fitted with thirty cartridge clips that could be emptied in about a half a minute, they were serious weapons. Although hidden by jackets, it was a good bet their choice of weapon for personal protection, should any good guy have the effrontery of shooting back, was an Australian Glock nine-millimeter. This seemed to be popular with the gun crowd.

The extremely loud, very angry buzz lasted just shy of a minute. The smell of cordite was overpowering. I had instantly dropped to the floor behind my desk and survived only because I lay absolutely prone, with every part of my body within twelve inches of the floor. I watched in horror as I saw my desk essentially sawed in two horizontally as uncountable bullets passed overhead. Above the buzz of the gunfire, a few screams were heard. The firing stopped, followed by a period of deafening silence interspersed with a pitiful moan now and then.

Slowly a few men started to move so they could take score. One agent was motionless, with a large pool of deep red growing beneath his head. Another was holding his left arm, which was showing exposed parts of broken bone, and yet he wasn't making a single sound. Either he was one of the toughest sons of bitches ever to live, or he was deep in shock. Three of the shooters were motionless, lying in variously shaped piles of death. Agent Hall had specifically told the team that he wanted one left alive for questioning. It seemed as if two were alive. One of the agents looked at his fellow team member with the head shot, turned to one of two living shooters, and with a short burst, accurately honored Hall's request. It is interesting how just seconds can separate a shot made in the interest of self-defense and one made to commit murder. Without a doubt, this was never to be part of the final report.

The office was a scene that was hard to take in. Every wall, the floor, the desks, even the ceiling, and of course several men, displayed bullet holes. The group that would have to document each and every hole was going to be busy for a long time. The bad guys hadn't done their homework; they had walked into a death trap. And frustrating at the moment, the good guys didn't even know who the bad guys were. Certainly, Gerald hadn't been anywhere around during the game. Neither Hall or I had any idea if the men were part of Hall's suspected hired hit men or were Gerald's men. I suspected the remaining live gunman was in for some unpleasant interrogation. While the general public walked around in complete bliss with respect to interrogation techniques, the CIA agents could do anything they wanted to get their information; it was as simple as that.

Hall placed a radio call shortly thereafter, and a couple of the ubiquitous black SUVs arrived, loaded up the dead agent, the wounded agent, and all five of the shooters, not showing much more respect to the remaining live one than the four dead. The agents drove off and it was over.

\* \* \*

# No Paperwork Needed...

I laid low for a few days after the gunfight at the OK Corral, a.k.a. our office. My first day back was a Wednesday, and I was hoping that everyone would show up, and we could have a meeting and get back to our simple loan business. The workforce Larry had called in, as if using a magic wand, had repaired all the damaged walls, ceiling tiles, windows, doorjambs, etc. The place smelled of fresh paint. The much-riddled floor was sporting a brand-new elegant carpet.

True, Gerald was still on the loose, but he no longer had his one million dollars or five of his men. Hall had pulled enough out of the one remaining shooter to find out that this had been Gerald's crew. The imported hitters had taken off, but not before extracting their pound of flesh and every remaining penny that Gerald possessed. Perhaps he would get on with his megalomaniac plans to terrorize the United States and leave me alone. I trusted in Agent Hall's ability to get more information out of the one living attacker. By noon, Larry, Kent, and Tom had all returned. While the immense power of the CIA had been reflected in the fact that the gunfight at our office wasn't even hinted at in the paper, somehow all the guys had heard about it and were as eager as I to get back to normal. We had no idea where Gerald was, but we knew where he wasn't, and that was fine with us.

I called Jeff Lancing and asked him to come by. He was obviously excited to get on with his plans. Moments after I placed the phone receiver in the cradle, there was a knock on the door.

"Come on in, Jeff."

"The place looks nice. Did you decide to repaint?"

# No Paperwork Needed...

"Yeah, something like that. Ryan tells me he gave you the name of a fellow who'll return your daughter for you. I don't want to know the name, but are you all set?"

"Yes. I'm paying one third up front and the balance when he delivers my daughter safely."

"So you have any of the details?"

"No. He just wanted as current a picture as I have of her and the address or description of where she could be found."

"How much?"

"He wants a total of thirty thousand, like I said—ten thousand up front and twenty thousand when she's returned."

We were again flush with operating capital from the one million Kent had returned to the business.

"You wanted fifty thousand. If your contractor is taking thirty thousand, that of course leaves you with just twenty. Is that enough for you to set up your entrapment scheme? You'll have to collect absolutely incontrovertible evidence of both your daughter's abuse and your ex-wife's attempts, and they'd better be over the top to get her back, if you stand a chance in court. That takes talent and equipment, and that takes money, so I ask you one more time, will the remaining twenty be sufficient?"

"OK, just to be on the safe side, can you loan me sixty thousand?"

"Sixty it is; drive by this afternoon, and the cash will be ready."

# No Paperwork Needed...

**Chapter Twenty**

Jeff Lancing drove by Larry and Trench's office to pick up the sixty large, and Trench took one last opportunity to ask Jeff if he was absolutely sure this was what he wanted to do. Jeff was told that if he walked out the door with the cash and made it no further than the sidewalk before he turned and walked back in, he would owe both the sixty and the interest. And if he couldn't pay, his troubles were just starting.

Jeff said he was sure, took the cash, walked out the door to his car, and drove away.

He drove to an agreed-upon location where he would get the first ten thousand to Phillip, as he now knew the name. Phillip had made arrangements for Jeff to place the cash, a picture of Debra, and a few other details that Jeff had written down in a small package. The package was then to be placed by a particular trash collection bin in the city park. Jeff was then to simply drive away. Jeff never would see Phillip.

Sam, a.k.a. Phillip, had been watching from a distance, and as soon as Jeff dropped the package and drove away, he retrieved and checked its contents. Everything he needed was there. Jeff was asked not to try to contact him in any way or for any reason. Phillip expected the job to take nine to ten days at the most. Jeff had been told not to worry; he would soon be holding his daughter.

Sam walked to his car, entered, and drove away. Back at his house, Jeff was left with the remaining fifty thousand and absolutely no guarantee whatsoever that he would ever see Phillip—if that was indeed his name—again. Jeff started the actual work of being prepared for his ex-wife's arrival.

# No Paperwork Needed...

Phillip wasn't his real name, of course. He changed names as often as most guys changed their shorts. His true name was Sam, but few people knew that. He would change his name once again prior to starting his mission. Sam drove to his apartment, parked the car in his garage, went inside, and reviewed his plans in absolute detail. It was real now; he had the first ten grand.

The next morning, Pete, aka Phillip, aka Sam, dressed, and taking nothing but the cash and the few items he had gotten from Jeff, backed his car out of the garage and headed for the strip of auto dealers. His first step was the proper car. The farther out the street, the sleazier the dealerships or car lots became. Sam would know what he wanted when he saw it.

His eyes caught the perfect vehicle at a dumpy little place called the Bargains Galore Lot. There it sat, a 2002 Pontiac Aztec. This was perhaps the penultimate getaway car. Since it was the single most hideous vehicle coming out of Detroit in decades, no one paid attention to the car, primarily because it was simply too painful to look at. Sam smiled to himself, thinking about what would happen if someone did see it; the report to the police would be that they had no idea what kind of car it was, but it was the ugliest thing they had ever seen. The downside was that the police would know the model instantly. The irony was that it was a dependable and versatile vehicle.

Sam parked about two blocks farther down the street and walked back to the lot. He was immediately approached by a man matching every single stereotype ever held about a used car dealer. He suggested Sam call him Big Al and shook Sam's hands so vigorously that some of Sam's filling were at risk. Sam expressed interest in the Aztec and was assured he had made an excellent choice;

the Aztec was perhaps the nicest car on the lot. Thus began the time-honored customer/car dealer dance. Sam listened for a short while and then said he would purchase the car. He walked to the small mid-lot office with the salesman. The car had a $2,850 sign in the window. Sam pulled out an envelope containing twenty-five hundred and said that was as high as he could go. The salesman said he would be skinned alive if he let the car go for anything less than twenty-seven fifty. Sam said he would have to look elsewhere and turned to go. Seeing twenty-five hundred in cold cash walk out the door was more than Big Al could handle; after all, that damn piece of junk had been on the lot for over four months.

Pointing out that this was going to be hard to explain to the owner of the lot, he said he would take the twenty-five hundred. He asked Sam for some identification so he could do the bill of sale, title, buyers name, entry, etc. Sam reached in his back pocket and then with an embarrassed look pointed out that he must have left his wallet at the bank that morning when he picked up the cash. He said he would go get the wallet and try to return with the cash within the next day or two. Once again, Big Al was about to watch his twenty-five hundred walk out the door. Al stopped Sam in midstride and mentioned that the ID wasn't that big a deal, it was only twenty-five hundred, after all. When Sam was asked for his name and address, he became Robert Hanson on the spot. After Big Al taped the temporary plates on the Aztec, Sam jumped in, said thanks, and drove his new car directly home and parked inside the garage. He set the alarm clock for eleven that night and jumped in bed.

Upon hearing the alarm, Sam got up, dressed, and made a strong cup of coffee. He went out to the garage and looked over his chosen car for the job. Damn, it was ugly. He pulled the light switch and checked for proper lighting all around the vehicle. Then he turned the key, set the turn signals first left, then right, and checked that all lamps were functioning. Placing a brick on the brake pedal allowed the brake lights to be verified. Lastly were the headlight bright and dim functions. All systems go. How many times had some enterprising criminal's vehicle been pulled over, leading to incarceration, due to a damned burned-out taillight?

The second-most important thing was to remember to take and use his pipe. The thing tasted absolutely horrible but was the perfect accessory. He had no idea why society in general seemed to instantly place a pipe smoker on a higher plane of social status. Men smoking a pipe just didn't seem to be the criminal type. At any rate, he never left on a job without what he had grown to think of as his good luck pipe.

He backed the Aztec out of the garage and drove with extreme caution to the location where he had parked his properly registered car earlier that day. He parked a few feet behind his actual car, and removing an adjustable tow bar assembly from his trunk, attached the Aztec to the rear of his car. Making sure to attach the proper tow lights to the rear of the Aztec, he carefully pulled the Aztec to his house. Watch every sign, signal all turns, stay just a bit below the speed limit—he told himself these things time and time again during the drive.

Arriving at his house, he disconnected the Aztec and parked it in the garage. He centered his everyday car in front of the house, locked it, and went back inside for a bit more sleep. He had reset the alarm clock for 3:00 a.m.

Again responding to the alarm clock, he redressed, once again picked up nothing but the few items he had received from Jeff including the remainder of the cash, took care of all matters around the house to allow for several days of absence, and walked to the garage. He backed the Aztec into the driveway, closed the garage door, backed into the street, set the trip odometer to zero, and left town.

As with the start of every job, he spent several hours going over his plan time and time again, sometimes adding a few steps, other times changing or removing a step or two. He had performed this service seven times before, but each and every time, it involved a situation that he truly believed was the right thing to do. He didn't think of himself as a kidnapper; he was a highly efficient child-placement service that had the ability to ignore the various legal nuances of a situation and quickly bring about the proper solution or placement.

So once again, he was off to correct a judicial error in an issue between an estranged couple. He almost choked at the use of "estranged." He had been in the middle of several estranged couples who were but a few social mores away from killing each other. He himself years ago had reached a point with his ex-wife that could indeed come under the heading of estranged. He joked with the boys at the bar that their relationship had degenerated to no more than hall sex. Upon walking by each other in the upstairs hall in the morning, they greeted each other with a bitter "fuck you!"

He had been driving for close to six hours, and it was time to stop for fuel, use the john, and get a bite to eat. He would soon stop for the day; he never drove more than eight hours a day. Tired people made mistakes. Watching the light reflections of the rear lamps in the truck-stop windows, he once again did his lamp checks, as he did at every stop. His day would end just short of five hundred miles toward his destination. Day one would be over.

# No Paperwork Needed...

He stopped at a small mom-and-pop motel. He registered under the name of Mack Peterson and wrote down a completely fictitious auto plate number on the registration slip. He mentioned that he didn't have a credit card, but laid out three hundred dollars in hundreds on the counter and said he wanted their best room before they could object to not holding a credit card. It worked every time. He was in the room, and the motel operators had no idea in hell who he was, where he came from, or where he was going. The three hundred cash would most likely never hit the books.

He set his watch alarm for 8:00 a.m. and upon awakening, put on his same clothes and started driving again. Mid-morning, he pulled into a shopping center just off the interstate. Finding a Sears store, he purchased a complete set of clothes, underwear and all. He drove on to a truck stop and used the men's room to change into the new clothing. He left the old clothing hanging by one of the trucker's showers. He then sat down for some breakfast, topped off the fuel, and headed on down the road. In another day or so, he would be at his destination.

\* \* \*

It had been a busy morning. First was the call from Agent Hall.

"Trench, it's Hall."

"Hello."

I had grown to dread Hall's calls. One never knew what might happen. More than once, a call had led to my jumping into a car within minutes and taking off to God knows where.

# No Paperwork Needed...

"I want to give you a bit of an update. We finally caught up with the owner of the boat that Gerald and his men took that day from the marina. No one could have been more surprised than the owner that his boat had been taken for a short cruise and had been used to commit a murder. It's starting to look like Gerald brazenly had simply taken the first boat he could find. And we've been unable to extract any information from the lone survivor of the office shooting. Hopefully we can do better soon; at the moment he's constantly in and out of consciousness."

I involuntarily shuddered a bit at the word *extract*. They hadn't been able to determine the name of the survivor yet, but whatever his name, I suspect he was in for some difficult days. Hall had mentioned it worked the same with all informants. They could either spill their guts right up front, avoiding a lot of pain, or finally slowly spit out the information while one step from death's door. The man who would never divulge his secrets could only be found in the movies.

"We're running out of options. I no longer think plan B would be effective. I think Gerald is calling his vendetta with you a push, and is on to bigger and better things. The woman he slipped away with at the Lawrence Livermore Labs wasn't Nancy Kundert. Whoever it was, she has about two hundred people scratching their heads as to how she passed herself off as Nancy. The real Ms. Kundert was on vacation while this all took place. I can only imagine her surprise upon being tackled by five agents the day she did show back up from vacation. That entire affair was like magic. We still have no idea whatsoever how they escaped, and now we have no idea how a fake Nancy Kundert got in."

"So what's next?"

# No Paperwork Needed...

"I have no idea. I suspect that Gerald and the mystery woman are holed up somewhere, busy building their destructive plaything. The woman has to have an in-depth knowledge about nuclear processes to have begun to fake her way into the labs in the first place. We either need to get something from the shooting survivor or get damned lucky."

"It sounds like the only person who came out of the Livermore event successfully was the real Nancy. I hope she enjoyed her vacation."

"She said she did. Funny thing though, she commented that she doesn't remember a single thing from the first couple of days. I guess a lot of drink, sand, and sunshine will do that."

"Yeah, or drugs," I said. Hall instantly dropped the line.

I slowly hung up the phone on my end, wondering what that was all about.

I turned to my next task. It was time to see if Kent had found out anything about the sabotage that was taking place at Jean Reynolds's up-and-coming pastry shop. I had given Kent the list of past and current workers on the shop's remodeling. I called him into the office.

"Kent, what have you found out about the Reynolds pastry shop problems?"

"Under a number of different guises, I obtained all the names of the workers and owners at the shop down the street, named Sweet Buns Pastry, by the way. I then one by one checked registrations to get plate numbers, thanks to Don Blondski at the cop shop. After following them around for a while, including staking out their houses or apartments, I came up absolutely empty-handed except for this."

"Except what?"

He handed me the list of names Jean Reynolds had created and the list he had developed while checking out everyone associated with Sweet Buns.

I looked them both over and said, "What are the chances that the Mullins on each list aren't related? An even better question would be, why in hell didn't the worker hire on under an assumed name? Look into these two, and I'll bet a nickel you have found the connection between Sweet Buns and Jean's new shop."

I wondered what goes through someone's mind, that he would use his real name in a situation like this. Time and time again it turns out that most small time criminals get caught because they do stupid things.

"You would win that nickel, but I'm way ahead of you.
 Tom and I waited outside the apartment of the Mullin working at Jean's shop. When he came out, Tom said hello  with his leather-covered slug, tossed him in the back of our car, and jumped in beside him. We took him over to Jean's shop, hauled him inside, and brought him around after tying him up. It didn't take long to get the full story. He is indeed the brother of the Mullin who is part owner of the Sweet Buns shop. They were worried about competition.

I told Tom I wanted Mullin to sit there for a while and think about what he'd done and to get his mindset corrected so it wouldn't happen again. Tom had the solution to keeping Mullins around for a while; he used a framing nail gun to

# No Paperwork Needed...

attach each of Mullin's feet to the floor. Three and one-half inch nails—wicked. He'll be on worker's comp for some time. Tom handed him a hacksaw. The idiot wanted to know if he was supposed to cut off his feet. I told him that would be one idea, but I was thinking that what he could do was slide the blade between the sole of his shoe and the floor and cut through the nail. At that point we left. I don't think Jean will have any more setbacks."

"Good, I'm going to call this solved. I'll contact Jean. Thanks, Kent."

I did just that. "Jean, it's Trench."

"Oh, hi. Did you find out who was damaging my shop?"

"Yes. You don't have to worry about that anymore. You'll need to replace a worker, but go ahead and get started again. You shouldn't have any more problems. And I don't want you to have problems with us either. You better speed up your schedule a bit and arrive over here on time with the repayment. I can't step much more out of line for you; you understand?"

"Trench, I do understand, and I'll honor my loan, I promise, and thank you so much."

Next on my mental list was to see what was happening with Mary Ellen Winestone, the gardener affair. I called Officer Don Blondski at the district police station. Don was on the line after two transfers.

"Officer Blondski."

"Hello, Don, it's Trench."

"Hello," he said, as warm as ever.

# No Paperwork Needed...

"Any more news on the Mary Ellen Winestone woman?"

"Why are you so damned interested in this woman? Never mind, I know you won't tell me. Nothing new on her; the robbery was an absolutely open and shut case. The gardener was found guilty a few days ago. First offense, so the judge gave him four years with three of them suspended. He'll be back in someone's garden in less than a year. However, the lady's bad luck seems to continue. Her husband was killed in a freak accident about a week ago. He forgot to set the safety locks on one of his car hoists, and according to the investigators, the hoist had a small hydraulic leak that allowed the hoist to lower slowly while he was under the car.

They think he finally noticed the leak, backed up quickly, and banged the shit out of his head, knocking himself out. He landed unconscious under one of the ramps and was still lying there when the hoist lowered itself all the way down, squashing his head flatter than a pancake. The coroner says he was dead instantly and has already closed the case, calling it accidental death. One of the officers still thinks it was somehow a successful murder. But he's the guy who considers every murder successful. If the victim's dead, the murder was successful; the perpetrator may not get away with the crime, but the murder itself was successful."

I felt it was time to tell him something to put his mind at ease. No need to let it fester to the point where he might start looking into things a bit deeper.

"Keep this to yourself, Don, but the reason I was wondering about this case is that one of Ms. Winestone's ex-maids was here looking for a bit of money to start a maid service of her own and gave me Winestone as a reference of her work skills. I think I'm going to say no; a lot of things seem to happen around her."

"That's for sure. OK, thanks for filling me in."

*So*, I thought to myself, *Mary pulled it off*. The two-timing gardener wasn't going to see the light of day for a year, the overpowering third wheel of a husband was completely out of the picture, and she had a ton of money coming her way in short order. The folks who say crime never pays have no idea what they're talking about. I gave Mary a quick call and told her I was up to date on her activities and that she needed to be sure to remember her obligation. She told me she was looking forward to our meeting, at which time she would pay her debt in full. And by the way, would I like to meet at her house and enjoy a bit of time in the sunroom and visit over a cup of Earl Gray tea? This lady was as cool as they come.

# No Paperwork Needed...

## Chapter Twenty-One

Kent told me that over the past couple of days, he had scheduled two more potential clients for the afternoon, and one of them was now here.

"Send him in," I said.

A medium build, average-looking man introduced himself as a Mr. Stanley Cornell.

"My name is Trench. Glad to meet you, Stanley, what can I do for you?"

Prior to saying a word, he placed two eight-by-ten photos on my desk. The top picture showed a cute verging on beautiful young lady who appeared to be about eighteen to twenty years old. When I set the picture aside and looked at the second one, I know I did a lousy job of restraining my reaction. What in God's name had *this* young girl gone through?

"That's my daughter, Angela," Mr. Cornell said. "As you can see, she was a beautiful and very happy young lady. Then she was raped and beaten by two boys, and you can see the result. I want the boys punished."

"I can see why, but I'm sorry, Stanley; we don't hire out for this kind of stuff. We lend money. Besides, this is a matter for the police."

"The boys' names are Jeffery Holmes and Tony Clark."

"Do you mean the Holmes and Clarks I think you mean?"

"Yes. Now you know why I would just be wasting my time to contact the police."

# No Paperwork Needed...

I couldn't help but think he was correct about that. Both the Holmes and Clark families had all the needed money, power, and influence to make anything go away. The rape and beating of the girl may have crossed some kind of line, but deep down I couldn't help but think that even in this, the boys would skate free.

"As I said, we lend money for a very high interest rate. What you do with the money isn't our business, but getting it paid back with all fees is our business. I assume you want to hire some guys to punish the boys. Again, that is your business. But I need to know how you're going to pay us back."

"Yes, I want the boys punished, and then I want all the money needed to pay the hospital bills and to pay for my daughter's upcoming surgeries, and lastly I want the money needed to pay you back. I want the boys told, as well as their fathers, that if the money isn't paid, the next two people punished will be the fathers themselves. To do this I need to hire some guys who can get this done—that is why I want the money. If it doesn't work out, then I'll sell my house to get you paid back."

"How much do you need?"

"I don't know anything about this kind of stuff, but I would rather borrow too much than too little. Would twenty thousand be OK?"

"Fine. Come by tomorrow and pick it up. But remember, this isn't a charity outfit. If you don't repay the proper amount on time, you and your daughter will share similar problems."

The last client I was to see today was a Doug Winters.

# No Paperwork Needed...

It all started with the normal introductions and questions and threats about repayment.

"You want ten thousand. How are you going to pay it back?"

"When I find my ex-business partner, I'll recover the money and pay you back out of that. If I can't find him, I'll start disposing of company physical assets and use that to pay you. One way or another, you'll get paid."

"Are you up to this kind of stuff? This won't be a normal, pleasant business meeting."

"I was a unit leader on a Navy Seal team and was in and out of several situations that make this seem like child's play."

Enough said. I had ten thousand in the office, so I handed him the cash, reminded him of the obligations, and told him good luck. A Navy Seal—I wish I could watch the re-union with his business partner.

# No Paperwork Needed...

**Chapter Twenty-Two**

Harry had spent the morning carefully looking over the day's racing form and wading through stacks of past performance guides. The standard six steps to "picking a winner"—recency, speed figures, race odds, career data, last finish, and running style—all meant very little to Harry. He simply had the knack. When at the track, keeping in mind his morning's study of the Race Card and Past Performance forms, he looked over the field and spotted the winner. He didn't know how he did it, but considerably more often than not, he did.

In days gone by, it had been, if not easier, at least more predictable to win via the expediency of cheating. These days, with some element of the FBI to be found at all tracks, and with state-level criminal background checks on everyone allowed in the stable areas from the water boys up to the owners and jockeys, tweaking things in your favor was a lot more difficult. In the past, manipulation of blood samples and use of drugs could give a real edge to winning the race. Harry had several people in his pocket in those days who allowed for a pre-drug introduction blood sample to later be exchanged with the after-race contaminated sample. The proper use and timing of drugs could make a loser out of a winner or a winner out of a loser. Today's multi-lock sample storage boxes, coded seals over the blood sample tubes, etc., made these surefire techniques almost impossible to implement.

Placing a winning bet now required some skill. Most bettors had a system, a surefire method for failure. Far better was a thorough knowledge of the available data and then that elusive and impossible to explain eye for the horses. This had put Harry in a tough spot. With his bullet-holed foot, thanks to that prick Tom, it was difficult to make it to the track to see the horses, so he hadn't been betting much. But now he was able to limp to the track, look things over, and have Doris run and place the bets. He was still in form, as most times he then had Doris run and gather the winnings.

As he looked over the field running a two-year-old filly race, an entry named Doughnut stood out for having a set of hips that proportionally appeared more massed than the rest of the body. Her PP results didn't stand out to any extent, with the exception of the gain in speed figures in her last race, which almost doubled the gain between any of her other past races. Allowing for one other horse to advance on her made her a good choice for a placing bet. Based on the pre-race odds, a placing would return just under two to one. He sent Doris to the window with two thousand and instructions. Post time was in two minutes. He felt good about the bet, but his joy was indeed dampened by the fact that every penny of the potential winnings would have to go to that fucking Trench.

Some eight minutes later, Doris was at the window picking up just shy of four thousand and placing Harry's next bet. In the meantime, Harry was thinking he had picked up two thousand, and the day was just starting. He wanted to leave the track with at least five thousand new in his pocket.

\* \* \*

Fifteen hundred miles away, Sam was pulling into Syracuse, New York, a smaller-size city of one hundred forty-five thousand hardy souls. Syracuse wasn't the warmest place on the planet.

First step was to find lodging for the night. He spent a few hours looking for a small mom-and-pop motel that would do for the night. He would stay in a different place each night. There was no reason to give the owners time to wonder about his not offering a credit card up front. He found a single level, small, U-shaped motel. The turquoise and off-pink paint job was a sure clue that this was the kind of place where not many questions would be asked. He performed his same 'no credit card but here is three hundred dollars and I want your best room' routine. Moments later, he was in the room. Later, he would go back out for a new set of clothes and some carry-in food and would start his location planning.

Once back in his room, he changed into his new clothes, and was off again to dispose of his old clothes. He chose a grouping of what appeared to be a collection of homeless people. Kindness had nothing to do with it; he knew that anyone in this group would never report the strange act to anyone. They would pick up the clothes and that would be that. He then searched out a fried chicken fast food joint and purchased three breasts, a pint of fake crab salad, and a large drink. As he drove back to his room, he couldn't help but notice how good the chicken smelled; he was hungry. Two breasts, some fake crab, and a large drink later, he turned his attention to the task at hand.

He had set an outside deadline of three days for leaving the city with Debra, Jeff Lancing's daughter, in hand. At his disposal were the last known address for Lancing's wife and a one-year-old picture of Debra. Without a picture of the wife, he could stake out the address and see her come and go several times and never know it was her. He had driven by the address, and it was a large apartment building with many people entering and exiting during the short time he watched. But he did have a picture of the daughter, so she was the one to watch for.

# No Paperwork Needed...

Plus, adults seemed to have an uncanny way of knowing they were being watched. The answer was the child.

Based on Debra's address and age, the most obvious school was named Lyncourt and was located five blocks from the apartment. That's where he would watch the kids come and go, play and exercise. He needed to know how she arrived at school, how she returned home, and anywhere she might go after school. This was difficult work. When the kids came out, they did so en masse. You had to look at each kid and do so very fast. He had a handful of visual clues to help, however. One, according to Jeff, she was small for her age and would indeed be one of the younger students. Obviously, he only needed to look at the females. Lastly, thanks to her mother and the smashed toes ordeal, she walked and ran with a slight limp. He had done other jobs with less than this to work with and wasn't concerned.

He had no intention of trying to pick her up today. He just wanted to spot her, see if this was indeed the correct school, and see which direction she headed, or who, how, and when someone picked her up. Given the profile Jeff had handed him about the mother, he'd bet Debra was on her own to walk the five blocks home each day. He had parked at a location close to the school where he could see all the kids leave the building, and also on the path most direct between the school and Debra's house.

He heard bells, and like a flash flood, out the children poured. This was going to be harder than he first thought. Out they came in huge, tightly massed bunches. His only hope was to apply his visual filters to the children that crossed the first intersection and headed his way. Child after child was glanced at, rejected—and then there she was! His every assumption had been dead on. He quickly started the car, pulled out, made two rights, drove down

# No Paperwork Needed...

the parallel street for three blocks, made a last right, parked, and jumped out. He quickly walked toward the corner and looked toward the school. With her limp she was a relatively slow walker for a child her age. She was still two full blocks away. He crossed the street and waited by some trees, playing with and eventually lighting his pipe. When Debra was abreast of him on the opposite side of the street, he slowly walked in the same direction as Debra. He took in every house, every driveway, every tree and hedge, every corner and alleyway. Tomorrow, with luck, at some location along this stretch of street, he would kidnap Debra.

He watched her walk all the way to her house, approach the door, open it, and step into what had become her own private hell. Sam didn't know it, but he was about to do one of the kindest things he had ever done for another person.

* * *

Jeff had no way of knowing how Phillip, as he knew him, was progressing, but he did know, if successful that he would be returning with Debra in another six to seven days. He could wait no longer to get set up for his wife's entrapment. It never once occurred to him that she might not come after the child. He alone knew her. She wanted the child as part of a sick mother-daughter arrangement and now more than ever; Debra was getting old enough to understand things were happening that shouldn't be happening and old enough to talk. His wife couldn't allow that.

Jeff had contacted the ICU surveillance company. He hoped to God they were better at their work than they were at dreaming up company names. He had explained that he needed to capture every bit of video and audio of

# No Paperwork Needed...

his ex-wife, should she show up—no matter where, in, or around the house. He explained that she had left a medium security mental health center without permission, and he was extremely worried about what she might do to herself, their daughter, or him. True, this was looking at the situation through rose-colored glasses, but the surveillance company might want to avoid being involved with a fucking full-blown sociopath hell-bent on murdering him and perhaps their daughter as well. The surveillance equipment rental and its installation were going to cost every bit as much as the kidnapping.

Watching the equipment installation was fascinating in itself. Absolutely everything was wireless and lithium battery powered. Jeff had but to click one button, and any one of thirty-three motion-sensing video cameras based upon both infrared and sound Doppler phenomena would arm themselves and transmit video to a master twenty-four-channel, digital memory storage device when triggered. Of course, an audio analog to digital transmission was made simultaneously. As one of the ICU technicians had stated, if a mouse farts anywhere near or in your house, you're going to know about it. The cameras were about the size of two dimes stacked upon each other. Each was held in place with a small piece of tape matching the color of the camera's surroundings. When finished, barring anyone who had watched them being installed, they simply couldn't be seen. Jeff was invited to test out the system in any way he saw fit. Try as he may, every single move, every single sound he made was recorded for later viewing in glorious high-definition color and crystal clear sound. It was nothing short of eerie.

Jeff had thought through the situation several times. Actually, he couldn't stop thinking about what might happen. He was absolutely certain she would show up to grab their daughter and do her level best to see that he wasn't around to ever try anything like this again. But the order of things would be critical. It many ways, it was very simple. First, he had to let her attack, shoot, stab, whatever. Second, he had to survive the attack; then, and as gently as possible, he had to subdue her. That was asking a lot, to take a bullet or a knife wound or whatever, survive, and yet have the strength and reflexes to disarm and subdue a person so irrationally mentally driven that normal pain or restraints would be of little consequence.

Every bit of this had to be on camera; at least, he was sure *that* had been covered. A light bullet resistant vest was a must, as was a wide array of various bandages, etc. It was strange trying to anticipate your own possible injuries and what would be required to patch things up a bit while waiting for help. For whatever reason, with the exception of trained killers, most people, even if they were out to kill someone, were hesitant to shoot their target in the head. It was most likely the image that bothered them. But with Karen, all bets were off. In fact, if she was in tune with her own reality, a head shot was most likely. In the most stressful of situations, it's interesting how the human mind can find mirth in things. What came to his mind next was the availability of a bulletproof baseball cap.

**Chapter Twenty-Three**

It had only taken Mr. Cornell a few days to find a couple of thugs who were up to the job of evening the score for Angela. Trench had suggested a few dives to start asking some subtle questions. Cornell explained in detail what he was after and at first didn't get much response. However, the before and after pictures of his daughter sealed the deal.

The goons needed to have things explained several times, but at last had details of the job down pat. Each boy was found and detained in turn at an abandoned shack. When both boys were present, that same evening they were to receive brutal beatings along the lines of what they had put Angela through. Prior to the beatings, each of the boys would be handed a note explaining the time, date, and location for the demanded money. The note made reference to the fact that if the money wasn't delivered, the boys would receive a second beating much more severe than the one they were about to receive, and that their fathers would also get to join in on the fun. It was very simple; the boys received their punishment via a beating, and the father's punishment was in the form of complete financial compensation. The boys said they understood and then, did indeed, receive the beating of their lives.

The boys were then delivered to their individual homes and dropped on the front steps. The goons drove away, completely confident their work was finished.

And, it was. The fathers, being cowards as most bullies truly are, immediately made arrangements to deliver their share of the demanded funds. They didn't bully with physical force, but rather via influence and financial repercussions, most times causing more grief than any playground roughness could ever cause. There was no way they were going to risk enduring a beating like their sons had received. Besides, the amount of money demanded was rather insignificant in the grand scheme of things.

They would pay the money, arrange for the best of medical treatment for their sons, and that would be that. No police, no fuss, no muss.

On the appointed day and time, the money was delivered to the proper location, precisely following instructions; the delivery stooges (there was no way the fathers were going to deliver the money themselves) then drove away.

A few hours later, Mr. Cornell himself drove to the location and picked up the bags of money. It was all there. What was a minor fine to the Holmes and Clark families meant the world to Mr. Cornell. He could pay his hospital bill, pay back the loan, and have the money to start his daughter's facial surgery to bring some confidence back into her life.

The next morning, he deposited the money, stopped by the hospital and wrote a check, and then drove over to Larry and Trench's place.

* * *

Mr. Cornell walked in and placed the loan amount and interest on my desk.

"Did it work out as you hoped for?" I asked.

"Yes. Here's your payment in full. I would never been able to do this without your help."

# No Paperwork Needed...

"Our pleasure, and I wish your daughter the best. They can work miracles these days. I'm sure she will soon be as beautiful as ever. Good luck."

With one more thanks, Mr. Cornell walked out of my world.

# No Paperwork Needed...

**Chapter Twenty-Four**

I answered the third phone call of the day. "Hello."

"Trench, It's Agent Forester. Remember me?"

"Like I could forget? What do you want?"

"Rumor has it that your Gerald situation has escalated into a real mess. Care to share any details?"

"Are you kidding? What the hell have you ever done for me? You need to stay on your best behavior. The CIA agents now know everything from the get-go about the Gerald situation, except that you wouldn't bump it up from Treasury level until the circumstances absolutely forced you to do so, and even then you did so without involving yourself in any way. Now that they know everything, you have no hold over me whatsoever, so my advice to you is to not piss me off. I have nothing to lose to hang you out to dry. When this is all resolved, then I'll at my discretion get back to you on issues involving any potential income tax issues. Not a minute sooner. Don't call me again. If you're lucky, you might hear from me again someday."

I hung up the phone feeling superior, but deep down I knew the minute things were resolved with Gerald, and Forester was no longer on the hook for any departmental misdirection, she would be all over me like a cheap suit.

Larry had asked me to get on with new business, and I knew he was right in asking. We couldn't survive on the status quo forever. I had told him about the last group of college kids, Larry, Moe, and Curly. Actually, the damn kids had an excellent idea, and Larry, like me, could see no way to lose. Not to mention, as distasteful as it was, this was a way to put our foot in the door of a legitimate business. I might end up having to squeal on myself to Mrs. Forester.

I called one of the numbers for the college kids and asked him to gather up the other two and come by my office. "We have decided to fund your start-up."

He responded in the manner of any true major corporate leader: "Holy shit, we'll be right there."

And they were.

"I'm going to ask you guys to go over your idea in detail with Larry. I want to hear it again myself. I'll be trying to get a handle on the amount of money that will be needed for the various steps; this will not be one of our normal loans. There will not be an interest rate. There will not be an expected payback date. We are funding your start up until the income can fund the remaining operation. For that, we legitimately own the lion's share of the company. And by lion's share, I mean one goddamned big lion—got it? I'll work with the numbers in my mind's eye as you once again explain your idea and plans."

We all walked into Larry's office and explain they did. For hours it was petabytes here, C++ there, NSAs, quad processors, data streams, object-oriented code, firewalls, USB programmer, etc. On and on it went. They never got more than twenty words out of their mouths before either Larry or I had another question. In the end, I didn't understand one damn thing more than I did at the start, other than some huge array of servers somewhere would hound the shit out of fat people for not losing weight fast enough.

As neither Larry or I had any idea what this stuff costs, I lied and told them I had an idea in mind of the needed

# No Paperwork Needed...

basic start-up capital and asked them what their thoughts were on the startup funds. We were told they had looked into this and felt they could get things going on a modest level and let the Internet posting grow the system from there for about seven hundred thousand. I thought Larry was going to choke to death. I, however, thought of how much of a better gamble this was than the seven-fifty we had advanced Gerald and got back only by the grace of God.

I turned to Larry and said, "Remember Gerald? I say yes. We'll be using money we had no reason to expect to ever see again."

The three kids walked out the door knowing that the next day they would have a seven hundred thousand dollar line of credit to draw from. They were told that the first time they couldn't acceptably justify an expenditure, the pain would begin.

We were on our way to being normal, respectable corporate level businessmen—in other words, bigger crooks than we had ever been before.

All in all, it was a pretty good day. No guns fired, no one hurt. I left the office telling myself I really needed to get ahold of Linda. It was past time for a date, and on top of that, I found myself missing her. I made it home, opened a beer, turned on some instrumental music, and forgetting that I was holding a beer, fell asleep on the couch.

# No Paperwork Needed...

**Chapter Twenty-Five**

Gerald had carefully examined the Lawrence Livermore Labs' public employee records. There was no detailed information to be found, but at this time, all he was looking for was a name and a position. He wanted a list of the female fissionable materials storage managers and supervisors. Once he had the names, he could go from there.

His number one partner in his unrelenting plan of US nuclear terrorism was Elena Vladimirovna Petrova, a former team member when he was in weapons research before leaving Russia. She, like him, could no longer stand the political environment that continued to allow the United States to walk all over the Soviet Union, treating them like a bunch of kids caught with their hands in the cookie jar. If his inept government wasn't going to do anything about the spread of US control of his country, he would. With Elena in hand, they made their way to the United States and began their step-by-step process to strike terror in the heart of America.

Together, they had all the needed skills to construct a small, portable, very powerful nuclear device that could reduce nearly any major city to rubble. After all, that's what they did for the Soviet government before they realized that the currently presiding government would never have the balls to use the devices.

They now had the backing of a strong financial provider, which meant they now had all three of the needed ingredients: knowledge, money, and contacts.

Elena was going to help with the materials. Gerald pored over the names he had pulled from the public archives and found five he deemed worth further investigation.

# No Paperwork Needed...

Now it became harder, but only by a little bit. Gerald assigned a name to each of his five underlings, with explicit instructions to find out as much as possible about their charge without the individual ever knowing that she was being watched.

Three names were scratched off the list in short order, their physical stature being so far from Elena's that there was no way Elena could impersonate them. The fourth one, a Ms. Nancy Kundert, looked uncannily like Elena. Gerald was tempted to skip looking at the data on the fifth name, but he hadn't gotten to where he was in life by making snap judgments or not taking advantage of all available data. Name five, however, proved to be impossible to use. Nancy Kundert it was.

Armed with Nancy's address, phone, job position, SSN, and just about anything else one could imagine, Gerald went to work. It didn't take long to discover she had booked travel plans for a couple of weeks hence. Perfect! She was going on vacation. According to the dates, her last day of work for a full week and two weekends would be Friday two weeks hence. Gerald made arrangements for his men to quietly pick her up later on that Friday night.

\* \* \*

Just past eight-thirty on the chosen Friday night, three of Gerald's men pulled up to the curb two houses down from Nancy Kundert's home. Two of the men walked to her door, one hiding on the small porch where he couldn't be seen and the other ringing the doorbell. Nancy answered the door and was instantly and violently pushed back by the first man through the door. He grabbed her shoulder, injected a medium dose of Versed, and spun her around so he could bear hug her from behind, trapping both of her arms at her sides. By this time the second man was through the door and plastered a wide piece of black duct tape across her mouth. She was now silent.

The second man grabbed and held her arms and shoved them around to her back, at which time the first man placed a fourteen-inch-long strong nylon tie strap around her wrists. Then he dropped to his knees and held her feet together as the second man in turn placed an identical strap around her ankles. Start to finish, the process had taken less than ten seconds, without a sound being made.

The third man in the car had by now moved the car in front of the house, opened the trunk, and walked to the house to let the two men in the house know it was clear and they could carry her to the car. This they did and dropped her in the trunk. They slammed the lid, entered the car, and drove away. It had all happened so fast, it was like Nancy had never existed.

Nancy was in a state of abject terror. Not a single word or sound had been made during her abduction. She was bounced around with every bump and turn, twice hitting her head on some hard metal object. But it was the infinite blackness that scared her the most. And why, oh why, did anyone want her? Of course, due to the injection of Versed, she would not remember any of this.

It seemed like hours before the car stopped, when it had actually been only a little over twenty minutes. The trunk was opened, and the garage light burned holes in her eyes. It wasn't that the garage light was so bright; it was that the closed trunk had been total darkness. She was picked up by two men, one grabbing her shoulders, and a second lifting her up by her feet. She was carried down some steps to a basement room and stretched out on a

# No Paperwork Needed...

flat table. She saw only two things before she went under: one, a man approaching her with a syringe, and two, a lady who in so many ways looked strangely like herself. Then there was only darkness.

With close to two full weeks to prepare for Nancy's arrival, Gerald had done splendidly. He and Elena had a finite list of tasks to accomplish to get Elena ready to successfully impersonate Nancy and enter the labs. Hair color, style, and length were easy. Facial coloring and marks weren't much of a challenge either. Body padding solved the overall size appearance; Elena was a trim lady. Teeth and voice were handled by simply keeping one's mouth shut. That left the retinal scans, fingerprints, and codes or passwords remaining.

The retinal scanning seen so often in spy and adventure movies was the simplest of the remaining three. A properly lit digital photograph taken with an at least fifteen-megapixel resolution camera and then image enhanced to proper opacity and reflectivity, sized correctly, and with a twenty-four-meg color density, was all that was needed. Print this out on a photo printer, any number of which can be purchased for less than seventy-five dollars, and you have the needed retinal scan. Simply hold the image at the proper distance from the scanning equipment, and the system responds as if it had scanned the correct eye.

The fingerprints were more difficult but not a deal breaker. Completely clear molds of Nancy's fingerprints had to be made. This, of course, was a two-step process, as the first strong latex fine grain rubber mold of the fingerprints was a negative. That is, on the molds, the ridges were where the valleys had been on Nancy's fingers and thumb and vice versa. The color of the first molds didn't matter, as they would only be used to produce a set of reverse or positive molds. These second molds had to be clear and tightly fit over Elena fingertips. It took three tries, but finally a comparison of Nancy's actual prints on a smooth glass surface and Elena's fingertip mold prints were indistinguishable. The last step during the job, of course, would be the application of an extremely light and mildly acidic oil to the molded tips to simulate the body's natural oil and sweat presence. Without any substance to transfer, there wouldn't be any prints.

That left the most difficult task of all, the pass or code words. These could be found in only one place, Nancy's mind. Sadly, there was no way to simply cut them out. Nancy was brought around. When she was fully aware, both Gerald and Elena did their best to persuade Nancy to reveal the needed codes. They would later try to obtain these via drugs anyway, but if the codes revealed via freewill matched the drug-extracted codes, one felt much more confident of their authenticity. Neither was surprised when Nancy refused. That is when the first of many drugs was injected.

Behavior and psychotropic drugs had been greatly improved by the pharmacological industry. The old drugs such as sodium pentothal were so crude compared to modern solutions. Before you start, an injection of midazolam, commonly known as Versed, erased most memory of the process from one's mind. The trick was the correct drug at the correct time in the correct amount. Improper use could easily lead to not obtaining the wanted information and permanent damage to the subject. Gerald couldn't have cared less about permanent damage, but he couldn't risk failure to obtain the information.

\* \* \*

# No Paperwork Needed...

It didn't take long to obtain all the information he needed. While inside her mind, he also pulled several pieces of information that might come in handy, should he through some problem, need to hold some information over Nancy's head. Gerald was indeed thorough. One last time, Nancy was put under, trussed up, and delivered back to her home, undressed, and placed in her bed. Gerald had considered simply killing her, but decided the confusion to be caused by her return would be a helpful delay.

The next day, Nancy awoke with a mild headache, looked at the clock, and with a startled awareness noted she had better hurry if she was going to make her flight.

# No Paperwork Needed...

**Chapter Twenty-Six**

The lone surviving shooter from the attempted hits at Larry and Trench's place of business had come out of his mild coma and appeared to be out for good. The next day, Agent Hall, with the backing of the CIA, had coerced the doctor to release him into Hall's care. He was transported to a bed in an interrogation room at the downtown federal building. Full nursing facilities were present, and his care could be assured. After all, one had to be in decent health to survive the rigors of sustained and intense interrogation.

Hall wasted little time. For several hours, the questions were presented in a quiet and gentle manner. That, of course, didn't work. So, the heat was turned up a bit. Literally, the heat. The subject was secured to the bed via leather arm and leg straps on each side. An efficient bed-sized heating pad  was located two layers below the bottom sheet, the temperature now set ten degrees higher.

Within fifteen minutes, the subject was starting to sweat and squirm a bit. It was obvious he was becoming uncomfortable. All the questions were asked by Hall and then translated into Russian for the subject. The few responses, of course, were translated from Russian to English for Hall's benefit. Every sound was recorded. The heated bed and repeated simple questions finally revealed his first name. They could call him Victor. Hall and company had no way of knowing if this was his true name, but they pretended it was, and Victor's reward was the lowering of the bed temperature by about five degrees. It was doubtful Victor even realized the change in temperature had been at the hands of the questioners.

# No Paperwork Needed...

Session after session like this took place. Question after question was asked. Lack of results led to additional temperature increases , and the rare piece of information gathered resulted in a slight cooling. Soon, however, the heating no longer led to any useful information. It was time for step two.

The background for step two was to assure Victor that they were seeking information about Gerald or his plans. They would catch Gerald and ask him these questions directly soon enough. All they wanted at this time was to know about Victor himself and what service he provided Gerald. It was important to give the subject small tasks, things that he wouldn't feel were all that important if they were revealed. If doing so bought him some relief, all the better. This, of course, was an abject lie on the interrogators' part. They didn't give a damn about Victor. The only goal was Gerald and Gerald's plans. Thus, the first question put to Victor was how long had he worked for Gerald. Victor mistakenly reasoned it wouldn't hurt to answer that question, and perhaps they might not be as hard on him as time went on. So he answered, and the CIA instantly knew Gerald had been working on his plans for at least that period of time. A little thing, but it was all the little things woven together that made up the complete picture.

The questions got a bit more to the point, and soon the process reached the point that any further information gained would need to be accomplished via nausea drugs. Intense nausea is truly one of the most debilitating sensations that a human being can experience. With the use of the nausea drugs, the emphasis of the questions ever so slowly shifted to Gerald. When one lies there so nauseated that he feels he's going to expel his entire insides, one tends to lose track of where the questions are headed. But even nausea drugs will not force most subjects to divulge deep-seated information. For that, psychotropic drugs are needed—step three.

The main drawback to drugs is that the subject will steadfastly report information as he or she perceives it. The color of a house could be red, but if the person experiencing the drugs gets it in his mind that the color is green, nothing on earth will change that. Under the absolutely most stressful of situations, he will report the house as being green. If drugs were 100 percent accurate and reliable, one would see their use in major legal trials. Why go through all the hassle of a courtroom trial if one could simply give the accused an injection, and moments later he would give you the story? They simply weren't that reliable—yet.

Keeping Victor on and off drugs for several days had given answers for many of the CIA's questions, but not the ones they desperately needed. They now knew that Gerald's helper was a Ms. Elena Vladimirovna Petrova. They knew she had been part of a weapons development team, along with Gerald, in Russia. They knew she and Gerald were indeed building their own nuclear device, which meant they could stop looking for one to be imported into the United States. They also knew how Gerald and Elena, who was Nancy's imposter, had escaped from the materials room at the labs. And with what.

Everything taken from the materials storage room was removed via Elena's mind. They didn't remove a single physical object; the only thing taken was information. That explained why the CIA couldn't find a thing missing from the room. The labs' infiltration had simply been a matter of information gathering  and misdirection; Gerald and Elena now knew where and to whom the last several plutonium shipments were made, and had succeeded in

# No Paperwork Needed...

sending the CIA off in the wrong direction in their investigation. God knows it worked. Hall shuddered when he thought of the huge number of man hours and resources wasted trying to figure out what the break-in had accomplished.

One huge tip did surface during the interrogation, however. Gerald and Elena had escaped via the room's thirty-two-foot ceiling. Victor disclosed the information that Gerald had used blackmail and a handsome payment to induce a lab staff member to be present in the ceiling crawl space, just waiting for Gerald and Elena's signal that they were ready to leave. At that time a ceiling panel was set aside, and a quarter-inch cable attached to a small, portable hoist was quickly lowered to the floor. Using the attached waist belts, both Gerald and Elena connected themselves to the cable. Ten seconds later they were above the ceiling, the removable panel was replaced, and several boxes were slid in place over the panel. Hall quickly made arrangements for an in-depth re-questioning of the entire lab's staff, focusing on the various maintenance and janitorial positions.

But they still didn't know the most important thing of all: where the hell Gerald and Elena were holed up building their toy. They didn't know for the simple reason that Victor didn't know.

To sum things up, Hall didn't know where the device was being built or more importantly, where it was going to be used. They were still stranded on square one. At this time the only hope was to find the third person, the lab employee who had helped with Gerald and Elena's escape.

# No Paperwork Needed...

## Chapter Twenty-Seven

It had taken the better part of two weeks for Doug Winters to track down his business partner, Roy Downey. He had the help of his office staff to fall back on in terms of Internet use, company credit card use, phone records, etc.

Doug was parked outside a rundown motel on the outskirts of Las Cruces, New Mexico. He smiled to himself at the lucky break he had gotten. As a perfect testament that greed knows no bounds, Roy had used one of the company credit cards to secure the room. Perhaps it hadn't been greed, but rather a simple mistake brought on by the relentless task of running. It appeared as if Roy never spent more than one night at a time in any one location. Regardless, according to the charge placed on the card, Roy was somewhere in the motel.

Doug entered the office. If possible, it was even seedier inside than on the outside. An old man with a cigarette dangling from the corner of his mouth walked to the desk and asked Doug if he needed a room for the night or just a few hours. Yes, this was a high-class joint indeed.

"Neither," Doug answered. "What I need is some information." At the same time, he took a fifty-dollar bill out of his wallet and placed it on the counter, but kept his hand firmly on the bill.

"Such as?" the old man said.

"Such as my business partner is in one of your rooms. His name is Roy Downey. I just want to surprise him."

"You're not going to cause trouble are you?"

# No Paperwork Needed...

"No. He's on a short trip, and I couldn't go, but at the last minute my schedule cleared, so I thought I would catch up and surprise him."

The clerk looked down at the fifty. Doug removed his hand, and the clerk told him room 122 as he snatched the bill.

Doug walked to room 122 and very quietly tried the door. Things were really going his way. The door wasn't locked. He burst in, and there was Roy on top of a gal who looked to be at least 40, perhaps 45. She looked as if they had been a tough 45 years.

Roy shouted, "What the hell?" And then it registered on him who had pushed his way into the room.

He was speechless, so Doug took up the conversation.

"Miss, I suggest you get up, gather your belongings, and leave. You aren't going to want to see this."

Roy started to talk and talk fast.

"I'm sorry, Doug. Really, I am. I've been absolutely sick about what I did and was going to call and tell you I was heading back with all the money. I don't know what I was thinking. I think the drugs were getting the better of me."

Roy had indeed started with some recreational drugs a few months ago, but to what extent this explained things, Doug had no idea, nor did Doug care. He didn't say another word until the whore had left.

"I want all the money and I want it now. You have thirty seconds to pull on some pants and start showing me the money. If not, I'm going to try a few of my old Navy Seal close-combat methods out on you. I'm sure I'm a bit out of practice, but I don't know if that's a good or bad thing for you."

In less than twenty seconds, Roy had pulled two bags from under the bed, opened them up, and dumped the contents on top of the sheets.

"Is that all of it? The ten thousand from the operations account and the three hundred thousand from the capital funds account?"

"Yes, every penny. Well, maybe I've spent about a thousand as I've been running around. But please, I truly was going to come back and return all of it. I've been a nervous wreck ever since I took the money. It isn't worth it."

"Give me your wallet." Roy didn't move. "I said, give me your wallet. Do it before I break your goddamned neck."

Roy handed over the wallet.

"Now your car keys."

Roy handed those over as well.

"OK. Now, I'm going to leave you so you can experience the feeling of complete abandonment, just as I did when you emptied the accounts and disappeared. Good luck. And if you ever try to contact me again, so help me God, it will be the last thing you ever do."

Three days later Doug was back home and opened new accounts at a different bank. He then turned around and withdrew the amount needed to pay the loan he had gotten from Larry and Trench. He said thanks and good-bye.

He drove directly to his apartment and before removing his jacket, turned on the DeLonghi and started to warm a cup.

# No Paperwork Needed...

## Chapter Twenty-Eight

Gerald and Elena were safely secluded in the large and extremely well-lit basement of the house Gerald had purchased under a false name the prior week. Laying the asked-for price in cash on the Realtor's desk bypassed many of the Realtor and lender scams and paperwork hassles. The two-story house was located in a modest and older section of town. All in all, it was an unassuming house in a middle-class area. With room to park both cars in the garage and the lack of newspaper or mail delivery, for the most part, it looked unoccupied. The last thing that would come to anyone's mind was that down in the basement, a device was being constructed that would have the power to remove a medium-sized city from the face of the earth.

This was Gerald's last stop prior to the placement of the device and its detonation. At last, the United States would be shown that a few devoted Russian citizens still had the balls to punish the great America for its heavy, unsolicited interference with his home country. Gerald had told Elena they were close enough to his final glory that it was time to dispose of the ugly American name. From this moment on, he would go by the name given him at birth: Nickoli.

Nickoli had acquired the single most needed material to create his device: money. He had months ago allied himself with a billionaire with strong ties to Russia, who despite all his personal gains, achieved in part because of the US economy, had a deep-seated hatred for the country. This alliance allowed Nickoli to obtain everything needed for the construction of his designed device.

Nickoli and Elena couldn't build a nuclear device from scratch, not due to a lack of skills, but rather from a lack of equipment and supply of basic materials. The needed

# No Paperwork Needed...

skills were present. Nickoli had been team leader and Elena the theoretical physicist and mathematician on Nickoli's small nuclear weapons design group. But, with the proper components, they indeed could assemble one.

In order of importance, the next item on the materials list was connections—first for the money and then for where to spend it to get what you wanted. With enough of these, and some paperwork, anything could be purchased.

Doing all the work themselves was out of the question. One couldn't keep watch on eBay for a functioning gas centrifuge or a sufficient quantity of uranium hexafluoride gas. That was just not going to happen. To be used as a functional core of a nuclear weapon, the uranium needed to be enriched to levels exceeding 90-percent purity in terms of the U-238 and U-235 isotopes. This isn't going to happen in the basement of a fifty-year-old house. The goal was plutonium-239 isotope, several pounds of the fissionable material.

Nickoli's list of connections was vast, coming from the many years of work in the small weapons design lab back home. He knew where the right amount of money—a huge amount of money—would acquire the needed plutonium-239. Even more important, he knew where he could get the plutonium machined into the exact shapes his design required.

Conventional techniques dictated that the plutonium be cast into a perfect sphere of precisely uniform density. This sphere, when violently compressed with absolute uniformity in terms of pressure and time, would lead to a chain reaction of heavy nuclei being bombarded by neutrons, splitting the matter into lighter elements and a huge amount of energy. The newly released neutrons would bombard additional heavy nuclei and because of the consistently uniform plutonium-239, the process would become self-sustaining, with the end result being the release of almost unimaginable amounts of energy in the form of light, heat, and nonvisible radiation. It was the intense heat and thus the almost instantaneous expansion of all air and surrounding materials that were at the heart of the explosion.

The trick was to compress the plutonium with the needed speed and consistency of pressure on a precise time line. This was most commonly accomplished by locating an explosive shell around the plutonium core. The individual explosive components of this layer of explosives are segmented wedges. The picture most often presented to represent this was a common soccer ball. This was a difficult task, the most difficult part of creating a properly functioning nuclear device.

Nickoli and his team had developed a different approach to the problem that required but one single explosive charge in the shape of a small sphere. Elena had produced the verifying mathematics behind this new process of core compression. Though requiring a level of mathematical manipulations of immense difficultly, nonetheless, Elena had shown on paper that Nickoli's approach would work. However, when Nickoli shared the proposal with the nuclear scientists and physicists that he and his team had been allowed to work with, even in light of Elena's work, he was told it would never work.

Nickoli, however, knew better. Working late and on weekends for months, he and Elena had built and demonstrated a working model, minus the fissionable material, of course, that had allowed them to take hundreds and hundreds of pressure, time, and temperature measurements that said it would work. If fissionable material had been present, it would have

# No Paperwork Needed...

indeed achieved fission—Nickoli, Elena, and all materials of all types in a radius of fifteen miles or so would have instantly been involuntarily converted to gas, heat, light, and ash.

Nickoli's design was based roughly on an onion: a layered device. The final size was slightly smaller in diameter than a basketball. At the center was a perfectly spherical densely compressed ball of high-grade semtex. At the center of the semtex was a monolithic silicone chip that functioned as the radio frequency receiver, which upon decoding a transmitted signal would verify the proper sequence of the twenty-four-bit enabling code. Once the proper code was received, the same chip would flash an ultra-small detonator. This in turn would ignite the semtex.

The burning of the semtex—all chemical-based explosions were nothing more than an ultra-fast burning of material—would result in an extremely fast explosion front that would drive the first layer of plutonium-239 outward at incredible speeds toward the second layer of plutonium. The casting and machining of the inner layer of plutonium had been done to assure an extremely uniform radius. This internal sphere was actually two hemispheres. Together, they were held at a constant distance from the outer machined two-inch-thick layer of plutonium by numerous copper standoffs.

The inner radius of the outer two pieces of plutonium perfectly matched the outer radius of the inner sphere. Various guides, along with a hard vacuum that would be pulled between the two layers of fissionable material, would keep the travel of the inner piece at the proper angles while it covered the one half of an inch it needed to travel. The inner piece would contact the outer piece with sufficient and uniform pressure that would in turn drive the outer layer into the outside retaining sphere at the proper matching pressure to ensure a chain neutron reaction, an atomic explosion.

When Nickoli had discussed the design parameters with the electronics technician commissioned to design and build the remote control device, the detonator, he was for the first time during the project at a loss for words to explain his needs. The remote control needed to have an operational range in excess of fifty miles. The technician had never received a request for that kind of range before and was puzzled. Nickoli finally let it go with the somewhat flimsy excuse that they had another idea they were working on, and it might involve the need for long-distance control, so they only wanted to purchase one remote. He couldn't figure out a way to explain that using the remote any closer than thirty miles would be extremely hazardous to one's health.

The machining and molding process of the plutonium wouldn't have been possible in terms of the needed precision years ago, except in the most elaborate of labs; but today's ultra-high precision, numerically controlled mills could handle the job with no problem, and they could be found almost anywhere. Of course, the correct data to program the mills had to be entered, but that was where once again Elena came into play with her unbounded knowledge of mathematics.

Lastly, all the internal parts were encased in a half-inch-thick, high-tensile strength, stainless steel, two-piece hemispherical sphere, with a bolting flange traveling the circumference.

Nickoli had had no problem obtaining the materials and machining he needed, thanks to his contacts. Most of his contacts instantly accepted his explanation that he was continuing his small weapons research under cover in

# No Paperwork Needed...

America because materials and processes were much easier to obtain. They were glad to help with theoretical research in the never-ending struggle against the capitalist United States.

The day came when the outer shell pieces were bolted together. It was finished. It sat there so cold and deadly on the table, just waiting for someone to transmit the enabling code. It gave Nickoli a sense of godlike power knowing that by moving three safety switches on the handheld remote and then pressing one button, he could release the full fury of hell.

# No Paperwork Needed...

## Chapter Twenty-Nine

It had been a slow morning at the office, and I didn't see my first client until around ten-thirty. That's when Cody Rider walked, or more correctly, hobbled into my office.

"Hello, Cody," I said, staring at his brand new crooked leg. "Your leg. I hope that's temporary."

"Hi. No, afraid not. The doctors tell me it'll get better, but never completely straighten out. It's bad enough that I'm finished riding the bulls. Damn it, I was well on my way to a championship."

"Cody, the entire world hates an asshole who jumps at the chance to say, 'I told you so,' but damn it, I did tell you so. Why anyone would jump on top of an eighteen-hundred-pound bull in the first place is beyond me. If you complete the ride, you get eight seconds of glory while risking a lifetime of pain or worse."

"I came here to pay my loan, not get lectured. Are you done?"

"Yes. I just hate to see a kid like you get hurt."

"In the first place, I knew the risks, and I knew the rewards. I made the decision that was right for me. In the second place, it wasn't a bull that got me, it was a ninety-five-year old lady looking through her steering wheel and driving about forty-five miles an hour in a grocery store parking lot that clipped me. She never even slowed down, let alone stopped."

"Oh. Well, never mind then. Where did you get the money to pay back the loan?"

# No Paperwork Needed...

"Just like I said. I sold my entire rig and horse to a young man who can't wait to jump into the rodeo game. He was so excited to be getting Cody Rider's rig that he offered me twenty-four thousand more than I paid when I bought it. Here's your money, plus the interest, as we agreed upon. That just about wipes me out, but at least we're even."

"Thanks. What're you going to do now?"

"I have a spot as color man on a small broadcasting network. After never getting hurt by the bulls in all my rides, I'll most likely get electrocuted when I touch the mike."

I handed him back twenty-one thousand. "Here, I want to split the interest with you. Use that to grab some kind of vehicle and save what little bit of money you have. Take care."

He said thanks and walked out the door. And like so many others, I never saw or heard of him again.

* * *

While Trench had been talking with Cody, some fifteen hundred miles across the country, Sam was making final preparations for picking up Jeff's daughter, Debra.

Sam had spent the morning picking up several supplies, never purchasing more than one or two items in any one store, to be used in the abduction of Debra. He purchased food and drink, a change of clothes for Debra, and a couple of age-appropriate books for the long drive back. Unlike the daily mileage restriction he placed upon himself on the drive out, the drive back would be a completely different process. Except for fuel, there would be no stopping. A stop at a camping outlet to purchase a small portable toilet solved the biggest issue with long, extended drives.

At precisely three o'clock that afternoon, Sam parked close to a small community park located along the route from the school to Debra's house. The two previous afternoons' surveillance of Debra and her walk home made him confident she would be along shortly. He exited the car and took up a position on a small park bench facing the sidewalk. Reading a newspaper and smoking his pipe, he appeared as benign as could be. He didn't have to wait long.

As Debra approached the bench, with a feigned look of mild surprise, Sam spoke out.

"Oh, hi, Debra, there you are."

Debra hesitated. She stammered a weak, "Hi."

"Your mom told me you would be walking by this park and so it would be a good place to find you. I have a big treat for you. You remember your daddy, Jeff, don't you?"

Jeff would indeed be Debra's weakness. In Debra's world, her father, Jeff, represented love and safety. She had wanted so desperately to go with her father, not her mother, when the court decisions were made.

"Yes," she said in an anticipatory voice. "Is my daddy here?"

"No, but your mom has told your dad it was OK for me to pick you up and take you to your dad to visit for a few days." As an afterthought, Sam took a bit of a gamble designed to help reassure Debra. If it backfired, all he had to do was skip the offer anyway. "If you want, we can stop at your house so you can ask your mom if it's OK."

Debra hesitated and then gave him the answer he wanted. "No, that's OK; I just want to see my daddy."

And just like that, a six-year old girl, filled with excitement at the thought of seeing her father, entered a van and drove off with a complete stranger. Sam wondered how many times a day this scenario was played out across the country with disastrous results. Sam turned at the next corner and used low-traffic side streets to distance himself from where he had picked up Debra. Upon exiting the city, he held to non-interstate roads for the first hundred miles or so, listening intently to the local radio stations. Not hearing a word about Debra's disappearance, he felt it was time to pick up the interstate and seriously make progress towards delivering Debra to her father and picking up his remaining twenty thousand dollars. He told Debra because of the higher speeds on the interstate, she would be much safer in the backseat. When she moved back, she was out of view, and as instructed, she buckled up. Sam pointed out the books to her and settled down for the long drive. He smiled to himself. Oh, how simple it had been.

* * *

Kent yelled in to me that there was a guy waiting to see me.

"Send him in," I replied.

In walked a young man who was best described as being completely nondescript.

# No Paperwork Needed...

"Hello, my name is Rusty Taggert. How do you do?" he said as he held out his hand.

*How refreshingly polite*, I thought, *this can't possibly be a college student.*

"My name is Trench. How are you, Rusty? What do you do—you're not a college student, are you?"

"No. Do I have to be, to get a loan?"

"Nope. As a matter of fact, your chances just skyrocketed. And why do you need a loan?"

"I want to open an upper-end foreign car service and repair center. I just graduated from an automotive technical school, and, well, I was the top graduate and truly do believe I have the skills to make it a success, sir."

"Congratulations. But I sense that what you are proposing would take a huge amount of money."

"Yes, sir, but acceptable labor rates and parts markup are very high these days, and these items are billed at even greater rates when you're working on a Volvo or Porsche or some other exotic such as an Aston Martin or the like. Do you know that oil changes for some of these cars can cost in excess of four to five hundred dollars?"

"That may be, but again, you'd be looking at a very large amount of startup  money. How would you pay it back?"

"Well, sir, I…"

"Hold it right there. If you call me 'sir' one more time, I'm going to throw your ass out of here. Understand?"

# No Paperwork Needed...

"Yes, sir, I mean, yes."

"OK, how are you going to pay it back?"

"Part of the prize for being top graduate is a monthly stipend for one year from a tool manufacturer. It isn't nearly enough to open a business, but it's supposed to be enough to go to a bank or other loan institution and borrow the money to get started, if that's what you choose to do."

"Let me know how that works for you."

"You're telling me. I never make it as far as showing my ideas and business plans and projections. I've done a ton of research, and nobody will even look at it. Would you like to see it?"

"No, but not because I'm not interested. It's just not the way we do things around here. You do understand how we do things? If we advance the loan, and you don't pay back the agreed amounts at the agreed times, we don't send you a past due notice; we simply drop by and break your arm. Are you still interested?"

"Yes. I have nowhere else to turn, and I'm absolutely confident I can succeed."

"Tell me more about paying back the loan."

"As I said, I'll be receiving a modest check once a month for one year. If you'll accept that as an ongoing payment, I feel confident my business will be established to the point that it can support the loan payment from that point on. Second, I only plan on purchasing very high-quality tools and service equipment, so if I need to close the business and sell out the inventory, I should be able to get a reasonable return on the items. Plus, I only need one or two somewhat extensive repairs a month to be able to send you a payment."

"Give me an example."

"OK. Pretend you're driving a non-turbo Porsche 911 variant and you hear a load growling noise start in the engine. Most likely you have just lost the camshaft intermediate bearing. This happens to about ten percent of the 911s if the owner isn't religious with oil levels and changes. The owner is now looking at anywhere from fourteen to sixteen thousand dollars in labor and parts. There are other horror stories as well. Losing pistons six and twelve on a V12 Aston Martin would cover my loan for half a year."

"When do you want to get started?"

"I've found an old garage that rents inexpensively. I have the money to do that. I need a sign and a phone number. The first parts and special tool orders will be determined by the cars that come in for service. I can live in the garage. I can get going on a shoestring until the first car comes in that requires some factory diagnostic machine, which costs several thousand. That's what I need the money for. I may have to repair ten of those cars to get the equipment cost back, but the day will come when I repair that type of car, and the income will belong to the shop—that being me, or you, I guess."

"OK, go rent your building and come by when you need some cash. The answer is yes, and I wish you well. Just remember the risks, and I don't mean the business risks."

"Thanks, and I'll remember."

# No Paperwork Needed...

I had finally gotten around to calling Linda. It took some convincing and an apology for such short notice, but I ended up with a date for that same night. I was to pick her up at seven-thirty.

# No Paperwork Needed...

**Chapter Thirty**

After stopping by my place, showering, and changing clothes, I was on my way to Linda's.

I parked in front and rang her doorbell. She answered, and moments later, I was sitting on the couch with a drink in my hand.

"Again, I'm sorry for taking so long to contact you. Things have been in such turmoil. The Gerald situation isn't one bit closer to a solution, and all hell is breaking out at the federal level. He's a nutcase and everyone truly believes he's soon going to set off a real live nuclear bomb somewhere in the country and take some city off the map. If they had any idea I had shared this with you, I'd be in such deep shit that my life would be over. As it is, I'm tearing myself apart that it was the money we loaned him that may well have been the first enabling step in this nightmare."

"Slow down. There was no way whatsoever you could have possibly known where that loan was going to lead. At this point do all you can do to help, and that's where it has to end."

"OK, I'll do my best to forget it all for tonight. I'm starving. You ready for some dinner?"

"Yes. What do you have in mind?"

"How does Chinese sound?"

"Fine. I'm told that the place out on East Forty-Fourth by the movie theater complex is good."

# No Paperwork Needed...

"Sounds just fine." And we were off. Some wine, hot tea, and an egg roll later, we were ready to order. Linda selected lemon chicken, and I chose black pepper shrimp. Both dishes were delicious. After we shared a fried ice cream, we were ready to go.

"What now?" Trench asked. "What would you like to do? We're right next door to a bunch of movie theaters."

"How about going back to my place? We could have some drinks, relax, and listen to some music. I have a second set of speakers in my bedroom."

I don't think another word was spoken until she was lying by my side under the covers. I had wanted this for so long; all the times I had spent like this in my imagination weren't even close to the real thing. She was so soft, warm, and giving. I wasn't ready for my reaction. I think I was falling in love. It was a long night, but even so, the morning came too soon.

The first call of the day was from Jean Reynolds. "You aren't having construction problems again, I hope?"

"No, not at all. As a matter of fact, my shop will officially open at six-thirty tomorrow morning. I'm calling to see if you, Larry, and Kent would like to drop by this afternoon to look the place over and have a bunch of pastry on me. I'm going to process the first batch through the new equipment to test temperature setting, timers, and stuff like that. How can anyone pass up all the free pastry he can possibly eat?"

"They can't. We'll be there. How does three o'clock sound?"

# No Paperwork Needed...

"Great. Don't eat until then; you're going to need the room."

At three sharp that afternoon, the three of us were sitting with a huge plate of piping hot pastries in the center of the small table.

"Well, dig in," Jean said.

And like the first time, many weeks ago, the pastry was almost beyond explanation. So rich, so flaky, so creamy— oh hell, it truly was unlike anything sweet I had ever tasted.

"Jean, this is absolutely fantastic. You're going to make a fortune. What are you doing to make this stuff, magic?"

"Extremely high-quality ingredients are part of the process. For example, the puff pastry is made with the highest quality flour, sweet butter, very cold ice water, and a dash of salt. It's a labor-intensive process, with the butter being softened via kneading, not melting. Everything is done cold or chilled. The butter pad is placed on the flour pad, which is folded over the butter and sealed and kneaded back to the flour pad's original size, then refolded and left to chill for at least thirty minutes. Then the process is repeated four more times. As I said, it's labor intensive and your hands get cold.

"If I'm making pie dough, I use half cold water and half cold vodka. That allows the dough to be moist enough to be properly worked and rolled, but the vodka evaporates off fast enough during baking for the dough or crust to end up very flaky. And then, after filling, you bake, but in your mind's eye, you must imagine baking not the pastry but the individual components one by one. The best temperature and time for one isn't the best temperature

# No Paperwork Needed...

and time for the next. First you do what's best for one component and then adjust things for what is best for the remaining baking of the next component. It gets a bit tricky, but it's worth it."

She smiled and said, "I'm sure that's more than you ever wanted to know, but I just love making my pastry."

I would never look at a turnover the same way again the rest of my life.

"I almost hate to bring this up, but are you making progress toward obtaining the money to service the loan?"

"Yes, I have various relatives coming in over the next week. They'll invest now that they can see it's up and going. I'll be able to get all your money and interest simply by selling my soul to them."

"Don't give it all away. If by being reasonable with the percentages, you come up a bit short, give us a call. Things can be worked out. Thanks so much for the treats. They're wonderful. You'll do well."

We left, but sending someone to Jean's pastry shop each morning to buy a round for the guys at the office pretty much became a habit.

# No Paperwork Needed...

**Chapter Thirty-One**

Agent Hall and a fifteen-member team had made their way back to Livermore, California. His task was to find the third man who had enabled Gerald and Elena to escape from the materials storage room. He needed a list of any potential staff who had access to above-ceiling areas of the lab complex. As he thought about the list of reasonable job duties, he came up with more and more possibilities. Electricians to service lighting systems, plumbers to service supply lines for fire suppression systems, maintenance staff for common physical plant work, and HVAC specialists for the various heating and cooling systems. The list seemed to grow and grow.

Upon visiting with three men from the lab's upper-level administration, he was presented with a list of possible staff positions and the men and women holding the positions. One hundred and thirty-seven names were on the list.

*I should have brought more men*, Hall thought as he left the meeting.

The names were more or less evenly divided among the CIA team. Hall instructed the team to instantly report any person who wasn't readily found. This was based upon the fear that their target would most likely disappear for a while, if not forever.

By mid-afternoon, Hall had the names of three people whom the agents hadn't been able to contact on first try. Hall picked his three best men and assigned a name to each. By the end of the day, only one couldn't be contacted. A Mr. Scott Berg was nowhere to be found. Hall obtained employment photos and Berg's complete personnel file from the lab's administration. All agents

# No Paperwork Needed...

were to continue with scheduled interviews, but the hunt was on for Scott Berg.

For days, Hall and two of his top men traced down every single hint, clue, or tip they could find on Berg. The man had apparently evaporated into thin air. Try as they may, they couldn't find him. Actually, they could have easily found him. They just hadn't looked in the correct place—the bottom of the local private fishing club's lake.

Hall's team continued to clear individual staff members left and right based upon the in-depth interviews. To date not one single person could be considered a suspect. No one was found with a drug habit, a gambling habit, any past run-ins with the law, not a single thing that didn't ring true. At one point Hall said that the group of targeted individuals was cleaner than the damn people who were questioning them.

And then, as happens so many times, serendipity stepped in. An older gentleman who was slowly trolling around on the fishing club's lake snagged a fish. A damned big one, it seemed. He stopped his trusty three-horsepower, twenty-five-year-old Johnson outboard and started to reel in his catch. He had never had a fish like this before, with absolutely no fight but heavier than hell. *This must be some kind of snag,* he thought, *it can't be a fish.* A moment later he received the shock of his life when he first noticed his snag was wearing glasses. The good news was that Scott Berg had been found. The bad news was that he wouldn't be too receptive to questioning.

The police were called, and the body was transported to the local morgue. Upon returning to the station house, one of the officers decided to look over his daily assignment sheet. On the back side was a photograph on which the CIA had posted a "Report Immediately" tag.

# No Paperwork Needed...

The officer stopped and stared at the man's image in the picture. Where had he seen that man? Christ! That's the body he had just delivered to the morgue.

In less than thirty minutes, Agent Hall was staring at the late Mr. Berg and questioning the local coroner. Mr. Berg had succumbed to a bullet placed in the center of his forehead, and the only thing found on his person was a safety deposit key.

Two hours later Hall was standing in a group of five men—himself, two other agents, the First Security Bank and Loan's vice president, and a line teller. The safety box was opened to reveal approximately two hundred thousand dollars and a small notebook. Hall grabbed the notebook and read through the entries with a fast first pass. Berg had obviously been uncertain of his relationship with Gerald and Elena and had jotted down every scrap of info he had overheard from the moment Gerald had approached him. Other notes pointed to the fact that Berg had a severe gambling problem and was very much in need of some serious money. And then Hall saw it. An address where Berg could contact Gerald if something came up at the lab that might be helpful to Gerald. Hall stared at the address for several minutes. After months of false leads, dead-ends, and purposeful misdirection's, Hall had an address.

He made a radio call to pass the address on to his home field office with the instruction to get the address to the most senior field agent of the few he had left behind. He requested that the agent do a visual surveillance of the property, but not to approach it in any way.

Hall pulled all his men off their assignments and left California for home. Along the way he received an in-flight call from the agent shadowing the address. The property looked completely abandoned, he was told, with no signs of occupation for a long time. He might be barking up the wrong tree, the agent said.

\* \* \*

Harry was walking better all the time. His foot still ached in the morning, and he had to be careful how much walking he did, but the little he could walk was done with a lot less pain and less effort to stay in a straight line. He had been able to make it up to the window and back a few times at the track and was pleased with the results. When things started hurting too much, he had Doris do the running. He would win, then lose, then win a couple of times in a row before losing again. Slowly he was building the amount of money he needed to get Trench and that psycho Tom off his back. He rarely made anything but single horse bets. The people who wanted to get rich in one bet chose things like a trifecta ticket. This never made sense to Harry; it was too much like betting against yourself.

But every so often, like with his standard single-horse betting, he would somehow see the finish, see which horses would cross the line first, second, and third. Sometimes he could so clearly see the order. When this happened, like all the other fools, he would place a trifecta bet. But he always made a single-horse bet for the same race to cover his potential trifecta loss. The lion's share of the time, he would break even, with his single-horse bet covering the trifecta loss. But now and then, he would approach the window after the race and stuff his pockets with scads of new money.

Today was one of his stallion days. He used that term to describe a day at the track that paid off. In his mind he added the money he had picked up today to the stash he had safely hidden at home and was pleased that the total would square him with Trench. Upon getting home, he gave Trench a call.

* * *

"Hello."

"Trench, this is Harry."

"Yes. What can I do for you?"

"What the fuck do you think you can do for me? Why don't you drive over here and get your damned money, all of it. I would bring it to you myself, but you might remember that asshole who works for you shot me in the foot."

"Come on, Harry. Don't hold a grudge. You know how it works. You're damned lucky Tom didn't cut off your foot and bring it back so he could shoot a hole through it at the office."

"Funny. Come get your money, and then I never want to see you again."

"OK, but I'll send Kent over to get it."

"Fine, just don't send Tom."

I hung up the phone. I knew we would see Harry again. The loan business only had two types of clients: those who would never come back again and those who could never stop coming back. Harry would be back.

* * *

# No Paperwork Needed...

Sam had been driving nonstop for many hours. Although tired, his energy was buoyed by the thought of delivering Debra to Jeff and picking up his twenty thousand dollars, an event that shouldn't be much more than an hour away. Debra had been the perfect passenger for the entire trip. She never questioned their eating in the car, sleeping in the car, even relieving herself in the car. She was getting more and more excited by the increasing closeness to seeing her father. Sam had been careful on the drive. He paid close attention to all his self-imposed rules. He got fuel at large truck stops where he was one of many cars. He checked all of his vehicle's lights. He made sure Debra had plenty to eat and drink and additional books and small toys to occupy her time. At one of the first stops on the trip back, he had purchased a portable DVD player and selected a handful of kid's movies. Debra always had something to do if not sleeping.

When Sam estimated he had around forty miles left, he called Jeff.

"Hello."

"Jeff, this is Phillip." Jeff would never learn that Phillip's true name was Sam.

"Oh thank God. I've been wondering when you would call. Where are you?"

"I'm about an hour out. Debra is with me, safe and sound. She's excited to see you. Do you know that small neighborhood park on Sixth Street between Apple and Maple?"

"Yes."

# No Paperwork Needed...

"Be there in one hour exactly, and make sure you have the remaining twenty thousand. That's important, Jeff. Without the twenty thousand, Debra leaves with me."

"I have the money."

"Good. What kind of car will you be driving to the park?"

"I have an older, green Oldsmobile Cutlass."

"Fine. Park the car on the north side of the park, get out, and walk to a park bench as far on the south side of the park as you can find. Wait there. Leave the car unlocked. Have the money in a plastic shopping bag and put it on the rear floorboard. Cover it with an old shirt or coat or something. I'll drive by with Debra. If I find the money in the car, I'll place Debra in your car and drive away. You'll never see me again. You'll never hear from me again. Is that all understood?"

"Yes."

"Jeff, one last thing. Debra seems to be so happy that she's away from her mom and is getting to see you. I only get involved in these matters if I think it's good for the kid. Don't ever let me find out that she's gone from one bad situation to another."

With that the phone went dead.

Jeff looked at the phone for a few moments, lost in thought. After all his planning, scheming, and efforts, he was within an hour of having his daughter back. He went downstairs and pried the lid off the salt tub of the house's water-softening system. The plastic bag containing the remainder of the loan proceeds he had gotten from Larry and Trench lay on top. How many times had he checked

# No Paperwork Needed...

that the money was still there in anticipation of regaining his daughter? It was silly, of course. After all, where was it going to go? But somehow it seemed to comfort him every time he looked; it was the key to her return. He grabbed the bag, picked up an old paint-stained sweatshirt from the laundry area, and headed for his car. He placed the plastic bag on the rear floorboard as instructed and covered it with the sweatshirt. He headed for the park.

After some extra driving simply to kill some time and fight his nervousness, as he didn't want to be either early or late, he parked on the north side of the park. Leaving the car unlocked, he proceeded to walk the entire length of the park and found a bench to sit on near the park's southern boundary. He could just barely make out his car, but was far enough away that it would be impossible to recognize anyone approaching the car. He had been sitting for only five minutes or so when someone did approach his car. Seconds later the person walked away from his car. He waited, straining as hard as possible to see what else may be going on, but couldn't detect anything. The wait continued. And continued.

After about ten minutes, Jeff came to the conclusion that the money had indeed been taken, but that Debra hadn't been delivered. Unable to sit still any longer, he started for his car. He walked at first, but soon he was running as fast as he could. He was within some one hundred feet when he noticed a small child sitting in the front seat. It was Debra! After all this time, it was Debra.

Jeff jumped in the front seat and turned toward her. Debra leaped into his arms and held him as tightly as a six-year-old could. Jeff returned the hug and held her for a good five minutes, softly repeating her name time and time again. He turned and faced forward, started the car, and said, "Let's go home."

Nothing was spoken during the drive home. Jeff wasn't sure how to explain to Debra what had happened over the past several days. He had no idea whatsoever how to explain what most likely would happen in the days to come.

\* \* \*

I picked up the ringing phone receiver. "Trench speaking."

"Hi, Trench. It's Jean Reynolds."

"Hi. How is your new business going?"

"Just great, Trench. And it's all due to you; well, maybe not all due to you. After all, I make the pastry, but without your loan, I would have never been given the chance."

"Our pleasure, but speaking about money—well, you know what I'm going to ask."

"Yep. And I'm pleased to tell you I have the full amount."

"That's great. How much of your soul did the relatives demand?"

"Well, none. It was kind of funny. When I first asked them for an investment before I came to you, they acted as if I weren't related. You couldn't count all the excuses why they couldn't help. But I had them over to show them the shop a couple days ago and stuffed them with pastry. They loved the shop, loved the pastry, and said they would be happy to help, but they would be doing so with very hard-earned money and thus would need a very high interest in the shop, plus some other assurances.

"As it turned out, an older lady sitting at the front of the shop must have had hearing like a fox, because she came up to me after the relatives had left. She told me the biggest mistake I would ever make in my life was to accept the funds from relatives. Not to mention, the suggested return rates were approaching usury. She suggested I could do better than that with a pack of loan sharks. I kind of grinned at that. We talked for about thirty minutes, and she left, but not before writing me a check for more than enough to cover your loan. It will also be enough to get some help and finish doing the nice things I wanted to do to the shop but couldn't afford.

"She's my new partner, and I'll pay her back at the rate of ten percent of my monthly profit, with an interest rate of five percent on the total amount; and then she receives a five-percent profit stipend for the remainder of the shop's existence. It was like a miracle. I called the relatives and told them thanks but no thanks. You should have heard the interest rates and percentage of ownership drop. What a greedy bunch."

"That's great, Jean, I truly am happy for you."

"Trench, do you remember when we first met and you tried my pastry for the first time? You suggested that my pastry just might be better than sex."

"I sure do."

"How would you like to drop over tonight around nine for a private pastry and coffee treat?"

# No Paperwork Needed...

"Jean, a couple of months ago, I would have been there before you could have hung up the phone. But since then I've met a woman I think I may truly be in love with. I'll stop by tomorrow and pick up the money, but I'm honored with your suggestion. I look forward to seeing you. Good night."

As I hung up the phone, I was amazed at my response. I was really falling for Linda. But at the heart of things, I still was nothing more than a male—I felt myself rising faster than any dough Jean had ever prepared.

The remainder of the week was completely without incident. The weekend was a complete blur. I spent the entire time at Linda's house. She had stocked up on food, drink, and a few movies. We didn't leave her house at any time during the weekend. Never had I been so happy; for some forty-eight hours all of the cares in my world didn't intrude.

The first call Monday morning was Debbie. She was bubbling with excitement.

"Trench, I made my first completely legal sale! It is now OK for me to sell five thousand dollars' worth of marijuana, and yet there are countless men and women still in prison for having sold fifty dollars' worth. What a world."

"Sounds like you're off to a great start. I assume it was retail shops that made a purchase like that, not an individual."

"It was a group of stores based in Colorado. I've since heard back from them, and I have a standing order for a monthly purchase five times that size. It's going to work,

# No Paperwork Needed...

Trench. I'll be over later this afternoon with my first payment."

"Great. Is anyone giving you a hard time? You aren't exactly selling Girl Scout cookies."

"True, I'm not, but my stuff is better for you. Thus far things have gone as smoothly as possible. I had a few public official types drop by and tell me what a menace I am to society. They said they would do everything possible to get the laws reversed and have me shut down. However, a few of those hinted that a decent supply of free samples might halt their efforts. Trench, I want to thank you. I'm still in touch with some of my graduating class, and only two of them have managed to find a job. I feel so lucky."

"It was our pleasure, Debbie. Please keep up with your payments; not everyone over here is as nice as me. See you this afternoon."

I didn't know it at the time, but Debbie was to meet every one of her payments. Due to her substantial income, she eventually worked her way onto the city council. Over time the marijuana laws continued to lighten as the council took to heart the revenue benefits of the ever-increasing tax levies. Everyone was happy.

# No Paperwork Needed...

## Chapter Thirty-Two

Tuesday midmorning, the trio of college kids walked in. They were carrying an equipment order a full three pages long.

"What's all this?" I asked.

"We have had our Big Brother Weight Watchers' Service online for just over two weeks. We have signed up over ten thousand clients. The funds you first advanced us are long gone, and we can't source any more in-house weight-mentoring data systems, otherwise known as smart scales, unless we send the current manufacturer three hundred thousand. Secondly, our two small servers are completely overwhelmed, and if we don't increase bandwidth and simultaneous access counts by a factor of at least one hundred, we're going to die before we get rolling."

"First off, for God's sake, find a better name than Big Brother Weight Watchers' Service. I've no idea what, but anything would be better. Second, not a single thing on this list means a damn thing to me. Are you sure it's needed?"

"Yes, we're sure it's needed," said John, one of the three. "We need a hundred-fold increase in server response, and while we aren't archiving—oh hell, you wouldn't understand anyway. Sorry, but the list just keeps growing and I wouldn't ask for it if we didn't need it.

"Fine—can you explain to me once again what this entire system does in terms of the client? I know it's all part of a remotely supervised weight loss system, and I know that anything that offers even a glimmer of hope in the weight loss field will make a ton of money; that's why Larry and I

# No Paperwork Needed...

invested. But I still don't know how it works from the individual's point of view."

"Sure, it's pretty simple. The user accesses our website and signs up for the service. They're shipped a USB data-sensitive scale that wirelessly transmits and receives data from or to their home computer; we also furnish the proper USB adapter used at the computer. They furnish us with their e-mail address and several other pieces of data. An important one is the tenor in which they wish to receive our server-generated e-mail messages. If our servers take note that the client hasn't stepped on the scale and thereby forced a weight measurement to be transmitted to their computer and passed on to their data profile on our servers, then they receive one, or many— their choice—e-mails telling them it's time to weigh. The tenor controls the tone of the e-mail. Anywhere from 'Oh my, I see you haven't weighed yet this morning; please do so now' to 'Get your fat ass on the scale now!' The daily data is logged and stored, and at any time the end user can ask the system to draw a graph of weight change over time, the system can point out trends, suggest menus and quantity changes if they enter food consumed data with the weights, give messages of encouragement or cautions, etc. The forced weighing and data logging is completely automatic; the local computer and our servers do it all."

Once again I thought of how much money this system was going to make. And, as opposed to snake oil and exotic plants, this might help someone.

"OK, I'll fund these purchase orders. Can I assume that this will carry you for a reasonable while?"

"Yes, but I hope not," John said.

# No Paperwork Needed...

"How's that?"

"The only reason we would need more money faster is that we're obtaining new clients even faster than we have planned for. That is a good thing. A good thing."

I started daydreaming about Linda and me storming down California One in a new Aston Martin DB9 Volante—top down.

\* \* \*

While Trench was lost in his daydream, Jeff was trapped in his own nightmare world of fear and depression. He had done his best to try to explain to Debra what had happened and why she was now with him. It wasn't a pleasant story, but even at the age of six, she was entitled to know what was going on. She wasn't bothered that her mother hadn't been asked if she could come or even that her mother didn't know where she had gone. Debra said she was happy to be with her daddy; he didn't hurt her. Jeff had no idea how to explain that his estranged wife would figure out where Debra was in no time and that she would be coming.

Jeff had spent endless hours trying to figure out just how, when, and with what Karen would arrive. Figuring out what a person might do isn't that difficult a task when the two parties involved have the same mind-set. But Karen was different. Seemingly normal actions to Karen would fall into the world of horrific imagination for Jeff. He absolutely had no idea what to expect.

He had stretched his imagination as far as it could go, coming up with scenario after scenario, in an attempt to prepare for her arrival and fulfilling her stone-cold promise to kill him if he ever took or even tried to take her daughter. It was a huge and almost insurmountable handicap to make sure Karen executed the first, but hopefully not lethal or debilitating, blow.

Jeff steeled himself and tried to explain what was about to unfold. He asked Debra if she understood that Mommy wasn't well, that she couldn't think about things correctly. He explained that she did things she thought were OK, but she only thought they were OK because she was sick. Mommy would never do the things she did if she weren't sick. In a child's uncanny manner to see through most things and get to the heart of the matter, Debra asked Jeff if that was why Mommy hurt her so much. Jeff was on the verge of tears as he answered yes. He told her Mommy had said that if Debra ever came to visit Daddy, that Mommy would come and do whatever she needed to take Debra away.

"Will she hurt me, Daddy?" Debra asked.

"No, Deb, we won't let that happen."

And then it was as if a light had been turned on. "Will she hurt you, Daddy?" she quickly asked.

"I think she will try, but I won't let that happen either," Jeff said, knowing this was a quasi-promise that he doubted very much he could keep.

"Debra," Jeff said, "Let's play a game. A game of magic. I'll hide downstairs, and I want you to run to any room you want and say whatever you want, and then go to any other room—any room you pick out—and again say whatever you want. Do this five times, and then come tell me you're done. I bet that I can, just like magic, tell you where you went and what you said. Does that sound fun?"

"Sounds kind of dorky, Daddy, but OK, if you want to play, I'll do it."

"OK, I'm going downstairs. Count to ten and then get started."

She did as she was asked and a short time later, she was at the top of the stairs telling Jeff she was done.

Jeff came up the stairs, and just as he said, he told her exactly which room she had been in and what she had said. Debra's eyes got bigger and bigger as Jeff in exact detail recalled her movements.

"Daddy, I don't think I believe in magic. How did you do that?" Of all of the things that Debra had said since Jeff held her in the car, this came closer to breaking his heart than anything else he had heard. He almost couldn't handle knowing she had lived such a tortured life that even at the tender age of six, she no longer believed in magic.

"Come over here and watch this." He entered a time and pressed the Auto Play button. The screen popped to life and displayed an image of Debra in the main living room. She was looking around and then quietly said she was going to the bedroom. The image displayed her movement walking away from the camera up to the second she left the room and instantly displayed her image shot from the front as one of the hall cameras took over. Her voice was heard saying she was now in the hall on the way to the bedroom. A few steps later, the first bedroom camera came online and displayed her walking into the bedroom itself. On and on it went, with every step she took and every sound she uttered being captured as time went on. Finally, she was shown at the top of the stairs telling Jeff she was done.

"What do you think of that?" Jeff asked.

"Wow, Daddy, you can see and hear everything."

"Yes, and that's one way we'll make sure that Mommy won't hurt anyone."

As it turned out, Jeff had no idea what was about to happen. Of all of his imagined possibilities, what actually took place wasn't remotely close to any one of them.

It was two days later that Jeff heard a quiet but insistent alarm sound. Someone was approaching the house. While the approach was indeed being captured on camera, Jeff took a quick look out one of the side windows of the farthest room from the main entrance door. It was Karen. Strangely, Jeff was as relieved as he was concerned. Good or bad, this was soon to be over.

Karen approached the house with an air of completely carefree confidence. She looked as if she were a representative of some neighborhood welcoming group. She stopped at the door and brushed several strands of her hair out of her eyes and back up where they belonged. She straightened her light jacket and rang the doorbell.

Jeff took a deep breath, walked to the door, unlocked it, and pulled it open as he stepped back several steps.

"Hello, Jeff."

"Karen."

# No Paperwork Needed...

"Jeff, I know you took Debra." *Actually*, Jeff thought, *she didn't know, but she was indeed correct.*

"And what makes you think that I did?"

"Don't fuck with me, Jeff. I've always been much smarter than you and have always been several steps ahead of you. I know damned well that you have Debra."

"Maybe I do."

"One last time, don't fuck with me, Jeff."

"Karen, she is here to stay. There is no way I'm going to allow you to take her and put her through any more of your sadistic tantrums."

"Allow? Allow? You seem to be forgetting that the court awarded me her care. You aren't in a position to allow anything. Where is she?"

"She's safe; you need know nothing more."

Karen turned and looked to her left. It always worked; Jeff looked in her same direction. When he turned back, she was holding a large pistol that for all the world looked like some kind of air-powered gun. He hadn't seen her remove it from her jacket, she did it so quickly.

"Jeff, where is Debra?"

"Do you think I would tell you?"

"Debra," Karen yelled, "you have to the count of three to come out, or I'm going to shoot your father. Do you hear me, Debra? After the count of three, if you aren't here, I'm going to shoot your father in the center of his face. You don't want that, do you? Here we go. One. Two..."

"Don't, Mommy. Don't," Debra screamed as she ran to the living room.

What happened next was far from anything Jeff had considered. The second Debra stopped in the center of the living room, Karen centered the air pistol on her and pulled the trigger. With a silent poof, a dart lodged itself in the center of Debra's small chest.

Debra looked at Jeff with an expression of puzzlement. Then ever so slowly, her eyes rolled into the back of her head, and she gracefully slumped to the floor.

"What the fuck did you do?" Jeff screamed.

"It seems obvious to me; I shot her."

"You fucking psycho, what is that, poison?"

"Don't be so melodramatic. It's a simple tranquilizer; she'll be out for a few hours. Now it's your turn. I believe I said something about shooting you in the face?"

Jeff wasn't the fastest thinker on his feet, but he did just fine.

"What is it about you that you enjoy doing this kind of stuff? Have you enjoyed all the pain you've inflicted on your own daughter?" Jeff was sure he already had enough of her visit recorded to guarantee a win in court, but the more, the better. Plus, he was stalling.

"I don't know if *enjoy* is the proper word, but stern punishment is effective. Debra was such a dear for days following her little hot seat on the electric stove. I didn't enjoy setting her on the stove, but on the other hand, it didn't bother me, as I knew it would help her behave. I see nothing wrong with proper punishment. I had asked her three times to pick up her bedroom. She now straightens things up the moment I ask."

"I have no idea how many times you've tortured Debra, but I do know of at least two other times. What did she do those times, spill a glass of milk?"

"Don't be silly. The toes and the nail in the hand were just punishments. I don't remember what they were for, but if not deserved, I wouldn't have punished her. But we're getting way off track. I guess you know why I don't mind admitting all this, don't you?"

"Yes, I know, but I suggest that you don't pull that trigger. You'll be sorry if you do."

"You know, if I were standing in your shoes, I bet I would be saying something just like that. You ready?"

"You are indeed one sick bitch. And soon the entire world will know. What if I told you that every move you've made since you started up my front walk and every sound as well has been recorded?"

"I would say you were a fool for letting me know about it. All it means is that after I kill you, I'll find the recorder and destroy it. I don't believe you anyway."

"Do you think I'm so damn stupid that the recording being made in this house is the only place things are being recorded? A second wireless recorder in a house about a thousand yards from here is making the identical recording."

# No Paperwork Needed...

For the first time, the unholy grin on her face slipped a bit. Jeff thought he had finally trumped her.

"As I said, I don't believe you. You aren't that clever."

"Maybe not, but if you look closely to your right up in the corner, you can just make out a small piece of tape. Go pull it down, and you'll find a small camera. There are thirty-two of them inside and outside the house."

Jeff knew this was his last hope. If she did indeed turn to look or even better, walk to the corner, it would be his last chance to attack. She did, and he did, hitting her full force, much like a defensive tackle. Down she went. Out of Jeff's back pocket came a small but heavy club. He swung with all his might. He could swear he heard something break, but he knew for sure he saw her eyes roll up. He then used a couple of nylon tie straps on her arms and legs. Jeff scooted over to Debra and lay beside her. She was breathing shallowly but steadily, and her pulse seemed fine.

He got up and walked over to Karen. She was stone-cold out. He had already picked up the gun she was holding and moved it to the kitchen. He searched her jacket for the air pistol she had shot Debra with. He found that, as well as three more syringe-type darts and a six-inch serrated knife. She had been well armed. He moved these items to the kitchen table as well. His next step was to call the ICU surveillance company and ask them to get a couple of men over to his house as fast as possible to download the digitally stored data from the recorder and make him five copies on standard VHS tapes. The call was answered, and they said they would be right over.

# No Paperwork Needed...

When the two surveillance technicians walked in the room, they came to a complete standstill and exchanged looks between themselves. They saw the crumpled and trussed-up woman in the corner whose head had obviously been bleeding profusely and the small girl lying in the middle of the room.

One said, "What the fuck?" and they headed back for the door.

"Wait," Jeff shouted. "Please, I'm not the bad guy here. Please go down and look at the recording. It'll tell you the entire story. When you've finished and made the copies I need, then please call the police. I'll be right here by my daughter. The police will confiscate every bit of the recording equipment; that's why I want the tape copies made before they arrive."

Jeff walked over to his daughter and sat down on the floor. The two technicians looked at each other, shrugged their shoulders, and headed for the basement. They were back up in about fifteen minutes.

"Holy shit. Do you know how lucky you are to still be alive? The tapes are recording as we speak and should be done in about ten minutes. We can't wait any longer; we have to phone the police."

"Fine. You can call the second you hand me the five tapes."

Jeff was handed the tapes just a few minutes later. He asked the technicians to place labels of signed certification on the tapes. That done, he left one tape for the police and stored the remaining tapes in various places. Two were placed in the water softener tub that had hidden the money he had used for the kidnapping.

# No Paperwork Needed...

"Please call an ambulance and then the police."

It didn't take long before all hell broke loose outside as three police cars and one ambulance arrived simultaneously. Debra was placed on a gurney and wheeled to the ambulance, as was Karen, along with her new handcuffs. The police started asking Jeff questions, but he suggested they first watch a tape. He placed it in his VHS player and pressed "Play". When it was finished, he asked if he could go to the hospital to be with his daughter. They said yes.

All that was left would be the court ruling on Debra's guardianship. That would be weeks in the future, but Jeff had no doubt of the outcome. It had all been such a daring move, but it had worked.

There was also the matter of successfully gaining control of Debra's trust so that Larry and Trench could be repaid. Jeff had lived through the Karen episode; hopefully he could do the same with the loan sharks.

# No Paperwork Needed...

## Chapter Thirty-Three

Rusty Taggert phoned.

"Hello, Rusty. I hope you're up to your armpits in car grease."

"I soon will be. I'm in the old garage. I'm sleeping on an old mattress on the floor, but I'm here. I'm phoning you on the new shop phone. I have three cars sitting in the garage with various problems. None of these will be high-dollar repairs, but it's a start, and I'll do everything possible to make these customers happy with my service. At this time, I don't need any additional tools or service equipment. Most auto shops and the mechanics have such a bad reputation. I don't understand. If they were simply honest, fair, and accurate with their repairs, they'd have more business than they would know what to do with. The last thing they need to resort to is being unfair or overcharging. Well, I'm off to change out a water pump on an old Fiat 128. Not that glamorous, but a start. I just wanted to verify that I have access to the needed funds if the next car in requires me to purchase some five-thousand-dollar diagnostic machine."

"I told you that you do. Don't worry. As long as we feel you are playing straight with us and making the payments that you agree to, all will be well. We'll help you get going. Hell, I might buy a car someday that would require your service. I better keep you in business."

"Thanks, Trench. I'll call when I need too. Bye."

Moments after Rusty's brief call, the phone rang again. It was Agent Hall with the CIA.

# No Paperwork Needed...

I let out a brief sigh; I had kind of put Gerald out of my mind.

"Hello, Hall."

"Trench, we've been watching the house where we think Gerald is holed up. We haven't seen him or seen anything, in fact, but things point to the house we have on stakeout."

"I hope you're right. Where are you?"

"Right here in town. Can you believe that? It's kind of one of those 'hiding in plain sight' things."

"Christ. What if he never leaves? What if he decides to set off the bomb you keep saying he built himself without making another move? How do you know the damn thing isn't ticking or whatever they do right now?"

"Well, the most accurate answer is that we don't know. But the guys back at National Headquarters who're paid to think things like this over tell me he'd want to detonate elsewhere. How the hell they think they know things like that is beyond me, but that's what I'm told. Also, they have Gerald down as someone who'll do everything in his power to not be part of the explosion; he's going to want to see just how much destruction and societal upset this will bring. He may even want to publicly take credit for the event. At any rate we're told the last thing to do is storm the house or tip our hand in any way. If we do, he just might press the button or flick the switch or do whatever in the hell he's going to do to set it off."

"So what are you going to do?"

# No Paperwork Needed...

"Watch. We're acting on other small clues, but our best bet is that he and Elena are in that house. If they come out, we'll follow them, and if we see the device is with him, both he and Elena will be taken out. We have a four-man sniper team on location. He's dead already, he just doesn't know it. We have no idea what his next move will be."

But inside the very house referred to in Hall and Trench's conversation, Gerald did indeed know his next move. Final decisions had been made. The residents of Fort Collins, Colorado, didn't know it, but their city had been scheduled for elimination. Gerald had given the choice of city a lot of thought. It couldn't be too big, because he wanted the psychological impact of a complete devastation and yet he wanted a significant body count. Fort Collins also had the advantage of being close to Denver, where the absolute horror of the explosion would enter the mind-set of over one million people—people who would tremble in fear, knowing they were spared by only some fifty miles.

Several weeks previous, long before the CIA started to watch the house, Gerald had traveled to Fort Collins and spent the day looking for the perfect spot to leave his present. One of the trash disposal bins on the CSU campus track and field area would be ground zero. Oh, how glorious it would be. He would be somewhere in a fifty-mile radius of the device, the actual direction determined by the day's wind.

Gerald had only one remaining decision. When. He wanted to allow himself two full days for the proper location of the device in his chosen spot and to establish his location of triggering and escape. He wasn't worried about leaving the safe house with the device and locating it in its final location, because the device had long since been removed. He smiled to himself as he thought of the agents who had kept up constant surveillance on the house. It had been Elena who had caught on to the surveillance; she had noticed the same nondescript car drive by one too many times and had started watching. She wasn't positive, but the proper action was to conclude they were being watched. He didn't care if they watched him or Elena. The day after completing the device, prior to the CIA surveillance, he had delivered it to a second in command during his trip to Fort Collins. They thought they were watching him, Elena and the bomb. They were right about him and Elena, but the thing that counted was long gone.

The day came. Gerald and Elena walked out of the house, holding hands, no less, into the bright and crisp brand new day. The agent assigned to watch the front door involuntarily blinked several times and quickly passed the word. "The front door. Repeat. The front door." Within seconds, no fewer than five sets of high-powered binoculars were trained on the couple. A quickly agreed-upon judgment was that neither person could possibly be carrying a nuclear device. They couldn't be carrying anything larger than a pack of cigarettes; it would have been seen. Agent Hall was on site and instantly issued the command to stand down. If a bullet were placed through each one of their heads at this time, the agents might never find the device. Hall had no choice but to once again simply let them walk away.

Gerald and Elena walked across the street and entered a car that had been parked there long before the surveillance had commenced. This car, like many others parked within a couple blocks of the house, had been searched time and time again. Hall knew that Gerald and Elena were leaving without the device. Of course, the device was the only thing that counted. Hall needed to try to keep track of Gerald's whereabouts, but he had to keep his main force on hand covering the house. One two-man agent team was dispatched to trail Gerald.

When Gerald pulled out of town, he knew beyond a shadow of a doubt that he was being followed. This, too, he had allowed for. Two fuel stops and several hours later, in the dark of the evening, Gerald pulled into another truck stop filling station. He and Elena walked inside and moved toward the restrooms. What the agents missed is that they had walked past the restrooms, down a short hall, across one of the truck repair bays, and out a small employee service back door. From there, it was less than two hundred feet to the planted car Gerald would use next. He started the car, turned, smiled at Elena, and pulled out, taking a county road running perpendicular to the interstate. After several minutes, the agent who had discreetly followed them in and toward the restroom area developed a real sense of concern. They were taking too long. Minutes later, he dashed back to his car and hesitantly pointed out that he had lost them. The agent in the car hung his head, wondering how in the fuck he was going to explain this to Hall.

An hour later, Gerald pulled into a small convenience store and phoned his second in command. He gave explicit instructions to locate the device exactly where he had planned. He was to locate the device just after noon three days hence. Gerald would detonate around ten in the evening, as he wanted to enjoy the brilliant flash in the night sky. His last instruction to the second in command was to make sure he was at least fifty miles away by ten o'clock. He didn't need to explain why. Gerald would watch the wind the next couple of days and place himself a good fifty miles upwind in time for the detonation. A few days to go and his dream for American despair would take place.

# No Paperwork Needed...

* * *

"What did you say?" Hall asked.

"I said, I'm sorry, sir, but we lost them."

Hall was white with rage. He hung up the phone without a word, more due to his inability to speak than not knowing what to say. For who knows how many times, they were once again back to square one. They didn't know if the device was still in the house for certain, even though that was the best guess, and once again they had no idea where Gerald was heading. They certainly had no idea they only had about seventy hours remaining before the detonation.

# No Paperwork Needed...

## Chapter Thirty-Four

The courtroom hearing was set for two o'clock that afternoon. Just over four hours to go. It had been a difficult and stressful past eight days. Debra remained unconscious for several hours after having been taken to the hospital. When she came around, she was nauseated and was given an antiemetic drug to help. After several hours, she was as bouncy as any six-year-old would be after being shot dead center in the chest by a strong tranquilizer. The attending physician pointed out casually that had the dart been two inches more to Debra's left, she would no longer be alive.

Karen didn't fare as well. She had a moderate concussion and had developed a large hematoma that was surgically corrected. She didn't come around until a day later than Debra. As only Karen could do, she had every one of the hospital staff feeling sorry for her and looking at Jeff with an intense distaste. She discussed the concepts of entrapment, premeditated violence, and harm, not to mention that honored tradition of self-protection. There wasn't a thing to say; without seeing the tapes, which would instantly set everyone straight, there wasn't a thing Jeff could do. Only he could see the evil that lurked toward the bottom of her deep, dark eyes.

The police, held in check by a court order advanced in Karen's favor, couldn't show the tapes to anyone. The tapes would be seen for the first time at the court hearing, if then. Jeff was under the impression that the attorneys had access to things like that to prepare for the presentation of evidence to the court. Somehow that got changed. You just stopped asking how, when Karen was involved.

# No Paperwork Needed...

Close to the hearing time, Jeff was allowed into the courtroom and saw Debra for the first time since she had left the hospital. She'd been sent to a child welfare center for her protection from both her mother and her father. He wasn't allowed to touch her, but when she saw him, she lit up like a light bulb. The light dimmed when Karen was ushered in, wearing a pair of handcuffs. The cuffs were demanded by the police, based upon reports from the officers who had responded to the call at Jeff's house.

Soon everyone was there except Karen's attorney. And then it dawned on Jeff. Karen didn't have or want an attorney. No one alive could do a better job of caring for her in this situation than Karen herself.

A door at the head of the courtroom opened, and a young woman walked through and took her place behind the bench. Great! Off to a nice start. A female steeped in the wave of women's rights. She turned and addressed Karen. "Ms.—oh, excuse me, I see you are divorced. Are you going by your maiden name?"

"No, Your Honor. He divorced me. I still love him and go by my married name, Karen Lancing."

One minute in and the first lie. How did she do it? Everyone in the courtroom took on an air of concern. This was going to be a long day.

"OK, Ms. Lancing, I don't see your attorney. Are you planning on representing yourself in this matter? That isn't a good idea."

"Yes, I am, Your Honor. I think only I have the ability to adequately describe the pain and suffering my daughter and I have been put through for the last eighteen months."

# No Paperwork Needed...

"Very well, Ms. Lancing." She turned to my side of the courtroom. "Mr. Lancing, your attorney may advance his case."

Jeff's attorney was Dan Johnson. Jeff had known him for years, and he had a good understanding of the situation. While not acting as Jeff's attorney, he had been present at the last court hearing when Jeff lost all access to Debra.

"Your Honor, I will beyond all doubt paint an accurate picture of Ms. Lancing. I'll show her for the sociopath she is, and—"

"Mr. Johnson, may I ask, are you a licensed psychiatrist?"

"No, Your Honor."

"Then find another word."

"Yes, Your Honor. We'll prove that Ms. Lancing doesn't seem capable of expressing normal emotions or making acceptable decisions in terms of child care. These actions have led to a very improper environment for the child. Indeed, they have led to pain and suffering that no person, regardless of age, should have to suffer. I would like to approach the bench with three sets of hospital documents that will show the pain—no, torture—that Debra has suffered at the hands of Ms. Lancing."

"You may approach the bench, Mr. Johnson, but leave the papers behind for a moment."

Dan approached the judge and was asked during a brief sidebar if there was any mention of abuse or suspected abuse in any of the medical reports. He had to answer no.

# No Paperwork Needed...

"Please step back. Mr. Johnson, I must rule that the documents are not relevant to the hearing. Please continue."

Other than lying about her name, Karen hadn't spoken a word, and Jeff was getting the shit kicked out of him.

"Your Honor, I would ask that you allow Mr. Lancing to briefly summarize the last few years of involvement with his ex-wife and daughter. You can then yourself ascertain the environment that Debra has been subjected to."

"I'll listen to what he has to say, Mr. Johnson, but when he is finished, I'm going to need much more than his statements."

Jeff stood and did his best to accurately describe the horror and frustration of the last two years. Not once did the judge show a hint of wonder or disbelief. He might as well have been speaking to a brick wall. And then it was Karen's turn.

Karen was Karen. She took only about a third of the time that Jeff had. When she was finished, the judge continued to stare at her for a few moments and then turned to my attorney.

"Mr. Johnson, unless you have anything else to present, I'm ready to pass my ruling."

"Yes, Your Honor. We have a set of video tapes taken by equipment Mr. Lancing had installed in his home in anticipation of Ms. Lancing's visit that will clearly—"

Even Jeff grimaced when Dan stated that the equipment had been installed in anticipation of Karen's visit.

# No Paperwork Needed...

"Excuse me, Mr. Johnson, did you say 'installed in anticipation of Ms. Lancing's visit?' "

"Well, yes, Your Honor. Mr. Lancing feared violence on his ex-wife's part and wanted to…"

"Before you say anymore, Mr. Johnson, I must warn you that this is starting to sound very much like premeditated entrapment."

"No, Your Honor, not premeditated entrapment—if anything, premeditated self-defense. Your Honor, Mr. Lancing has been the victim of unending improper and outright judicial judgment errors. With all due respect, Your Honor, you yourself just sat through one of Ms. Lancing's utterly convincing performances, and it would appear that you bought it hook, line, and sinker."

"Careful, Mr. Johnson."

"Yes, Your Honor. But that is exactly what is happening to Mr. Lancing every time he attempts to seek relief from the judicial system. I ask you—no, I implore you—to watch the video tape we have to present. I have two witnesses with no relationship to either Mr. or Ms. Lancing who will testify to the absolute authenticity of these tapes. Please, I implore you in the interest of finally bringing some justice to Mr. Lancing, watch these tapes. They don't need to be exposed to the court in general if you don't wish; they can be watched in chambers. But please, as you would rule on any piece of evidence, view this tape."

"I cannot imagine that I would come to any other conclusion than to rule them inadmissible and seriously consider taking Mr. Lancing to task for entrapment, but based upon your impassioned plea, yes, I will at least start to watch the tape in chambers. All present are not allowed to leave or have any communication with one another during this brief adjournment."

The judge was handed a tape by Dan, and she moved to her chambers. The tapes were about seven minutes in length. The judge was in chambers for over twenty minutes. She returned to the bench.

"Mr. Johnson, please present your witnesses testifying to the fact that this tape is an accurate recording and done in the actual time frame as displayed on the tape."

"Yes, Your Honor." He called the two technicians from the ICU surveillance company to stand forward.

Jeff thought even the judge grimaced at the company's name. After several questions as to their employment and expertise to be passing judgment on the tapes, she asked the magic question.

"Do you both certify the authenticity of these recorded tapes, both video and audio?"

"Yes, Your Honor," they said in unison.

"You may step back."

"Ms. Lancing, do you have any further witnesses or comments?"

"Yes," Karen said. She turned to Jeff and said, "This isn't over, you mother fucker. I'll find a day when I can get to both you and that fucking daughter of yours, and you both will die at my hands."

The judge beat her bench with the gavel.

# No Paperwork Needed...

"Ms. Lancing, you are remanded to the local police to be held for an upcoming trial on attempted murder, aggravated assault, child endangerment, and lying in my court. Remove her. Mr. Lancing, it's with the deepest regret and apology that I ask you for forgiveness on the judicial system's past errors and hereby award full custody of the minor Debra Lancing to you and your care. This hearing is concluded."

One last gavel blow, and Debra was mine. It had indeed all been worth it.

\* \* \*

Jeff asked Dan to obtain and make available all the needed court documents he would need to present to the attorney who represented the trust held in his and Debra's name, so Jeff could take over the trust. As far as he knew, the only qualification he was lacking, but had obtained, was the court ruling showing him as the sole and legal guardian of Debra. About a week later, he was sitting in front of a large desk watching an attorney carefully read through all of the trust's caveats. The attorney finally called his secretary in and asked her to witness his signature and sign her own name as witness. He filled out and signed a couple of other forms and handed one of them to Jeff.

"Take this to the First Federal Land and Trust Bank, and you'll have full access to the account. Use it wisely; it sounds as if this little girl has been through enough."

Jeff went by the bank and withdrew enough to pay Larry and Trench, plus enough to cover a fantastic trip to Disneyland for Debra. If he worked hard, he might be able to bring a little magic back into her life.

# No Paperwork Needed...

That very afternoon, Jeff stopped by Larry and Trench's office, walked in, and handed Trench the cash.

"Trench, I can't thank you enough. I know you took a big risk with this money. As you told me, there were a thousand things that could go wrong with the plan, but I felt I had no choice but to try. Plus, it worked. I have Debra back, I've been granted full guardianship, and Debra and I are on our way to see Mickey Mouse."

"Just every so often, Jeff, I feel good about what we do around here. This is one of those times. Have a wonderful trip, and I wish both you and Debra a very happy life."

And once again, some nice people walked out of my life forever.

# No Paperwork Needed...

## Chapter Thirty-Five

Gerald was about three hundred miles and two and a half days away from his dream of many years coming to fruition. Since that day so long ago when his grandfather was imprisoned at the request of the current US ambassador to Russia, he had dreamed of his great nation taking a stand and no longer letting US whims dictate Russian policy. His grandfather had done nothing more than ruffle the feathers of the ambassador, but it was taken as a real threat, and the current Russian authorities would bend over backward for the United States. Off to prison his grandfather went. In retrospect, the issue with his grandfather currently had little to do with his desire to punish America. But without a doubt, it had planted the seed of his hatred.

But that was a long time ago, and for many years since, Gerald had been working on developing and completing his plan to make a Russian statement to the United States that would never be forgotten. Everything had gone well. Sure, there had been some bumps in the road after he got mixed up with that loan company that gave him the seed money to bring in someone with real money. It had taken literally millions of dollars to get to this point. But loan company fiasco had not impacted his plans to any real extent.

As he drove along, he and Elena discussed the old days back home and their dislike for America. But Gerald spent most of the time trying to present his thoughts on the post-detonation period, as America reacted to a city within their own borders being vaporized, completely removed from existence, along with all its inhabitants.

"It will be glorious, Elena. The light will be seen for hundreds of miles. For anyone closer than twenty miles

# No Paperwork Needed...

away, it will be the last thing they ever see. The force of the energy conversion will be massive. They always relate the force of a nuclear explosion to so many tons of TNT, but that is so misleading. Why am I telling you this? You know the actual yield and results better than I do. Just think. Aside from the instantly formed crater, the countryside will be swept absolutely clean for many, many miles. I estimate the total death toll at better than four hundred thousand. Thirty to forty thousand people die each year in traffic deaths. There is never a word said. But kill ten times that number in seconds, and you'll hear about it."

On and on he went. Elena had heard all this so many times. She was also proud to be part of the statement they were about to make, but she didn't revel in it. She didn't gloat. She felt sadness, but she believed the end in this case did justify the means. Russia had to stop lying down like some kind of drunken whore. They needed to make a strong statement, and this indeed would be like shouting from the rooftops.

Later that day, Gerald and Elena pulled into Denver. According to the weather reports, the wind was out of the south, blowing from Denver toward Fort Collins. Good. If the wind held tomorrow evening, Gerald could flip the three switches and press the button while in Denver. Gerald and Elena took a room at a Hampton Inn on Federal Boulevard. He asked for the top floor and a room facing to the north. If he passed sentence on the United States from his room, he wanted to be able to clearly see. He registered for three nights and proudly paid under his given name, Nickoli.

Nickoli and Elena had dinner at a close-by sports bar and then returned to the room.

# No Paperwork Needed...

* * *

Many months ago, Elena had hoped that Nickoli would express interest in forming a romantic relationship with her. Actually, she had wished this the entire time they worked together back in Russia, but he never once expressed any such interest. But one night several weeks ago, Nickoli simply walked over to her and started to remove her blouse. Without a word he continued to undress her, and then he removed all of his clothes. He had led her by the hand into her bedroom and more or less shoved her on the bed. He climbed on top and without a word being spoken, took her.

When finished, he stood up and walked to the shower. He dressed and came back to her bedroom and casually started speaking of a work detail they had been discussing the night before. Ever since then, from time to time, he would grab her, and in minutes she would find herself under him on the bed, the floor, the couch, whatever seemed to be convenient to him, always without a word being spoken. He got a bit rougher with her each time. She soon could tell she was the furthest thing from his mind each time he took her. It was the device and the detonation that were on his mind during the act; lately, he started to speak of it as he were coming to orgasm.

She knew it would most likely be even worse in the room tonight and during the day tomorrow. She was developing a real fear and strong dislike for the process.

He continued to discuss the detonation, and with glee to re-evaluate the death toll. She, too, continued to think of the death toll,I but with ever-increasing regret.

She was awakened the next morning by him once more climbing on top of her. When finished, he showered and dressed. He ordered in breakfast for the two of them and started in again about the glory he was presenting to his home country later that very day. He checked the weather, mainly the wind strength and direction, several times during the morning and early afternoon. The wind wasn't changing, and their current location would indeed be just fine for the detonation.

As the afternoon wore on, Elena more and more questioned what she was doing. It finally did seem so real. It was no longer a game or fantasy. She was about to be part of an event that stretched the imagination in terms of horror, pain, and suffering. But there was nothing she could do. She made the mistake of casually mentioning to Nickoli that she was starting to question their decision to detonate the bomb. Nickoli's expression went from wonder to rage. He reached out and grabbed her by the neck, and holding her tight, struck her several times with his clenched fist in the face. Her split lip was pouring blood, and her left eye instantly started to close. This aroused him sexually, and he shoved her down on the floor, ripped off her skirt and panties, and thrust himself into her. He violently and quickly reached climax, stood up, kicked her in the face, and walked off. He didn't know that his actions helped Elena make a huge decision.

About an hour later, Nickoli told Elena he was going down to the lounge to have a drink. He had the balls to suggest she had better not come along, as she wasn't looking all that pretty. He was laughing as he walked out the door.

As quickly as possible, Elena gathered up an in-room note pad and pen. She wrote out the following message:

"CIA:

# No Paperwork Needed...

"My name is Elena. I'm the woman who has been with a man you know as Gerald, whom you have been trying to find, as you suspect he is going to detonate a small nuclear device on American soil. His real name is Nickoli. This is indeed going to happen—tonight,10:00 p.m. The device is located on the CSU campus in Fort Collins, Colorado. It can be found by a trash collection bin on the outdoor track and field site. We are located in room 1702 of the Hampton Inn on Federal Blvd. in Denver. That is where Nickolil will be triggering the bomb. Again, he will be pressing the button at 10:00 p.m. tonight. I'm passing this note to one of the hotel's service staff, as he will not let me out of the room. For God's sake, please hurry."

Elena folded the note and opened the room door. Looking both directions up and down the hall, she soon spotted a hotel maid exiting a room several doors down. She called for the maid and frantically motioned for her to come to her. The maid did.

When she arrived, Elena grasped her and placed the folded note tightly in her hand. She stared as deeply as possible into the maid's eyes and quickly told her to go to one of the management offices and make a call to the CIA and read the note to them word for word.

"Don't mention this to anyone else. Give them your home phone number and then instantly go home. I beg you with all that is holy to do exactly this. The lives of close to half a million people are at risk. The CIA will see to it that they get your job back for leaving early, or any job you want, for that matter. You must do this. Promise me you'll do this. Nod your head yes. Don't read the note until you are talking to the CIA. Don't give up calling until someone at the CIA takes you seriously. Now go."

# No Paperwork Needed...

Elena stepped back into the room, knowing that for the next seven or so hours, all she could do was wonder.

Elena had walked a fine line between writing the note as quickly as possible, as she had no idea when Nickoli might return, and still including enough detail to convince the CIA that the note was for real and had to be taken seriously.

Time would tell.

# No Paperwork Needed...

## Chapter Thirty-Six

It was just shortly after five o'clock MST that afternoon when Agent Hall's phone rang. He answered with the traditional, "Agent Hall speaking."

"Agent Hall, this is Senior Field Agent Roberts calling from the Denver regional center. I have a message I need to read to you. A copy is being faxed and e-mailed as well as we speak."

After the Agent read the letter he asked, "You are listed as the lead agent on this matter. What can we do to help?"

Hall was slow to answer. He thought of the many times they had felt they were so close to Gerald, or Nickoli actually, and he had slipped away each time. Five hours to go. This time, no matter what, he had to be stopped. They had just one more chance.

"Please stand by. I'm going to get to Denver as fast as possible. To save time I would like to use your field staff. How many agents can you summon?"

"We have almost twenty-five agents based out of the Denver office. I can have them all rounded up in less than thirty minutes."

"Fine, get twenty of them to the CSU campus in Fort Collins as fast as possible. Put a team leader in charge, and when you've done that, contact me with the team leader info. I'll be boarding a helicopter and then a jet within minutes. I'll let you know in flight my touchdown in Denver. I expect you to be waiting with transportation. I'll have our best bomb technicians and the federal government's Nuclear Emergency Support Team—NEST—in route to Fort Collins, God help them. You'll hear from me again shortly."

Hall could think of several reasons why he should be in Denver, but at the same time could think of several reasons why he should be in Fort Collins. That decision could wait for a short while. He needed to get going toward either as fast as possible. Just fifteen minutes later, the jet broke ground and headed toward Denver.

In flight, Hall placed a three-way call to his second in command and the senior field agent in Denver.

"OK, how the hell do we handle this? We only have one chance. If Nickoli senses anything, he'll simply press the button. It seems to boil down to either finding the device and disarming it so it doesn't matter if he presses the button, or keeping him from pressing the button in the first place."

The Denver senior agent responded. "I think we should pursue both approaches and add a third—that is, things are OK if we can't disarm the device and he does indeed detonate the thing."

"What the fuck are you saying? How do you move close to four hundred thousand people to a minimum of fifty miles away in less than seven hours?"

"You don't; you move the device to a location that's better than fifty miles away from a single person and hopefully out of range for remote triggering. Then the disarming can happen without being under the gun. Nickoli could be temporarily spared and forced to guide in the disarming of the device. It would be better to be safe on all counts;

prevent him from pressing the button, but make sure that if he does, it leads to little harm."

"I take back everything I was thinking about you. That's brilliant. My explosive team and NEST will be on-site in minutes, as will a team out of Denver. Find that fucking device. If the explosive team gives you the OK, get it on a jet and get it to somewhere in Nevada, one of the old nuclear test sites. Drop it off and get the fuck out of there. Wait as long as you can to still have time to safely complete the job. Use that time to do your absolute best to see if anyone is watching the device who could tell Nickoli to trigger now. That would take a hell of a commitment on someone's part, because if it's triggered while under observation, the observer is toast. Have my explosive team contact me with what's been done with the device. I'll go to Denver and find Nickoli. We'll do our best to take him down and keep him from pressing the button, but if he does, let's hope it's out of range for successful triggering. If not out of range and the device is triggered, then it's imperative that the detonation take place out of harm's way. According to the note, you still have six to seven hours to accomplish the task."

"OK, let us know if and when you've disabled Nickoli."

Better than two hours passed before an update came from any of the teams. Then the lead agent from the team searching for the device in Fort Collins checked in.

"We have secured the site. There is no indication of the device being watched. Either no one was tasked with that duty, or if he was, he has decided to put a hell of a lot of distance between himself and the device. Do you want us to secure the device? Should we have the explosives team try to render it untriggerable, or do you want to send it to Nevada? That's still possible given the original time line, but things are getting very tight."

"The decision is in the hands of the explosives team. I have no idea how they would know if trying to open it up would trigger the thing or not, but unless they're positive it can be safely done, get it on a fast plane to Nevada."

Twenty minutes later, Hall was told that the device was on its way to Nevada. This wasn't without risks as well. Remotely activated motion triggering or atmospheric triggering might be in place. The explosives team ruled out atmospheric triggering, however, because close examination didn't reveal a pressure equalization or atmospheric pressure monitoring port of any type. The motion triggering was a crapshoot, but the consensus of opinion was that no such circuit was in place. Having the circuit in place opened up too many possibilities for a premature triggering, and all indications pointed to a well-planned and staged event. Nickoli wouldn't want things taken out of his control by the box being bumped into by a garbage truck. Everything said Nickoli wanted the pleasure of pressing the button.

The device was placed in a Faraday cage, a triple-layer-thick copper box, to aid in the prevention of transmitted or received radio' signals. It was placed on a helicopter, flown to the Loveland-Fort Collins Front Range Municipal Airport, and placed on a Lockheed F-22 Raptor. The pilot quickly advanced the throttles to achieve the 1,500 mile-per-hour, mach-two velocity the aircraft could sustain. Creech Air Force Base at the north end of the 15,000-square-mile Nevada Test and Training Range Complex was just thirty minutes away at this speed. A CH-47 Chinook helicopter would be standing by to take the device to an abandoned above-ground test site. There it would rest safely until it was analyzed and disabled, and the remote triggering device, along with Nickoli, was neutralized.

The Chinook had returned to base and a flock of observation helicopters had scoured the area for better than an hour. Three individuals had been terrified when a military helicopter landed close to them, and they were none too gently grabbed and tossed in and flown off. All observation helicopters were called back to base, and the area was considered secure. Hall was notified of the situation. He was now completely free to attempt to close in and subdue Nickoli.

Nickoli was at that moment listening to Elena beg him to stop the detonation. He had a maniacal look on his face as he told Elena he had looked forward to their watching the glow of the explosion together. He was sorry for her traitorous change of heart. He reached inside his suit jacket and removed a small pistol. He placed a bullet in the center of Elena's forehead. He didn't want her interfering in any way when it was time to press the button.

He walked to a fast-food joint next door and purchased a couple of cheeseburgers, an order of french fries, and a large soda.

When he got back to the room, he placed a chair by the window he would use to view his handiwork. He put the food and drink on a small table he had pulled next to the chair and then sat down. It wouldn't be long now.

The cheeseburgers tasted great, and the fries were nice and hot and salty, just like they should be. The soda fixed that. In fact, the soda worked a bit too well. Shortly he found himself needing to urinate.

# No Paperwork Needed...

What he didn't know was that every single sound he made was being monitored, recorded, and analyzed by the CIA agents who had taken up the rooms on each side of his. When the team in the room closest to his bathroom heard him urinating, the team waiting in the hall stormed his room. They had correctly assumed he wouldn't be holding the trigger device while he was holding his dick. The first agent saw a cigarette-sized device on the table by the remaining french fries. It had what looked like three switches and a button. He dove for it and placed it in his pocket. Nickoli burst out of the bathroom with a pistol in his hand and aimed at the first agent he spotted. It was the last thing he did. No fewer than three agents placed a tight grouping of bullet holes around his heart. One would have thought they were at a marksmanship contest. Nickoli was dead before he hit the floor.

The radio call to Hall was short and sweet. "We have the remote trigger, and both Elena and Nickoli are down: Elena at Nickoli's hand and Nickoli at ours."

Hall acknowledged the radio call, placed the radio on his small desk in the command center van, and sat back. Thinking over the operation from the first relay of Elena's message, Hall shuddered with thoughts of how it could have gone. They had been so lucky. The device could have had any number of triggers that would have made moving or disarming it impossible. A remote spotter easily could have been watching the bomb, and one radio call to Nickoli would have resulted in an instant detonation. The times given for the placement of the device and detonation could have been changed at any time. On and on. Yes, they had been very lucky.

But the biggest piece of luck of all had been Elena's change of mind about being part of the impending atrocity and risking her life to lead them to both the device and

# No Paperwork Needed...

Nickoli. Had she not contacted the CIA, the city of Fort Collins and four hundred thousand souls would no longer be in existence. From so many viewpoints, the CIA had failed miserably. Elena couldn't be thanked for her change of heart. He did, however, have the name and number of the room service maid at the Hampton Inn who had been the next most important person in preventing the disaster. He would see to it she was well taken care of. His next call was placed to Trench.

"Trench, it's Agent Hall."

*Oh no*, I thought. *Am I to be used as bait again*?

"Yes," I answered with trepidation.

"Gerald—by the way, his real name is Nickoli—has been stopped and his device captured. Both Nickoli and his female partner, Elena, are dead, and the device is sitting in the middle of one of the old above-ground nuclear test sites in Nevada."

"How? When? Last I knew, you had no idea what to do next."

"Elena had a change of heart and arranged for us to be contacted with the info we needed to stop things. If she hadn't, the only way we would have ever found the device is when it was detonated. In her own way, she was a bit of a hero. Bottom line, it's over. Well, over except for one thing."

I thought, *oh shit, here we go.*

"What?"

# No Paperwork Needed...

"We need to figure out what to do about you, Larry, Tom, and the rest of your merry band of fuck ups."

"Please remember we had no idea what Gerald, or Nickoli, was up to when we lent him the money, and we were the ones who put you onto the fact that he was going to be playing with a nuclear device. And lastly, we risked our lives several times in an attempt to help you capture him."

"I remember; that's the only reason a bunch of guys haven't already knocked on your door and let you try out a personalized pair of handcuffs. The higher-ups are going to debrief the shit out of me over the next couple of weeks. I suggest you make yourself scarce, because if you don't, they're going to call you in for questions. Let me run interference for you, and while we both know it can't be done, I'll try to put you in a good light. Take that Linda gal for a trip or something. I'll contact you when things have calmed down. But if it means anything, I myself want to thank you for all you have done. I'll see what I can do for you. Bye."

# No Paperwork Needed...

## Chapter Thirty-Seven

I decided to do just that. I would call Linda shortly, but first I needed to check things out with Larry. I knocked on his door frame.

"Larry, can I talk to you for a few minutes?"

"Sure, I want to talk to you as well."

"First, the Gerald thing is over. Both he and his female co-terrorist are dead. The bomb is sitting on an above-ground nuclear test site in Nevada. The CIA has the remote trigger as well. They'll be taking their time to study and disarm the device. I still have no idea what will happen, but Agent Hall said he was going to go to bat for us."

"Thank God. Trench, this has been hard on me. As you know, I've more or less handed you the reins on the operation ever since I've been back. I want to finish the process. I want out, Trench. I'm turning everything over to you. I would ask that you send me twenty-five percent of the monthly profits, but other than that, it's all yours. I just don't want to be involved anymore. I'm going to go to a small place I have on the Baja and try to drink myself to death with margaritas. Do you remember that little gal named Pam who works at the Whistle Stop diner just south of here? Well, she's going with me."

"That sounds great, Larry. We all knew your heart was no longer in this. When are you taking off?"

"Not real sure. Why?"

# No Paperwork Needed...

"I wanted to take a couple of weeks off and take a trip with Linda. Agent Hall suggested it might be best if I couldn't be found for a while."

"No problem. It'll take that long or longer to get ready to leave. Have a good time. Let me know when you're back, and I'll hand you the keys. You know, I'm still not sure you've completely paid back the five hundred dollar loan I made to you so very long ago," he said with a smile.

I called Linda. I said hello, and then with no delay asked about her joining me for a two-week trip. I thought heading to the California coast would be just the ticket. She said she could turn her shop over to her sister for a couple of weeks, and she would love to go.

I still had one big surprise coming. Later that afternoon, the three college kids that Larry and I were in business with came in.

"Don't tell me you guys need more money already?"

"Oh, we've spent a bunch more money on equipment and services, but we used current income to do so. And here's your share of the profits to date."

They handed a check to me for three hundred thousand and gave me another one for Larry in the same amount. I instantly knew what I was going to do with it. I called Linda back and asked if she could be ready to leave tomorrow morning; she said that would be tight, but she would be ready.

"Pack very little stuff, we won't have much room in the car."

# No Paperwork Needed...

"What are you talking about? That Lincoln SUV of yours will haul a household of stuff."

"Who says we'll be taking the Lincoln?"

I picked her up the next morning in the Lincoln. She gave me a strange look. "I thought you said we wouldn't be taking the Lincoln?"

"I did say that, and we won't be after a while."

We drove during the day, stopping constantly for this and that. We had a few drinks each afternoon, a fantastic dinner each evening, and made love most of the night. The trip was going to be wonderful. When we pulled through Chicago, I made my way to Napleton's Aston Martin. There I traded in my Lincoln for a new DB9 Volante Convertible. The Aston Martin was so beautiful, more or less a form of mechanical sex. I laid cash on the desk, signed a few papers, and we were on our way to California.

A few days later, as we approached Denver on I-70, I felt a huge unease rise in my body. I couldn't help but think about all the people some fifty miles to the north who came within a few hours and one woman's conscience of being vaporized. They would never know. Their lives would continue on with the daily moments of joy and grief—happy about a new job or a dollar-an-hour raise, cussing and screaming about a scraped fender at a stoplight incident—all the while in complete ignorance of how close they came to nonexistence.

We were going to stop in Denver, but I couldn't make myself do so. We drove on west of I-70 up into the mountains, through the Eisenhower Tunnel, and continued on west. I wanted to put every single aspect of the Gerald and Fort Collins event out of my mind.

Four lazy days later, we were heading north on Highway One in California, stopping constantly to enjoy scenery and sun. Each day was like a bit of heaven. We drove with the top down on the Aston, listening to its incredible V-12, forty-eight-valve engine exhaust growl fighting with the Linn 280-watt music system for supremacy. Around noon we enjoyed an Italian-like lunch of cheese, bread, cold meat, and wine. In the late afternoon, we would grab one room, two bottles of wine, and watch the sun go down. The day would end being lost in love. But as all good things must come to an end, there came a day when we knew we had to make our way back home to our own world.

The Monday after our return, I went to the office and had a long visit with Larry. He handed me a few documents. We shook hands, he said good-bye and walked out the door. I asked if it would be OK to call if I needed any help or advice in the future. He said sure, but he didn't want to know anything about the day-to-day operations. He said if he wanted to be part of the operation and know what was going on, he wouldn't leave in the first place. Fair enough.

I called Agent Hall that afternoon.

"Hello, Hall. It's Trench. Are we in trouble?"

"Several folks wanted to see you make some serious amends for your business practices; my agents and I prevailed, but just barely. The Treasury Department got involved, and an agent named Forester wanted your head for some reason. I don't know what you did to piss her off, but you have a real fan there. I asked her what she knew about you and the Gerald affair, and she replied 'not much,' but she was sure your business led to a lot of untaxed income that the Treasury Department should be aware of so they could arrange for tax collection. I told her I would talk with you about it, at which time she said never mind. I suspect there is more going on than I know about, but I'm willing to let that go as well. Bottom line, you're off the hook, but if I were you, I would clean up my act a bit."

"Not to worry; I'm well on my way to becoming an admired corporate business leader. Thanks for everything, Hall. Take care."

I hung up the phone, shaking my head in disbelief. It was just like in the movies. The agents had turned their heads, and I simply walked away. I would let the loan business slowly fade away, as income from the business investment continued to grow. But in the meantime, it was business as usual.

Later that day, a young man stumbled in, reeking of pot, wanting to borrow ten thousand to hire some muscle to convince his father it was time for him to release his trust. He was twenty-two years old and was tired of working.

Goddamn it. Another college kid…

# EPILOGUE

The black letters on the glass door read:

## Carlena Martin

## Janitorial Services Manager

Carlena was very happy with her position with the C.I.A. She was supervising and scheduling a staff of eighty-seven workers dedicated to the appearance, cleanliness, and proper stocking of supplies of the massive C.I.A. headquarters in Langley.

She was earning six-fold the income she had ever received in the past. Not bad, not bad at all for someone whose only experience had been as a part-time maid working at a hotel in Denver, Colorado.

And all she had to do was keep one little note to herself.

\* \* \*

The team of nuclear scientists and weapons design specialists had grown in excess of twenty-five members.

In the past two months, as they studied, planned, argued, and overall failed to achieve any real progress, they had time and time again steadfastly refused to seriously consider what was turning out to be the only viable option for the device that had been delivered to the Nevada above-ground test site.

# No Paperwork Needed...

They could not come up with any method to try to dismantle the device that did not come with so many unknowns that any discussed attempt was simply madness.

No, what had to be done was a well-planned destruction. And, any destruction could very well lead to a detonation of the device itself. They simply had no way of knowing what was going on inside that stainless steel ball, and any type of X-ray process was out of the question.

The final decision was made to destroy the captured device by an underground detonation of a much smaller nuclear device placed at its side.

Various test ban treaties had to be addressed. The political aspects of the plan started to outweigh the scientific and engineering work required.

But, three weeks later, the team leader was ready to press the button.

3...2...1...0  the destruction device did indeed trigger the captured device. Never before had the weapons experts experienced such a massive yield from so small a device.

For all his planning, Nickoli may well have not survived the blast from his hotel room in Denver.

* * *

And as for Trench and Linda, time will tell...

Printed in the USA
CPSIA information can be obtained
at www.ICGtesting.com
LVHW042015200724
785997LV00029B/86